IF BOOKS COULD KILL

A Bibliophile Mystery

Kate Carlisle

AN OBSIDIAN MYSTERY

OBSIDIAN

Published by New American Library, a division of
Penguin Group (USA) Inc., 375 Hudson Street,
New York, New York 10014, USA
Penguin Group (Canada), 90 Eglinton Avenue East, Suite 700, Toronto,
Ontario M4P 2Y3, Canada (a division of Pearson Penguin Canada Inc.)
Penguin Books Ltd., 80 Strand, London WC2R 0RL, England
Penguin Ireland, 25 St. Stephen's Green, Dublin 2,
Ireland (a division of Penguin Books Ltd.)
Penguin Group (Australia), 250 Camberwell Road, Camberwell, Victoria 3124,
Australia (a division of Pearson Australia Group Pty. Ltd.)
Penguin Books India Pvt. Ltd., 11 Community Centre, Panchsheel Park,
New Delhi – 110 017, India
Penguin Group (NZ), 67 Apollo Drive, Rosedale, North Shore 0632,
New Zealand (a division of Pearson New Zealand Ltd.)
Penguin Books (South Africa) (Pty.) Ltd., 24 Sturdee Avenue,
Rosebank, Johannesburg 2196, South Africa

Penguin Books Ltd., Registered Offices:
80 Strand, London WC2R 0RL, England

First published by Obsidian, an imprint of New American Library,
a division of Penguin Group (USA) Inc.

First Printing, February 2010
10 9 8 7 6 5 4 3 2 1

Praise for
Homicide in Hardcover

"This first in a new series is going to launch Carlisle to a bestselling position and have readers looking forward to the next installment of delightfully eccentric characters, droll dialogue, and a meticulously planned crime. Bibliophile heroine Brooklyn Wainwright is brilliant, feisty, and funny."   —*Romantic Times*

"Let's just say it up front—I really enjoyed this book. For once I am very happy this is part of a series because I want more. This book is unusual in that it has both a strong mystery *and* unique, well-created characters.... Thank goodness for Kate Carlisle."   —Front Street Reviews

"Kate Carlisle. Remember that name. I have the feeling you'll be seeing it a lot in years to come. Carlisle bursts onto the publication scene with ... a bibliophile mystery that kicks off what I hope will be a very long-running series."   —Romance Novel TV

"I found Brooklyn to be an engaging character to follow and I'm looking forward to her next adventure, which, I suspect, may take place in Edinburgh. Don't miss this delightful debut. *Recommended*."
                                  —I Love a Mystery newsletter

"The bare bones of the book are quite good and the story is pleasantly readable.... The premise was interesting. Bookbinding and restoration are a new path in the glutted concept-cozy genre." —Reviewing the Evidence

"A fun, fast-paced mystery that is laugh-out-loud funny. Even better, it keeps you guessing to the very end. Sure to be one of the best books of the year."
        —Susan Mallery, *New York Times* bestselling author
                                                    of *Sunset Bay*

continued ...

This book is dedicated to my mother, Patricia Campbell Beaver, whose good humor and love of life have always inspired me. I love you, Mom.

Acknowledgments

Heartfelt thanks to Maureen Child for great advice, fabulous ideas and unflagging support, and to Susan Mallery for her plotting genius and wise counsel. Thanks also to Christine Rimmer and Teresa Southwick, all part of the most amazing plot group ever. Gracias, my friends. Drinks are on me!

Once again, I am amazed and inspired by book artist Wendy Poma, who has the lovely ability to make an esoteric art seem approachable and downright fun.

Many thanks to my literary agent, Christina Hogrebe of the Jane Rotrosen Agency, whose intelligence, charm and enthusiasm for my work make me the envy of all my friends.

I am so grateful to my new editor, the extraordinary Ellen Edwards, for taking Brooklyn—and me—under her wing. Thank you! Thanks, as well, to everyone at NAL who worked so hard to help Brooklyn hit it out of the park her first time up at bat.

I'm also indebted to P. J. Nunn and Breakthrough Promotions for helping to put this newbie author on the map. You are the best!

To the bookbinders, librarians and readers who have let me know how much they love Brooklyn, your support means so much to me.

To the Banditas, y'all rock!

Finally, a big, fat thank-you to my darling husband, Don, who makes me laugh and believes in me, always.

Chapter 1

If my life were a book, I would have masking tape holding my hinges together. My pages would be loose, my edges tattered and my boards exposed, the front flyleaf torn and the leather mottled and moth-eaten. I'd have to take myself apart and put myself back together, as any good book restoration expert would do.

I had just finished my first glass of India Pale Ale in the pub of the Edinburgh hotel I'd checked into an hour earlier, and it seemed as good a time as any to throw myself a pity party and reflect on the strange turns my life had taken recently. I wasn't happy about it. I needed to get back on track. And it occurred to me, why not treat myself as I would a damaged book? Study the twists and turns and knots and smudges that had left me short-tempered and befuddled. And threadbare. Then I could dust off my pages, resew the torn folds, trim the frays and smooth out the dents. And be my happy self again. Trust me, nobody liked a grumpy bookbinder.

"You look like you could use another, love, and quickly," the waitress said, placing a second glass of ale on the table to replace the one I'd just swilled.

Great. Just in case I'd imagined things were okay with me, a kind stranger was here to assure me that I was indeed a total mess.

I smiled at her, an older woman with short, curly gray hair and a teasing grin, and said lightly, "I don't look that bad, do I?"

She studied me for a moment. "Aye, you do, love. And for that, the IPA's on the house."

"Thanks a lot," I said with a rueful laugh, then explained, "It's just jet lag. I'll be fine in twenty-four hours."

She nodded judiciously. "Of course it's jet lag if you say so." Her eyes narrowed as she studied me. "But my woman's intuition thinks 'tis a man you're mulling over."

I laughed a bit desperately. "Truly, I'm not."

She raised an eyebrow. "Then you'll be returning the IPA?"

"No." I gripped the beer I'd been craving for the last six hours of my transatlantic flight. "No, I'm sorry. I'm going to need this."

Her eyes twinkled gaily. "Aye, I knew it." She tapped the side of her head. "Can't another woman tell when one of her ilk is suffering, then? And isn't it always about a man. Damn their skins!"

"Order up, Mary!" the bartender shouted.

"Haud yer wheesht!" she yelled over her shoulder, then smiled sweetly at me. "Enjoy your luncheon and take good care." She turned and marched to the bar, where she bared her teeth at the burly bartender as she collected a tray of drinks.

I wasn't an expert in the Scottish dialect, but I believed she'd just suggested to her boss that he shove a sock in his piehole.

I chuckled as I checked my wristwatch, then paid the bill. Barely an hour in Edinburgh and I'd fallen in love with the people all over again.

I'd arrived at the Royal Thistle Hotel after flying

nonstop from San Francisco to London, then catching a quick shuttle flight north. I'd checked in, unpacked my bags and headed straight for the hotel pub to grab a sandwich and a beer. Now I was ready for a brisk walk out in the cold March air. In travel, I believed in hitting the ground running.

I was here to attend the annual Edinburgh Book Fair and was looking forward to visiting with friends and colleagues I hadn't seen in a while. I would be giving a few workshops, and there would be thousands of beautiful books and fine bindings to study and drool over. With any luck, I'd find one or two bargains to snag for my very own. I expected lots of good conversation and much pub crawling in one of the most delightful cities on the planet.

I should've been elated. Instead, I was sad and feeling a little overwhelmed, knowing that Abraham Karastovsky, the man who first taught me bookbinding years ago, the man I'd worked with most of my life and always considered a mix of beloved uncle and benevolent dictator, wouldn't be in Edinburgh with me.

I'd known him since I was eight years old, when he'd repaired a favorite book my brothers had ruined. Fascinated with what he'd done, I'd gone back every day to watch him work in his small bindery, pestering him so much that he'd finally brought me on as his apprentice.

Now Abraham was gone, senselessly murdered last month, and I felt an emptiness I'd never experienced before. It didn't help that the man had left me the lion's share of his estate, some six million dollars, give or take a million. And while it gave me a secret thrill to know that in his will, he'd called me the daughter of his heart, I hated that I'd benefited so greatly from his death. After all, I was now rich beyond my wildest dreams and all it had cost was Abraham's life.

"Brooklyn?"

I whipped around, then jumped up when I spied an old friend walking briskly toward me. "Helen!"

Helen Chin grinned as she glided confidently through the bar, her glossy black hair cut in a short, sassy bob. She'd always been demure and soft-spoken, a brilliant, petite Asian woman with lustrous long hair and a shy smile. The haircut and the confidence were major changes since the last time I saw her. That had to have been over two years ago, when we'd both taught spring classes in Lyon, France, at the Institut d'Histoire du Livre. But we'd first met and bonded while teaching summer courses at the University of Texas at Austin. A hurricane had come through, blowing the roof off the dormitory we were staying in. Nothing forges a friendship better than sharing trail mix and toothpaste while sleeping on cots in a crowded, smelly gymnasium for a week.

I gave her a tight hug. She felt thinner than I remembered.

"I saw your name in the program," she said, and clasped my arms with both hands. "I'm so glad you're here."

"I wouldn't miss it." I took a closer look at her, checking out the new hairstyle, her pretty red jacket, black pants and shiny black shoes. "You look amazing, and you've lost weight. Are you moonlighting as a supermodel?"

"Oh, right," she said with a laugh.

"Seriously, you look great."

"Well, you don't have to sound so surprised," she said lightly, but I could sense the defensiveness underneath.

"Silly," I said, avoiding the bait as I hugged her again. I casually looked around. "So where's Martin?"

She waved her hand dismissively. "He's here somewhere, but it doesn't matter. I might as well tell you I've filed for divorce."

I hoped my eyes weren't bugging out of my head as I said, "No way! I'm so sorry."

She gave me a pointed look. "Oh, please." Then she slipped her arm through mine and we walked through the lobby. "You're not sorry and neither am I."

"How's Martin taking it?"

"Not well, as you might expect." She shook her head in disgust. "He was as big a jerk as everyone said, and I'm thrilled to be rid of him."

I squeezed her arm. "Okay. Then I'm doubly happy for you and not sorry at all."

Helen was right. I'd never liked Martin Warrington, and I wasn't the only one. When she'd announced her engagement in Lyon, I hadn't understood how such a smart woman could marry such an annoying man. Then I figured, with my own stellar record of bad choices and broken engagements, I was hardly one to criticize.

At the time, I was more sorry for myself than for her, because I knew we wouldn't be able to be friends once she married Martin. He didn't like me any more than I liked him, probably because I'd tried to talk Helen out of marrying him and he'd caught wind of it.

"So where have you been hiding?" I asked. "I didn't see you in Lisbon."

"Martin didn't like me attending the book fairs." She shook her head in irritation. "He said I flirted too much."

Translation: Helen was a nice person; Martin was a toad.

"Did you happen to mention that attending book fairs is part of your job?"

"Don't get me started," she said, puffing out a breath. "I lost ten pounds worrying about it but came to realize there's no making sense of it. Let's just say I was a moron to put up with it as long as I did. And now I'm determined to have a fabulous time while I'm here."

"Good." I hugged her again. "I've missed you."

"I've missed you, too." She giggled. "And I have so much to tell you."

"Really? Let's hear it. What's going on with you?"

"You won't believe it," she said, moving closer to whisper in my ear. "I'm in love."

"What?"

"Shhh!" She waved her hand at me. "Nobody knows. We've kept it very hush-hush. It's crazy, but I've never been so happy."

She did look happy, and I was glad for her. Trust me. Anyone who had put up with Martin all this time deserved to be happy.

"Okay, we definitely have to talk," I said, clutching her arm. "We can go up to my room. I'll order drinks."

"I can't," she said, pouting. "I'm off to meet a client. But look, a bunch of us are doing the ghost tour later. Join us. It'll be a hoot. We can have a drink afterward, just you and me, and catch up."

I caught someone moving in my peripheral vision.

"Hello, Martin," I said loudly to alert Helen. He'd literally sneaked up on us, probably to overhear our conversation. What a creep. I hoped he hadn't heard our plans, because I refused to spend any more time with him than was absolutely necessary.

"Hello, Brooklyn," he said, giving me a smile I didn't trust for a second.

I supposed some women would consider him handsome. He was tall and lean and wore white linen pants with a beige linen jacket. He looked elegantly rumpled, with boyish blond good looks and an easy grin. He owned a bookstore somewhere in London, and I always figured he had some family money tucked away. He was feckless and disdainful of most of humanity. I'd seen the way he treated Helen and I didn't like it. I didn't like him.

The smile disappeared as he confronted Helen. "I told you I'd meet you on the conference level."

"And I told you I'd try to make it but probably wouldn't be able to," Helen said defiantly.

"We have to talk now." He pushed up the sleeves of his linen jacket.

"I'm off to meet a client," she said as she glanced at her wristwatch. "I can try to see you at two thirty."

He tapped his elegantly shod foot as red blotches of annoyance cropped up on his cheeks. He shot a quick glance at me, then said to Helen, "I'm meeting with the president of King's College at two and will be tied up all afternoon."

Well, la-di-da. Was he trying to impress me?

"I'm sorry, Martin," she said, but she didn't sound at all remorseful. "Maybe tomorrow."

His face puckered up as though he'd bitten into a lemon; then he flashed me a venomous look as if it were my fault his wife was insolent. "I can see you're in a mood. I'll speak with you later this afternoon."

We both watched him stalk away.

"Gosh, I've put you in a mood," I said, using air quotes as I tried to lighten the moment. "Sorry."

"Yes, it's all your fault." She shook her head and tried to laugh. "What a pill."

"You handled him well."

"I've had some practice," she said. "He makes it hard to be nice. Now, where were we? Oh, the ghost tour. Please say you'll come?"

"Definitely. It sounds like fun."

"Wonderful. I'll add your name to the reservations."

"Great." We arranged a time and place to meet. Then she gave me a hug and took off, leaving me with a decision to make. It would be smart to take a nap, because I was starting to feel dizzy and sleep deprived, but I wanted to see and breathe in a bit of the city first.

I headed for the wide double doors but spied a sundries store tucked into the far corner of the lobby. I made the detour, walked in and found a candy bar for sustenance and a pack of cinnamon gum for clean breath. As I stepped up to the counter to pay, a tall, heavyset man pushed me aside, slapping a newspaper on the counter and reaching in his pocket for change.

"Hey!"

He ignored me completely as he fished for coins.

I knew him. Perry McDougall, a pompous ass who thought he was smarter and better than everyone on the planet. Perry was one of Abraham's contemporaries. He owned a rare-book store in Glasgow and fancied himself a scholar, specializing in Scottish history and the Georgian and Regency periods of the British monarchy. He'd always been a rude, angry man. Guess that hadn't changed.

"Excuse me," I said, getting more annoyed by the second. He hadn't even glanced at me. In Perry's world, only Perry mattered.

He took his change and folded the paper under his arm.

"I said excuse me," I said more loudly. "You need to learn to wait your turn."

He turned and sniffed at me. "I beg your pardon?"

"You can beg all you want, but it doesn't mean you get to push people out of the way who were here first."

He looked at me as if I'd soiled his shoes. "What are you raving on about, you silly wench?"

Blame the two beers and an extreme case of jet lag, but I moved up close to him and said, "I'll show you raving, pal." Then, without thinking, I grabbed his newspaper and waved it at his face.

He recoiled and I realized I'd lost what was left of my mind.

"Sorry," I said, and handed his paper back to him.

His mouth opened and closed like a trout's, but he finally said, "You're a crazed bitch."

"Oh, I'm a bitch because rude people piss me off? At least I said I was sorry. But not you. You're just a big bully." I slammed a pound note on the counter to cover the cost of the gum, the chocolate and the hissy fit, and walked out.

"I know you!" he shouted after me. "You worked with Karastovsky. I'll make sure you never work again, missy."

Oh, crap. I rushed across the lobby and escaped through the automatic doors. What was wrong with me? I never confronted people. Was this part of my new weirdness? Was I going to turn into a crazy old crone and mutter to myself? Would I scare small children wherever I went?

Maybe.

But as I walked down the short drive in front of the hotel, I smiled and started to laugh. It felt good to yell at that rude bastard. And why was standing up for myself such a bad thing? As far as his warning shot went, he had no power over who hired me. Still, it gave me a chill to think he would try to threaten my career. I pulled my jacket tighter and raised the collar as a brisk wind blew across my neck.

I forced all thoughts of rude Perry out of my head so I could appreciate one of my favorite places in the world. As I approached the Royal Mile, I drew in the fresh air of Edinburgh and got my first real up-close taste of the ancient city.

The Royal Thistle Hotel was perched on a slope half a block down from St. Giles' Cathedral in the heart of the Royal Mile. The afternoon air was cold and clear, the sky a deep blue with the occasional white puff of cloud. It was a perfect day for a solitary stroll. I turned left toward Edinburgh Castle, breathing in the scents and absorbing the sounds. I stared at the proliferation of souvenir shops selling everything from tartans and kilts to whisky, to ashtrays and coasters and shot glasses, to cashmere shawls and fisherman knit sweaters.

As I walked along the smooth stone sidewalk, I tried to tune out my angry run-ins with both Perry and Martin. I stared at the window display at the Scotch Whisky Heritage Centre and laughed at myself for thinking I could actually handle a taste of Scotch right now, with jet lag tugging at me. I'd fall flat on my face and never make it back to the hotel. I made a mental note to stop back here in a day or so. I didn't usually drink Scotch, but when in Scotland, a wee dram seemed the way to go.

It sounded as if I had an addictive personality, and I was okay with that. The thing was, I could just as likely be swayed by a piece of chocolate or a beautiful book or a twice-baked potato as I was by a shot of good Scotch. The only obsession I didn't seem to possess was the shopping gene, much to the dismay of my best friend, Robin Tully.

Thinking of Robin made me smile, as I was reminded that she would be here tomorrow to lead a small group on a tour of Scotland. Besides being a talented sculptor, Robin owned a small travel company called Wisdom Quest. Most of her clients were Fellowship friends who sought out sacred places throughout the world where they could soak up the mysteries and magic while getting their auras polished and their portals tweaked.

The Fellowship—officially, the Fellowship for Spiritual Enlightenment and Higher Artistic Consciousness— was the commune in Sonoma County where my parents had raised me and my five siblings. It was where I first met Robin. It wasn't much of a commune anymore since its members had discovered capitalism and commerce in a big, fun way and become rich off the California wine boom. But everyone was still close and supported one another, as small town people tended to do.

I reached the fork at the top of the Royal Mile and crossed the cobblestone street to head up to the castle. I stopped and took a deep breath of clean air to clear away the prickly feelings. I gazed back at the picturesque, mile-long High Street that meandered down to the Palace of Holyroodhouse, the queen's official summer residence.

The city had changed in the three years since I'd been here. For one thing, there were more Starbucks now, including the one that shared the block with the venerable St. Giles' Cathedral. And the Royal Thistle Hotel had expanded recently to include a luxurious health spa—not that I was complaining about that. I just hoped my favorite pubs were still in business. I had my priorities, after all.

I took my time hiking up the last block toward the castle. Halfway there I stopped, distracted by one store window that displayed an astonishing jumble of tartan kilts and sporrans. For some reason, they reminded me of big, brash Abraham. The last time we'd attended the Edinburgh Book Fair together, he'd worn his full kilt ensemble to the Saturday-night gala. Much to the delight of the crowd, he'd danced the jig and felt so unfettered that he declared he was going to wear a skirt from then on.

I chuckled at the memory, then realized my eyes were moist. I had to breathe in some air as the full force of jet lag hit me—or maybe it was simply the acceptance that Abraham was truly gone. Either way, it was time for that nap.

Without warning I was grabbed from behind, lifted off the ground and twirled around.

I screamed and swore loudly at my assailant. Then I realized who it was and swore even more.

"Despite that mouth of yours, you're more beautiful than ever," he said.

"Kyle McVee, you idiot!" I cried, and hugged him hard.

"Ah, you've missed me," he crowed as he held me snugly in his arms.

"No, I didn't miss you," I said, burying my face in the crook of his delicious-smelling neck. "You're a cad and a rat fink, remember? The Bad Boy Bookseller of Belgravia. I curse your name every morning."

"I love you, too, my sweet," he said with a laugh. "Besides, I've mellowed."

"Really," I said.

"Yes, I'm quite housebroken these days, not a rat at all." He kissed me full on the lips. "Mm, you've still got the sexiest mouth on four continents."

"Oh, stop it." I stood back and looked at the man who'd broken my heart three—or was it four?—years ago. My breath almost caught as I stared. Kyle McVee was simply beautiful. Tall, elegant, with a wicked grin and dark eyes that sparkled with charm and humor, he had the look of an angel but was an unapologetic devil through and through. He was yet another living example of my pitiful taste in men.

Maybe I did have a sad habit of picking the most unsuitable men, but I certainly chose the prettiest ones.

"It's wonderful to see you," he said, nuzzling my neck. "Mmm, and you smell good enough to eat. Let's go back to my hotel room, what do you say?"

"In your dreams," I said with a laugh. "How dare you proposition me in the middle of the street?"

"Because you're still a darling girl," he said, then backed up and looked me over.

I straightened my shirt and jacket and tried to find

some trace of decorum, but it was useless. My cheeks heated up at his blatant perusal. I tried to remind myself that if I'd been so *darling*, why had he felt so compelled to cheat on me more than once during the six months we dated while I lived in London? A simple question.

I knew the answer: He couldn't help himself. Kyle came from money, lots of money. Among other things, his family owned a respected London book publishing company. He had a collection of rare books that matched any museum collection in the world. He enjoyed the business of buying and selling and trading, and especially enjoyed the bed-hopping and screwing around that came with being the prettiest, wealthiest man in a business that catered to smart, wealthy people.

"What are you up to?" he asked.

"I was enjoying a quiet walk to the castle."

"How boring," he said, pulling me across the street. "Join me at the pub and we'll have a snug chat."

"Hmm. Thanks, but no."

"Come on, babe. It's been too long. We've got catching up to do."

"Don't you have someone else to torment?"

"There's no one more fun to torment than you."

"Oh, don't I feel special," I said.

He leaned closer. "Besides, I've something to show you that'll knock your socks off."

"I've already seen it," I said dryly.

His eyes widened. "Minx! Damn it! I insist we skip the pub and go back to my room."

"You haven't changed," I said, reluctantly enjoying his silliness.

"Why should I?" he said with a wink.

I laughed again and realized I'd missed him. He'd always been a relentless charmer. It had been my mistake for thinking he'd taken our relationship seriously, my mistake to allow the pain to overwhelm me. I'd felt so betrayed, it had taken me months to get over it. And now, gazing up at him, trying to recall the pain and anger, I couldn't. Truth be told, he was just too adorable to hate.

"Come on, now," he said, pulling me closer to the pub's doorway. "I really do have something to show you. It's fate that I stumbled upon you here."

"All right," I said, as if it mattered what I thought, since we were halfway inside the Ensign Ewart pub.

I'd been inside the pub before, three years ago. It was a serious drinking spot for locals who showed up to enjoy the traditional music the bar featured several nights a week. Despite its location directly next door to the castle, the pub didn't cater to tourists, much to the dismay of anyone who might wander in after a day of sightseeing and expect a charming Scots welcome.

The room was relatively small and cozy, with dark wood posts and beams across the low, flat ceiling. Kyle ordered two pints at the bar, and we found a quiet corner nook and sat side by side. Kyle removed his gray cashmere sports jacket and laid it on the bench next to him.

I stared at the pint. "I should've had a Pepsi."

"Heresy," he said.

"Jet lag's catching up to me," I explained as I settled into the small space. "But you're right. It would be a waste to drink anything but beer in a place like this."

"That's my little soldier."

"So what did you want to show me?"

"Straight to business then," Kyle said, and pulled a small, wrapped parcel from his satchel. "I need your expertise."

He handed me the item and I held it, felt it, determining its size, weight and shape without opening it.

"I'd say it's a book." I handed it back to him.

"Brilliant, darling, but I'm serious. I want you to look at it."

I unwrapped the brown paper to find a small book covered in tissue. I peeled back the fragile paper and stared at the perfect little book. The leather cover was red goatskin, otherwise known as morocco, heavily gilded and well preserved. It felt warm in my hand as I weighed it, then turned it to study the words on the spine. *Love Poems to a Flaxen'd Quean* by Robert Burns.

"Beautiful," I murmured.

The front cover was dominated by a gold Scottish wheel surrounded on four sides by Solomon's seals, or pentagrams, thought to ward off the powers of evil. Gilded thistle, holly berries and rose vines made up the graceful border around the edges.

"Cathcart?" I wondered aloud, turning the book in my hand.

"Oh, well-done," Kyle said, sitting back.

It was an easy guess. The sheer overabundance of gilding, together with the combination of Scottish wheel, pentagrams, thistle and holly, were the distinctive markings of William Cathcart, an illustrious eighteenth-century Edinburgh publisher and bookbinder.

I took a sip of beer, then put the glass on the table and returned to the book, carefully opening to the title page. It was hand-dated 1786. On the flyleaf was an inscription, faded and barely legible, but I could make out the words: *Many thanks and cheers to my friend and comrade William.* It was signed by Robert Burns.

Robert Burns?

I looked at Kyle. "Is this a joke?"

"No," he said lightly, but his lips had thinned and his eyes were narrow. "It's not a joke. It's real. But that's not for me to say. I need you to authenticate it."

"Me? I can't."

"Of course you can," he said brusquely. "You're a leading authority on book fraud. You uncovered that scam with the fake Steinbeck. Your reputation is—"

"No, no," I said quickly. "I mean, I would need a laboratory to test the ink and the binding, the underpinnings. And my tools. I brought my travel tools but I don't have everything here. I don't think . . ."

"I can set you up somewhere. Could you do it?"

I stared at the book again. "Well, of course. Except for the signature. You'd need a lab to test the ink and a historian and a handwriting expert and—"

"I'll pay you, of course."

"Of course." I nodded absently. My mind was already considering the practicalities of working in a strange lab in another country. I'd done it before. The details were no big deal. All that mattered was getting answers, and those could be found only inside this book. And oh, how I was tempted. Judging by his expression, the man sitting next to me knew it, too.

Kyle sipped his beer in moody silence while I studied the rare treasure in my hand. Even without the inscription of possibly the most famous Scottish poet who ever lived, this book was an excellent example of William Cathcart's genius. The condition was mint, although the outer joints were slightly rubbed and the gilding was pale along the spine.

"If that signature is real, this should be in a museum," I said, handing the book back to him.

"No, no, you hold on to it," he said. "Maybe you'll have a chance to study it more."

I gladly held on to the book. "Where did you get it?"

He exhaled heavily. "Cathcart is an ancestor. The book belongs to my family. Legend has it he created only ten copies of this edition, so it's rare indeed."

"Indeed," I echoed.

"This is the only one inscribed, that I'm aware of." He chewed on his bottom lip.

"What else?"

He eyed me, then admitted, "It's not just the book itself that concerns me."

I sat back. "What do you mean?"

He took the book from me and opened it to the text. "I told you only ten of this edition were published. The others have disappeared. Believe me, I've searched high and low, asked around, advertised."

"They probably went into private collections."

"Maybe." He frowned.

"What's wrong?"

"It's the poems themselves." He sighed. "There are poems in this book that I've never seen published anywhere else. And if you Google the book's title, it doesn't show up at all."

It was my turn to frown. "That can't be true."

"Look." He thumbed through to a particular page and held it open for me to see. "To this day, I can't find a trace of this poem in any other edition. And you know as well as I that books of poetry by Robert Burns are ubiquitous in Britain. They're everywhere. But not this one."

For the first time, I looked beyond the title page and found that although the spine was maybe an inch thick, there were only ten or twelve poems in the whole book. Each heavy page contained a few lines each. I began to read the first one, entitled "I've Loved a Flaxen'd Quean." I'd read Robert Burns before and knew his words could get bawdy, but I was frankly surprised by the highly erotic images Burns inspired in this particular poem, seemingly devoted to a beauty named Sophie. At least, that was what I could glean from the heavy Scots dialect.

"It's a beautiful book," I said. "But I'd need a glossary to understand all the words."

He chuckled. "It's impossible to read without one."

"It's all pretty stirring stuff, though. He must've loved her very much."

"Ah, yes, and that's the problem."

"Why?" I snickered. "Was she really a queen?"

"Funny you should ask." He took a long sip of beer before continuing. "In this case, the word *quean* is old Scots dialect, meaning a pretty young girl. But there were rumors, frantically quashed, naturally, that Robbie Burns had a sizzling affair with Princess Augusta Sophia, the daughter of George the Third."

"Sounds exciting."

"Doesn't it just," he said wryly. "According to some accounts, the princess spent the season in Edinburgh in 1785, then returned to London and, shortly thereafter, gave birth to a son."

"Okay, wait, jet lag must be catching up to me." I took a sip of beer as though it would help me concentrate. "Are you seriously talking about George the Third, *The Madness of King George* George? That George?"

"That's the one."

"You're saying his daughter had an affair with Robert Burns?"

"So it would seem."

I thought about it, then nodded. "So what's the problem?"

"What's the—" he shouted, then hushed himself. "We're talking about Robert Burns, for God's sake. They called him Rab the Ranter. He was a poor farmer and a troublemaker, and he appealed to the same class of people. He wrote a poem called 'The Fornicator.' Another he devoted 'To a Louse.' He would've been booted out of Holyrood on his ass."

I waited for his rant to finish, then said, "So you're saying he didn't have an affair with the princess?"

"No," he whispered. "I'm saying he did and the news was squelched at the highest levels of power."

I squinted at him. "I admit I'm a little slow today, but are you implying that the monarchy frowned on the bad boy of Scotland diddling the pure English rose?"

He laughed. "Exactly. It's highly titillating stuff."

"Especially in that time." I sat back. "The English must've hated that rumor."

"Oh, indeed, because they made sure there was never a whisper of controversy."

"Really?" I turned the book in my hand. "Well, that's fun, isn't it?"

"That's one way to put it." He pointed to the book. "I'll guarantee they won't be happy to know this book is still in circulation."

"But that's silly. Who cares?"

He sat back with his pint. "Ah, my naive Yankee love."

"You're saying they would care?"

"Most greatly."

"Two hundred years later? Why?"

"It's a stain on the monarchy. If nothing else, it's bad PR."

"Well, I understand that," I said, nodding. "So you think they hushed it up? Paid Burns to stay away?"

"At the very least."

"And at the most?"

He ran his finger dramatically across his neck.

I slapped his knee. "That's ridiculous." I opened the book, felt the paper. The pub was too dark to study it closely, so I couldn't conclude much. And before I got too wrapped up in the book and the history, I had to remind myself that Kyle had been known to flirt with the truth in more than just his love life. He could flatter and cajole and twist the truth if it meant making an extra buck in bookselling, as well. I wanted more information before I would agree to work on the book.

"So who's 'they'?" I asked finally.

He folded his arms across his chest. "My guess would be Queen Charlotte, George's wife. History has it that she watched those princesses like a mother hen."

"So God forbid one of her darlings might bring home a scruffy Scottish lad who called himself a poet."

"Exactly."

"And this book . . ."

"Could blow the lid open."

I sighed. "And you figured I'm always up for bringing shame and embarrassment to the British royal family."

"It's what makes you my favorite girl."

"Yeah, right," I said. "Look, Kyle, I don't know squat about Robert Burns or the history of that era. I can help you authenticate the book itself, verify that it's a genuine Cathcart, maybe even find a way to validate the inscription. But you're on your own as far as the content goes."

"I thought as much." He downed the last of his pint, took the book from me and studied it. "I just wanted you to be aware of what you're getting yourself into if you agree to help me with this project."

I rubbed my forehead, trying to brush away the fuzzies from my brain. "What's that supposed to mean?"

He shrugged. "There may be some people who would rather the book weren't authenticated."

I leaned back to look at him more carefully. "You're saying they wouldn't want the specific mythology of the book to be known."

"*Exactement*," he said in a perfect French accent, then signaled the barmaid over to order another round.

"None for me," I said.

"You're sure?" Kyle asked.

"Absolutely." When the barmaid left, I wrapped the book back in the tissue paper and slipped it into my purse. "I guess I should ask how much trouble I could get into over this book."

His mouth curved in a frown. "I hope you won't live to regret that question."

"I was kidding," I said, "but you're not. What is it?"

He waved off my concern but I knew him, knew he was hiding something.

"What are you not telling me?" I asked.

He pursed his lips. "I suppose there is a bit more to the story."

I sat back with a thud. "You're killing me."

"Yes, well, this is where it gets a bit sticky."

"Sticky?" All sorts of alarms went off in my foggy brain. "Okay, spill it."

Kyle avoided eye contact by grabbing my hand and playing with my fingers. "I was thinking of presenting a paper on the book this week."

"That's cool." I nodded encouragingly. "I'll try to be there."

The barmaid brought his pint and he took it eagerly. After a long drink, he said, "I'm not doing it."

"But this would make an awesome presentation."

"I thought so, too," he said. "But it seems someone disagrees."

"Who?"

"I've no idea. But since I first mentioned the book, I've received a number of strange phone calls and several poison-pen letters."

"Poison-pen letters? How weird."

"Yes, quite." He glanced anxiously around the pub. "Some are fairly brutal, in fact. You might even say life threatening."

"Oh, my God." I grabbed hold of his fidgety hands. "Did you show them to the police?"

"No." He hesitated, then added, "I threw them away."

"Kyle!"

He held up his hand to stop me from saying more. "I know it was stupid, but I figured it was all a sick joke." He chuckled without mirth. "But then yesterday . . ." He shook his head.

The fact that he'd actually bothered to call the police was alarming in and of itself. "What, Kyle? What happened yesterday?"

His smile was nearly apologetic. "Seems someone tried to kill me."

Chapter 2

"That's not one bit funny."

"Tell me about it," Kyle muttered.

I rubbed his arm consolingly, hoping to get him to spill the whole story. Kyle had a tendency to dole out information in bits and pieces, as control freaks often did. I could relate. "What happened?"

He breathed in deeply, as though the extra air might give him courage. "I was crossing the street in front of the hotel. There was no traffic, and suddenly this car gunned its engine and aimed straight for me. I barely made it back to the sidewalk when the driver veered the car right at me. I knew I was a dead man. But then he swerved back and took off."

"I don't suppose you could see who was driving."

"No." Frustrated, he raked his hand through his hair.

"What kind of car?"

"A Mercedes. Big. Probably S-Class. Black, with darkened windows. The hotel uses them to chauffeur people in from the airport."

"Someone might've stolen it from the hotel," I murmured.

"Quite possibly."

"So it would be impossible to track down."

"Exactly," he said, slumping back against the padded banquette.

"And you talked to the police."

"They can't do anything." He tapped his fingers on the table. "One of the valets saw everything, thank God. He was more shaken than I was. He called the cops and told them as much as he knew, which was about as much as I knew."

"Did you tell them about the book?"

He snorted in disgust. "Oh, that'll go over well. Someone's trying to kill me because I dared suggest that Rabbie Burns shagged a Sassenach princess back in the day. I'd be laughed out of the city."

"What did you say? Saucy what?"

He chuckled. "Sassenach. It's what the Scots call the English when they're riled up. It's from the word *Saxon*, I believe."

"Saxon? Like the ancient Saxons?"

"That's right."

"Wow, some people know how to hold a grudge."

"We British seem to excel at it," he said.

I shifted in my seat to face him. "Okay, so the police don't know about the book. Now, what if this whole thing with the car was just a mistake? Maybe they accidentally hit the gas instead of the brake. It happens."

"You're suggesting coincidence?"

I shrugged helplessly.

"So I just happened to discuss this admittedly controversial book with a few scholarly experts, and within hours, someone happens to aim his car at me? Oh, I like that."

I smacked his knee again. "Maybe you pissed someone off for a different reason. Are you sleeping with someone's wife? Did you cheat on your taxes?"

"Now you're just trying to make me feel better."

I laughed, as he'd expected me to.

He gulped the last of his beer. "Perhaps walking around with this book in my bag is making me paranoid."

"Not to worry," I said. "Because now it's in *my* bag." As soon as the words left my mouth I could feel the paranoia shifting from his shoulders to mine.

He smacked his forehead. "That was shortsighted of me. I don't want to put you in any danger. Give it back."

"No, no," I said, shaking off my anxiety. "I'm not worried. No one knows I have it, right? It's you I'm concerned about."

"Thank you, darling," he said, squeezing my hand before letting it go. "But it's not necessary. I'll be careful."

"You'd better be."

The bartender walked over and asked if he could refill our drinks. Kyle ordered a third pint. I passed.

"Suppose we go at this from another angle," I said when the bartender left. "Who are these scholarly experts you discussed the book with?"

"I've shown it to only three people. Perry McDougall was the first."

"Perry?" The guy who'd cut me off in the store. "Why'd you show it to Perry?"

He was taken aback by my antipathy. "Because he's a scholarly expert," he said defensively. "If anyone can verify such rumors, it would be Perry."

"But he's such a jerk." I briefly explained my run-in with Perry at the hotel store.

"I'm sorry," he said, and gave me a quick hug. "I suppose he is a bit of a boor, but he's an expert in the field. And he and I get along well. Or we used to, before this happened."

"Why? What did he say?"

He sighed. "He was outraged, insisted the book was blasphemous and a fake besides. He told me I'd better not show the book to anyone else or I'd find myself in more than a spot of trouble."

"So he threatened you." My eyes narrowed. "Now I wish I'd slugged him."

"There's my girl," he said with a grin, then waved my concerns aside. "That's just Perry. He tends to think the world revolves around him."

The bartender returned with Kyle's ale. Kyle thanked him and took a long sip.

"You honestly don't think Perry was threatening you?" I persisted.

"He's just Scottish," he explained.

"Unfair," I said with a laugh. "I've met plenty of happy Scotsmen. He's not one of them."

"True," Kyle said. "I've seen him go off on other people, but it was never like this. He turned purple, right before my eyes. Warned me that if I dared discuss the erotic poems or the Princess Augusta Sophia connection, there would be dire consequences."

"*Dire* consequences?"

"Yes. He didn't explain what he meant. Just, well, he threw me out of his room." Kyle looked more upset by this than by the attempt on his life. I understood his pain. He was considered the golden boy of the British book trade, slick and charming, accustomed to being adored by everyone.

"I'd like to know what he looks like when he's truly angry," I said. "Since he basically looks pissed off most of the time."

"It's not attractive," he muttered.

"But you don't think he was threatening you? Sounds like he was to me."

"Perry's volatile, but he's not generally murderous." He crossed his arms. "I knew the book would be controversial, but I imagined people would be excited, not furious. I just wanted to stir up some interest from a few key buyers. I certainly never expected to become a target."

"I say Perry is the most likely suspect."

He frowned thoughtfully, then threw his arm around me and rested his temple against mine. "Maybe I'm imagining the whole thing, Brooks."

"It's not your imagination that someone tried to run you down, Kyle," I said. "You have a witness. The hotel valet."

"True," he allowed.

I patted his chest companionably. "Now, who are the other two you showed the book to?"

A quiet trilling sound erupted from Kyle's jacket pocket. He looked disoriented for a second, then pulled away and quickly scrambled for his cell phone. "Yes, hello? No. Yes. Damn it. Fine. Right, five minutes." He hung up the phone and slid it back into his pocket.

"Everything okay?" I asked.

"Um, yes. No. Yes." He looked as confused as he sounded. He shook his head, glanced around the pub. "I'm being an ass. Sorry. I've got to run."

Kyle stood up, then leaned over and kissed me on both cheeks and stroked my hair. "You'll take care of yourself."

"I will, but—"

"And the book. Look after it for me."

"Of course. Maybe we can—"

"Yes," he said with conviction. "Yes, we can. I'll call your room later and we'll set up a time to talk some more. Love you, darling. Ta."

And with that, he rushed off, leaving me alone with the book and the tab.

On the way back to the hotel, I stopped at a bookstore and purchased a paperback copy of Robert Burns's selected poems, specifically because it included some history of the time and a glossary to help translate Burns's old Scottish dialect.

Next door was a convenience store, where I bought three bags of Cadbury Chocolate Buttons and two large bottles of water. As I walked back to the hotel, I thought about Kyle. The book fair women I knew had always called him the Bad Boy Bookseller, and yes, the moniker was completely deserved. He was charming and slick and he'd always managed to slip and slide through relationships and love affairs, leaving a trail of brokenhearted women in his wake. And yet, everyone loved him. It helped that he was gorgeous and wealthy.

But today I realized that while he still had that same charm about him, he was right to say that he'd mellowed a bit. I didn't know if it was because of the attempt on his life or if he was just growing up. Whatever it was, I liked it. I liked him. Then again, I didn't have to date him, did I?

Back at the hotel, I went straight to the front desk and asked for a safe-deposit box. Once Kyle's book was safely tucked away and I had the key zipped securely inside my purse, it was time to head for my room. I was beyond tired and starting to see double as I crossed the lobby and turned down the wide hall to the bank of elevators.

"Oh, no, they'll let any piece of trash in here these days."

I recognized that shrill, grating voice. Heat flared up my neck like a bad rash, and my stomach twisted in a knot as I turned.

"Minka," I said through clenched teeth.

Minka LaBoeuf, my archenemy and worst nightmare, approached me slowly, her hips gyrating alluringly—if you were a water buffalo. I grew concerned for the fragile antique furniture nearby. One wayward thrust of those hips could destroy any one of the elegant Georgian side tables that lined the wide hall.

Back in college she'd tried to incapacitate me by stabbing my hand with a skiving knife. She'd been a pain in my ass ever since.

Of all the hotels in all the world, she had to walk into mine.

"What are you doing here?" I asked before I could stop myself.

"Working," she said proudly. Her leopard-skin spandex top emphasized her hefty breasts along with several rolls of stomach fat. "For one of the most brilliant men in Scotland."

"A pimp?"

"Do you see me laughing?" she asked frostily. "You're not funny."

"You've never had a sense of humor," I said, pounding the button to hurry the elevator along.

"Perry McDougall is the top expert in Regency and Georgian—"

"Wait, you're working for Perry McDougall?"

"Yes," she said smugly, apparently mistaking my horror for admiration. "He specifically requested me to be his assistant this week."

I was speechless. Knowing Perry actually thought this Goth twit was capable of even a smidge of competence in the workplace lowered my estimation of Perry even further, if that was possible.

"Aren't you going to say anything?" she said.

"Wowie?"

She smiled tightly. "You're just jealous."

"Better not screw up," I said. "I've heard that Perry stuffs incompetent assistants into his haggis and eats them for breakfast."

"That's disgusting."

"I'm just telling you what I heard." The elevator doors opened and I gratefully walked inside alone.

"I'm warning you right now," she said, slapping her hand against the side of the door to keep it from closing. "Stay out of my way."

I held up both hands in surrender. "I'm trying, but you can't seem to let me go."

"Bitch," she said viciously.

"Ouch," I said as the doors closed. I couldn't believe I'd run into her before I'd had time to recover from jet lag. I sagged against the wall as the lift climbed to the third floor—second floor, to those in the UK—and dropped me off.

I'd requested the lowest floor available for two reasons. First, I could always take the stairs if the lifts were too busy, as they invariably were during a crowded event like the book festival. And second, living in San Francisco had given me a healthy respect for earthquakes. The last one I went through wasn't even that powerful, but my sixth-floor loft apartment had felt like it would topple over if the rumbling and shaking had lasted much longer. I had no idea when the last earthquake had hit Scotland, if ever, but I wasn't taking any chances.

A housekeeping cart was set up next door to my room and a young blond maid in uniform was knocking on the door.

"Housekeeping," she announced in a chirpy, high-pitched accent.

I was thankful she was turned away from me, because she seemed like the friendly sort and I was no longer capable of making small talk. I opened the door to my room, slipped the Do Not Disturb sign to the outside of the door, then shuffled inside, kicked off my shoes, set the alarm and was asleep before my head hit the pillow.

*   *   *

Four hours later, the alarm woke me up. I was disoriented and groggy but I knew I needed to get up right then or I'd sleep for another twenty-four hours. I hated jet lag, and the beers hadn't helped my cause, but if I had it to do over again, I would've imbibed anyway.

I turned the spigot in the shower and was shocked to see a healthy stream of water pour down. I'd been steeling myself for the usual dribs and drabs of British showers, but now I hopped in and almost sighed with pleasure. The warm water felt wonderful, and, unbidden, the events of much earlier that day flashed through my mind.

I'd boarded the plane in San Francisco and taken my seat in first class. I'd never flown in the first-class section before, so I'd felt a little self-conscious. But now that I had some extra money, thanks to Abraham, I'd decided to live large and upgrade.

Settling into the wide leather seat, I'd pulled a magazine out of my bag and shoved the bag under the seat in front of me. The cheerful flight attendant asked me if I would like coffee, tea, juice or champagne, plus a croissant or muffin. I placed my order for coffee with cream and she brought it in a real cup and saucer. With real cream in a porcelain creamer.

Then she handed me a menu and asked me to select my breakfast, which would be served once we were in the air.

Okay, I'll say it: First class is really nice. Besides all the amenities and great seats, the flight attendants are a lot perkier.

"Ah, you've beaten me to it, I see," said a man with a British accent. I would've known that smooth voice anywhere.

Derek Stone? Here? On my plane? Impossible.

I looked up and stared into his gorgeous blue-eyed gaze. I had to stifle a ridiculously immature sigh.

"Don't you look fresh and pretty?" he said. The simple words sounded unbelievably sexy when spoken in that debonair British accent of his. I'd managed to grow rather fond of that accent during Abraham's murder investigation. Despite the fact that Derek had first accused me of the crime, he'd changed his tune and we'd become quite friendly by the time the killer's identity was discovered.

"What in the hell are you doing here?" I said.

He grinned. "There's that little ray of sunshine I've missed so much."

I felt my cheeks redden. "Sorry, it's still a little early and you've caught me by surprise." To say the least.

"I know, so I forgive you your pique."

"Thank you, I think."

"You're welcome." He threw his coat over the seat, then opened his briefcase. "Won't we have a lovely flight together."

"You're sitting here?"

"I most certainly am," he said with an amused smile. He pulled a newspaper out of the briefcase, then stowed the case and his coat in the overhead luggage compartment and sat down next to me.

The flight attendant hurried over and Derek ordered coffee, which she brought immediately.

I continued to stare stupidly at him. Despite the aroma of freshly roasted coffee, it was Derek's scent that permeated my brain. I imagined a rain-washed forest mixed with spicy citrus and a hint of—oh, dear God—leather. Was I really going to have to fly halfway around the world with those smells assaulting me every time I inhaled? I wanted to bury my face in his soft wool sweater. He was the sexiest, most masculine creature I'd ever met. And the most annoying. What was wrong with me?

"Isn't this cozy?" he said, grinning as though he could read my admittedly transparent mind.

"You could've warned me we'd be on the same flight."

"And deny myself the pleasure of seeing your expression of stunned joy? Never."

"I plan to sleep for the next eight hours or so."

"Cozier and cozier," he murmured.

A few minutes later, the flight attendant cleared away the coffee service and the plane pulled away from the gate. Derek grabbed my hand and held it securely as we taxied down the runway.

"I'm not a nervous flier," I said.

He shifted closer so we were pressed shoulder-to-shoulder, then gazed into my eyes. "I am."

I shut off the shower and just as sternly shut off the memories. Grabbing a towel from the wonderfully warm towel rack, I dried off. I pulled a can of Pepsi from the minibar and popped it open, hoping the caffeine would help perk up my system. I blew my hair dry, put on some makeup and dressed for the chilly evening outdoors in warm tights, jeans, boots and my short down jacket.

I left my room and stepped into the empty lift to go downstairs. Despite much mental protesting, my recalcitrant mind dragged me back to earlier that day.

We landed at Heathrow and disembarked. Derek and I walked down the breezeway toward customs, holding hands. I was slightly disoriented from the flight but happy and laughing at his droll commentary. When we reached the long line, he wished me good luck at the book fair, then warmly kissed my cheek and said good-bye. A British citizen, he didn't have to wait in the long passport section with us poor tourists. I waved as he walked away, then watched him stop, think for a moment and turn back.

"This is unacceptable," he said as he came up close, tugged me even closer and kissed me for real. My brain shut down and my senses took over. All I could feel was heat, pressure, electricity. The kiss was hot, thorough, openmouthed. My heart stumbled in my chest as I dropped my bag and wrapped my arms around him.

I vaguely heard a passing woman whisper, "Oh, my."

"Damn it, I'll miss you," Derek muttered, his forehead pressed against mine.

"Mm." I was too stunned to say anything intelligible.

He gently ran his finger along my jaw, then chucked my chin. He grinned, kissed me once more, fast and hard and meticulously. Then he turned and left me for good. I watched him go, sighed a little, and picked up my bag and joined the line for customs, while he strolled down the European Union members' ramp and out of the airport.

I emerged a mere twenty minutes later and headed for the next terminal to catch the shuttle flight to Edinburgh.

Imagine my surprise when I saw Derek still waiting curbside forty or so yards away. I smiled with delight and hurried over to him, just as a dark-haired woman jumped out of a shiny new silver Jaguar and rushed to hug him. Derek laughed as he grabbed her and kissed her, then tossed his bag in the Jaguar's trunk. They chatted companion-

ably as the woman opened the rear door to allow
Derek to greet an adorable toddler who bore a
striking resemblance to him. Derek then helped
the woman into the car and jogged around to the
driver's side, jumped in and whisked his little family away.

The hotel elevator stopped and my memories jolted to
a halt. The doors opened but I had to take a minute to
breathe and settle myself. I refused to feel devastated
by Derek's betrayal, but I could go with livid. Or pissed
off, or furious, not to mention being completely embarrassed and annoyed with myself.

Stepping out of the elevator, I managed a few steps
but had to stop again. I leaned against the wall and tried
to find my composure.

This was me, facing the well-established fact that I
had lousy taste in men. My family was so right about
that. Maybe I would just hire a matchmaker or some
other third party to choose for me, since I was utterly incapable of making healthy choices. Or better yet, maybe
I'd give up men altogether. Who needed this kind of
grief?

Forcing a smile I didn't feel, I walked to the lobby.

"Brooklyn, here we are," Helen cried out gaily from
halfway across the large space. She was standing with
four other women and I recognized one, Kimberly, a
book history teacher we'd met in Lyon. We gave each
other hugs as Helen introduced the others. Then the
whole group walked out of the hotel and headed for the
High Street. Another group of six was already waiting in
front of St. Giles' for the ghost tour to begin.

A lanky young man wearing a garishly striped wool
scarf and matching skullcap introduced himself as Liam
and announced that he would be our guide for the evening. He began with a bit of the condensed history of how

Edinburgh was established and told us some cringeworthy facts about the place we'd be touring tonight, just a few hundred yards away down a narrow passageway between two tall buildings.

"Now gather close," Liam said, his tone turning somber. "Take a good, long look at your friends and loved ones here with you tonight. Study their faces, for you may not see them ever again once we've stirred up the ghosts of Mary King's Close."

Everyone laughed and he scowled. "'Tisn't a thing to scoff at. We've already had reports of a missing couple tonight."

Lost to a pub, no doubt, I told myself. In good humor, we all descended the steep, narrow steps of Mary King's Close. I shivered as we huddled around a narrow doorway while Liam fumbled for his keys. The thick wood door opened with an eerie screech and he led us into the bowels of an ancient building set against the slopes of the Old Town.

We walked single file down a dark, narrow hall, then through a low archway into a tiny room, maybe eight feet square. The only light came from Liam's dim flashlight, and we gathered close around him. He held the light under his chin so that his face was distorted and the shadow of his head was projected onto the low ceiling above him.

It was an old trick but effective. A few women giggled as Liam explained that this small space was once home to a family of six. He waved his flashlight at the far wall, where a narrow counter held a small bucket and various dry goods, indicating the family's kitchen area.

A female mannequin stood by the counter, dressed in what I assumed was typical servants' clothing in seventeenth-century Scotland. A roughly hewn wooden baby's cradle sat on the floor next to her feet.

I noticed one of the men in our group was too tall to

stand upright, and I was beginning to feel a bit claustro-phobic myself.

Liam turned and ducked his head to get through a small doorway that led down another passageway. As we followed, he told us that in 1645, after many years of people dumping raw human waste and sewage out the windows to trickle down the steep narrow stairways and collect in Nor' Loch at the bottom of the Old Town, bubonic plague finally hit Edinburgh.

His voice was grave as he related grisly tales of wealthy homeowners above stairs bricking off the lower floors, trapping and suffocating the sickly servants below in an attempt to stop the plague's spread.

"Thousands died throughout the city," he said dole-fully. "And ghosts still haunt the dark, cramped spaces, such as the one in which we stand tonight."

I shuddered as I ducked my head to enter yet an-other oppressively dark, airless room. Here, pallets were laid on the straw-strewn floor to indicate the family's cramped sleeping area. Two pint-sized mannequins dressed as children lay on the lumpy bedding. Liam ex-plained that the pallets were pulled up during the day and the space became the family's sitting room.

I heard something skitter across the floor and gasped.

"What was that?" a woman asked.

Somebody else whispered, "Shut up."

I wrapped my arms around my middle in an effort to bring back some warmth. My hands were as cold as ice cubes.

Liam aimed his flashlight around the space and I could see a rickety rocking chair near the compact hearth. Sit-ting in the rocking chair was a dummy dressed like a woman, holding an infant in her arms while her husband lay sleeping near the hearth.

The smell of mildew filled the air, and I couldn't

understand how anyone had managed to live in that cramped little room. My feet stuck to the moldy straw on the floor as Liam explained that the straw was used to soak up the moisture that seeped from the walls and low ceiling.

Fabulous. I was beginning to feel trapped, and was wondering if I was courageous enough to make my way back out to the street by myself, when Helen screamed.

I jumped. The shrill sound echoed off the thick walls and reverberated in my ears.

"What's wrong?" I asked, grabbing her arm.

But she couldn't stop screaming, so I shook her. Then another woman screamed.

"What the hell is wrong?" I shouted, then followed the direction of Helen's gaze. Liam's flashlight beam rested on the mannequin lying in the straw by the hearth.

But it wasn't a mannequin. I recognized the man's elegant gray cashmere jacket and the sweep of dark hair.

It was Kyle McVee. His head lay in a puddle of dark liquid, and I had no doubt it was blood. He was dead.

I let out my own piercing scream. The flashlight went off and the room was plunged into blackness.

Chapter 3

The room erupted into a chaotic mass of confused wails and more screaming. I felt sick and knew I might pass out if I didn't escape, so I scrambled in the direction of the doorway and almost slipped on the slick straw. Someone in the crowd pushed me forward and I protested loudly.

"Sorry," he muttered. "Keep going."

"I'm going." I managed to find the narrow door and stumbled back along the passage toward the outside. The pounding footsteps and screaming behind me made me fear I'd be trampled at any second.

Liam called out, "Don't panic." His flashlight was back on and that helped marginally. He held it high and I could make out the little room we'd come through earlier. I hit my head going through the low doorway, but didn't care as I recognized the same dank passageway we'd gone through before and knew it led to the outer door.

I wrenched the door open and stepped outside onto the narrow step of the close, where I gratefully sucked in clean air. As more of the group made it outside, I moved up the steps to allow room.

"Ah, this is good timing," a man said from several steps above me.

I turned and gasped. "What are you doing here?"

"Looking for you," Derek said, coming closer and brushing my hair away from my face. "You don't look happy, darling. Ghost tour too much for you?"

"You're kidding," I said, staring at him in disbelief.

"I never kid," he said soberly.

"How did you find me?" I whispered.

He might've answered. It didn't matter. I was so relieved to see him, I launched myself into his arms.

"That's more like it," Derek said as he caught me, then had to struggle to keep his balance on the treacherously steep stairs. "Hell, woman."

It took him a moment to realize I was sobbing.

"There, now," he soothed as he moved to lean against the wall. We clutched each other tightly for a moment before I was able to speak.

"It's Kyle," I said, and my eyes overflowed with tears again.

"What's Kyle?"

"He . . . he's dead. I know it. There . . . there's a lot of blood." I pointed to the door. "In there."

"Wait." He pulled back. "What're you saying? There's a dead body in there?"

I nodded.

"Christ," he muttered as he pulled out his cell phone to call the police.

I listened as he greeted the person who answered the phone as if they were old friends. I supposed criminal investigator types stuck together. I still didn't know what Derek was doing here in Scotland, skulking around in Mary King's Close, but this wasn't the time to ask. Instead, I rubbed my arms and stared at the open doorway that led into that stifling servants' quarters.

Derek finished the phone call and put his arm around me. "Tell me again who this person was."

"An old friend," I said. "I just saw him earlier today. We went to the pub and . . . and . . ."

"A friend?" Derek repeated, pulling me closer.

"Yes," I muttered, sniffling into his worn leather bomber jacket. I hated feeling safe in his arms, knowing he was a scoundrel and a cheat. I should've pushed him away, but damn it, did he always have to smell so good?

It didn't matter how wonderful he smelled or felt, or how perfect his timing might be. He was involved with someone else, someone with a baby who looked just like him. He had a family. So what the hell was I doing clinging to him like a lovelorn leech?

I pulled back finally, desperate to catch my breath, stop crying and shape up. And focus. Someone had killed Kyle McVee, and other than the killer, I might've been the last person to talk to him. I needed to figure out my next move.

"Thank you for the use of your jacket," I said, self-consciously wiping teardrops off the smooth leather.

"Always a pleasure," he said. "You're not going to pass out, are you?"

"No," I said irritably, knowing I'd come close to it. "How did you find me?"

"The hotel concierge was quite helpful. He made your reservations."

"Oh, good." I frowned. "But what are you doing in Scotland?"

"Can I get some help here?" Liam called.

"Helen!" I cried, as Liam and another man struggled to keep a sobbing Helen standing upright.

Derek moved forward and grabbed one of Helen's arms and helped her up a few steps, then got her to sit down on the cold stone stairs. I sat next to her and put my arm around her. She burst into loud tears and threw herself against me.

Derek, meanwhile, corralled everyone in the tour group and warned them to stay close by until the police arrived. Most sat on the stairs of the close, but some stood leaning against either side of the tenement walls. No one questioned Derek's authority. He sounded very much like the British Royal Navy commander I knew he used to be.

He took Liam aside and assigned him the job of watching the group to make sure nobody left the area. Liam nodded briskly, exceedingly flattered to be of service. Derek took the young man's flashlight and disappeared back inside the building.

Sirens filled the night air. I continued to try to comfort Helen, but she wouldn't be calmed down. She was bent over, her head practically in my lap. Every few seconds she moaned and her body shook in agony. All I could do was rub her back and feel helpless.

"Helen, the police are going to be here in a minute," I said. "You should try to sit up."

She groaned but managed to pull herself into a sitting position, then leaned heavily against me and rocked.

"Oh, God," she whispered. "Oh, God."

Kyle was my old beau and I'd loved him once upon a time. I still did, I guess, and I'd like to think he loved me, too, in his own way. We'd spent a warm, comfortable hour that afternoon talking and reminiscing. He'd shared his troubles and asked for my help and I'd agreed without question or condition.

But there was no way I could've reacted to his death with the same intensity of emotion that Helen was showing. Did that make me a cold person? Had the two previous murder victims I'd seen up close inured me to violent death?

I didn't think so. Something else was going on here.

"Helen, were you close to Kyle?" I asked quietly.

She sniffled and rubbed her nose, then whispered, "I can't tell you."

I stared at her. What the hell?

The sirens were close enough that I put my hands over my ears to block the noise. The police cars stopped at the top of the stairway leading to Mary King's Close. Car doors slammed and boots thudded downstairs, just as Derek reappeared and stepped outside.

"Commander," a deep voice shouted out.

"Hello, Angus," Derek called. "Down here."

I watched the two men shake hands and slap each other's backs. Old friends and possibly colleagues, it seemed. Then Derek turned and said to the group scattered up and down the close, "Ladies and gentlemen, this is Detective Inspector Angus MacLeod. He'll be in charge of the investigation. Please give him your attention."

"Aye, the commander has the right of it," the detective inspector said, taking over. "Now, you'll be wanting to line up along the stairway wall to give my unit as wide a pathway up and down as possible. Each of you'll speak to one of my men stationed at the top of the close."

Several of the group jumped into line and made their way up the stairs to get the procedure moving.

MacLeod continued. "We'll need to see some identification, so if you've left your hotel or home without it, we'll be accompanying you back there to get it."

"Can't we bring it by the station in the morning?" Liam asked.

"No," MacLeod said in a cheery voice.

"Will this take long?" one of the men asked, his voice bordering on petulant. Not a good sign.

MacLeod smiled. "Ah, well, we're not after keeping you all night, but there are questions that must be asked when foul play is suspected, and these things can't be rushed. I thank you in advance for your cooperation."

All I could think was, Angus MacLeod was a hunk. Literally. Big and burly, at least six feet, four inches tall, with boyish, sandy blond hair, the man had muscles on his muscles. I could picture him strutting about in a kilt, brandishing a claymore and looking for trouble.

Derek Stone met my gaze and grinned as if he knew what I was thinking. The man had friends in the strangest places. He and MacLeod began to talk in hushed tones as they stepped inside the building together.

"I don't think I can do this," Helen whispered.

"I can help you," I said, clutching her hand.

"Not yet," she said. "I . . . I don't think I can move yet."

"That's okay. There's no hurry."

"Oh, God, he's just lying there in that horrible place, cold and alone." She buried her face in her hands and wept silently.

"Helen," I said gently. "You know Kyle and I were old friends, right? We talked this afternoon. I don't think you'd be betraying any secrets if you wanted to tell me why you're so upset."

She blinked away tears to look at me. "He told me he ran into an old friend, and that's why he was running late." She sniffled. "It was you?"

"Yes," I said. "We ran into each other up by the castle, so we stopped at a pub and had a beer together."

"That sounds wonderful," she said wistfully. "He was such a loving, friendly person."

Ah. Friendly, yes. Especially when he was trying to coax you out of your pants. And no, I didn't think that qualified as speaking unkindly of the dead. On the contrary, Kyle had often said that his skill at removing a lady's clothing was one of his most admirable abilities.

"You know we used to date, right?" I said cautiously.

She hesitated, then let out a tiny sob. "I'd forgotten."

I persisted. "I'm going to assume from your reaction to his death that you two were involved?"

She choked back a sob. "We were in love. We were going to be married."

It was my turn to choke. Was she kidding? Sure, I loved Kyle, but I'd suspected all along that he was a total player. Of course, I'd thought at the time that I was special enough to be the exception, so I was in no position to judge Helen.

"Kyle asked you to marry him?" I asked. "He proposed?"

"We were in love," she repeated softly, as though that were all anyone needed to know. It wasn't.

"Ladies," Detective Inspector MacLeod said from directly behind us.

Helen clutched my hand.

Damn. I'd been so wrapped up in Helen's shocking disclosure that I hadn't noticed him sneaking up on us. For such a big guy, he sure moved quietly. Thank goodness we were whispering. How much could he have heard?

"I couldn't help but overhear your conversation."

Crap. I rubbed Helen's cold hand, hoping I hadn't gotten her into too much trouble.

"Miss?" he said, looking at me.

Why was he looking at me?

"I heard you say you met with the deceased this afternoon."

Oh, crap again. "Yes, sir?"

"I'll speak with you now, if you please."

Me? What did I do? I had to pry my hand away from Helen's before I could stand. MacLeod helped me up as if I weighed almost nothing. Once I was standing, I still had to lean back to look up at him. The man was extra large. His eyes were the type that twinkled when he talked, but I doubted he'd be jolly enough to let me slide simply because I happened to know his old buddy Derek.

And speaking of his old buddy, where was Derek? Figured he'd disappear when I needed him most. It wasn't the first time he'd left me to fend for myself with the cops.

MacLeod allowed me to go before him up the stairs of the close, but he kept his hand on my elbow the entire time. It should've been comforting but felt more like he was coaxing a turkey to the chopping block.

When we reached the area at the top of the close, I saw Derek talking to one of the investigators. As I walked past in MacLeod's wake, Derek shook his head in resignation. Hey, it wasn't my fault I seemed to find dead people on a regular basis.

Angus MacLeod led me inside a nearby office building where, apparently, a few offices had been commandeered for the investigation. We walked down a short hall to an open office and he indicated a chair in front of a mahogany desk. "Please do have a seat, Ms. . . ."

"Wainwright. Brooklyn Wainwright."

"Ah, yes, Ms. Wainwright. You know our Commander Stone, I understand."

"Yes, I do," I said, starting to sit. "We're acquaintances from—"

"A previous murder investigation in which you were also the prime suspect."

My butt had barely hit the chair before I bounced back up and blurted, "*Also* the prime suspect? What's that supposed to mean?"

And what kind of stupid question was that? I knew exactly what he was insinuating, and I wasn't happy about it. How had I become the prime suspect again? It was so unfair. This probably wasn't the best time to throw a tantrum, but I wanted to pout and kick something.

"It simply means that you have some experience with murder," he said a little too cheerfully.

My inner alarm meter rose quickly. "No, I don't. I

mean, yes, I've been unfortunate enough to have come across a few victims of murder, but I have no experience with murder personally. I mean, I'm not a . . . Well, I would never . . ." Oh, God, I just needed to shut up.

"Please sit down, Ms. Wainwright," he said again.

I stared at the threadbare visitor's chair, then glanced at him. He had already seated himself in the deluxe boss's chair behind the intimidating desk, clearly in charge. This wasn't looking at all friendly. Good thing he wasn't really carrying a claymore.

Did he think I did it? That this was a slam dunk? Was he picturing this investigation all wrapped up with a bow on top? I pulled my jacket a little tighter around me, feeling a distinct chill in the air.

"Fine." I sighed as I sat. I could learn to hate the police, despite my sincerest efforts to love my neighbor and all that.

"Thank you," he said. "Now, what I meant by experience was that you, Ms. Wainwright, of all people, may be the most accommodating of witnesses, having been on both sides of a similar situation in the past, and thus able to shine a clear light on the sad events of this evening."

My eyes narrowed. His dialect was almost lyrical, his words were lovely and I should've been charmed, but I had this twitchy feeling that it was all a bunch of smoke he was blowing up my kilt. Not that I was wearing a kilt, but really, wasn't he just flattering me before his hench men showed up and dragged me away in shackles?

"So . . . you want my help?" I ventured.

He smiled brightly. "Aye, now you've got the right of it."

I took a deep breath and channeled my mother, trying for one of her cheery Sunny Bunny smiles. I would've succeeded were it not for the sudden nervous tic in my cheek. "Okay, sure. Of course I can help. What would you like to know?"

He asked questions and I answered, telling him everything that had taken place from the beginning of the tour until the police arrived on the scene. I tried to remember everyone's comments, every room we walked into, Helen's first screams, then mine, then me racing out of there and straight into Derek's arms.

"You can imagine my shock," I said, "when Derek Stone appeared out of the blue, just as the body was discovered."

I hastened to add, "Not that I'm accusing him of murder or anything."

He barked out a laugh. "Of course not." He was remarkably boyish and cute when he smiled. Nevertheless, he didn't take the bait and rush off to arrest Derek. Instead, he sat back in his chair, folded his hands together and asked, "What was your relationship with the deceased?"

"Kyle and I were old friends," I said. "Good friends. Okay, we used to date. But it's been almost four years since we broke up."

"I see."

"We stayed friends, though," I said quickly. "I ran into him this afternoon and we had a beer together."

"Where was this?" he asked as he wrote notes in a small tablet.

"The Ensign Ewart."

He excused himself and left the room but was back a minute later. I assumed he must've sent someone to check out my Ensign Ewart story.

"What did the two of you talk about?" he asked.

"Books, of course," I said. "And also, Kyle was in some trouble and asked me to help."

MacLeod leaned forward. "Trouble? What sort of trouble?"

There was a knock on the door and MacLeod swore under his breath. He jumped up and opened it, listened to his man, then closed the door and returned to his chair behind the desk. He folded his hands together and stared at me through narrowed eyes.

"What?" I finally demanded.

He shook his head. "It's nothing. We have a witness who saw you and the victim at the Ensign Ewart earlier today."

"I just told you I was there," I snapped, then exhaled heavily. "Sorry. I'm a little stressed out."

"No harm done," he said, and probably meant it. He seemed a cheerful sort. He checked his notepad, then said, "You were saying that Mr. McVee thought he was in some bit of trouble?"

I debated how much to tell him and decided on the whole truth, since he'd be checking up on everything I told him anyway. "Kyle said someone had tried to kill him. Tried to run him down with a car. It happened right outside the hotel."

"Which hotel would that be?"

"Oh, sorry. The Royal Thistle, we're all staying there for the book fair."

He wrote it down in his notebook. "And 'we' would be the antiquarian book fair people."

I nodded and he continued to write, then asked, "Did Mr. McVee tell you why he thought someone was trying to kill him?"

"Yes, he did." And he'd been right. Someone had been after him and they'd succeeded. My mind flashed back to a picture of Kyle in the pub, laughing and teasing, then flipped to see him curled up on the hearth in that awful, dark room. My stomach clenched in pain and I shook my head to get rid of that dreadful image.

"And . . . ?" MacLeod coaxed. "I know it's difficult, but please go on."

"Yes, it is difficult. Sorry." I gulped in air. I couldn't lose it now. Not in front of the police. No, I'd have to wait until later to have a nice little psychotic break. "Kyle thought someone was trying to stop him from showcasing a . . ." I hesitated, asking myself how much I was willing to reveal about the Burns book. Would anyone believe it? Did that matter? I owed it to Kyle to tell the whole truth. I inhaled, exhaled, focused, became one with the Bodhisattva warrior within, as my upbringing on the commune had taught me to do, and said, "Kyle had a special book he was going to present at the fair. There was some history behind it, and some dispute over—"

Somebody knocked on the door and blew my whole inner-warrior pretense to hell.

"Enter," MacLeod called.

One of the police investigators opened the door. He was dressed in a white jumpsuit with disposable white cloth booties over his shoes. In his hand he held a large manila envelope. "Sir, we believe we've found the murder weapon."

MacLeod gave his subordinate a severe frown as he jumped out of his chair. "Outside, McGill." To me, he said politely, "Pardon me, won't you, Ms. Wainwright? I shouldn't be long."

"No problemo."

The door closed and I muttered, "Don't mind me. I'll just sit here and envision my life in a Scottish brig."

Would they force-feed me haggis? I wondered. Would there be portions of rum for the condemned? Oh, God. Rum always gave me a headache.

With my elbows resting on my knees, I rubbed my face. I was frustrated and scared, and really wished I'd brought the bag of chocolate with me. How had I gotten myself involved in another murder investigation? In a foreign country, no less? Should I have called the American embassy before spilling the beans to the chief cop?

And Kyle, my darling Kyle, was dead. My eyes burned

as I realized his worst suspicions had come to pass. And as far as I knew, the only person who had as much knowledge of Kyle's book as I did was Perry McDougall.

Had Perry killed Kyle? It wouldn't surprise me. Kyle had claimed that Perry threatened him.

Kyle had also said that two other people besides Perry knew about the Robert Burns book, but he'd never told me who. If he and Helen were as close as she insisted they were, he might've told her about the book and the story behind it. But I didn't think Kyle was the type to upset Helen with talk of death threats.

Helen's reaction to Kyle's death had been so painful and over-the-top, it convinced me that she really had thought Kyle would marry her. Call me cynical, but I couldn't believe he would've gone through with it. He was an incorrigible player and cute as could be, but dangerous to a woman's heart. Poor Helen. I knew I shouldn't talk, but the woman had seriously atrocious taste in men. First she'd married that jerk Martin, and now she thought she'd be marrying bad boy Kyle? Not too smart.

Again, I didn't have a whole lot of room to criticize, especially since I'd been led on by Kyle, too. But I never would've fallen for Martin, so as far as I was concerned, that made me a genius compared to my friend.

I shifted in my chair, wondering where MacLeod had run off to. Was Helen being interrogated somewhere nearby? If so, was she telling the cops that she and Kyle were to have been married? And had she honestly bought into the fantasy that they would live happily ever after? Apparently, yes.

I rubbed my eyes, feeling more tired than ever. Who was I to judge Helen, just because Kyle had never promised me anything more than a good time? Why wouldn't he propose marriage to Helen? She was sweet and smart and very pretty. And very rich. Couldn't forget that. But

Kyle was rich in his own right, so I didn't think money would be much of a motivator for him.

Of course, Martin had money, too, so that probably hadn't been a consideration when he asked Helen to marry him. I'd always thought Helen appealed to Martin because he'd mistaken her easygoing nature for subservience.

Now I wondered if maybe it was Helen on the other end of the phone call Kyle had received. He'd certainly run out of the pub in a hurry, and maybe that was a sign that he really did have warm feelings for her. I hoped so. I'd like to think that Helen had been happy with Kyle after putting up with Martin for as long as she did.

I would have to remember to tell MacLeod about that phone call Kyle received. The police would be able to check Kyle's cell phone. Sadly, they probably wouldn't let me in on who'd called.

The door opened and MacLeod came back in.

"Sorry to keep you waiting," he said, his expression falling somewhere between disapproval and condemnation. He laid that same manila envelope on the desk, then reached into his pants pocket, pulled out a rubber glove and snapped it onto his left hand.

"Can you identify this, please?" he asked as he pulled a blood-splotched hammer out of the envelope and dangled it carefully between two fingers. The look he gave me turned my toes to ice.

"It appears to be a hammer," I said cautiously, then took a slow breath. "Is that the murder weapon?"

"Why don't you look at it a little more closely?" he suggested, and moved the hammer so I could see it from several different angles. Icy tendrils slithered from my toes up to my spine and into my neck so quickly, I thought I might freeze and shatter into a thousand pieces.

The hammer was a familiar style. Too familiar. Unlike a typical hammer, this one was lightweight, with a shorter handle, a longer claw with a blunt end, and a smaller, dome-shaped nose.

A bookbinder's hammer.

There were initials engraved at the base. I didn't have to look any closer to recognize them.

The initials were BW.

The hammer was mine.

Chapter 4

I coughed to clear my suddenly dry throat. "It's a . . . a bookbinder's hammer."

He looked at it more closely. "Odd sort of shape."

"Yes." I took another breath. "Its shorter length and lighter weight allow for more accuracy and efficiency when pounding and rounding the spine of a book."

Did my words sound as dully rote to him as they did to me?

"Thank you for the information." He peered at the object, then pointed to something he saw near the edge. "There seems to be a design here on the end. Or are those initials? BW? Ach."

Now he was just showing off. He knew they were mine. Spots began to circle and fade in and out of my field of vision. I took a huge gulp of air and let it go. I refused to further disgrace myself by fainting.

"Ms. Wainwright, have you ever seen this hammer before?"

"Yes, of course. It's mine. It was a gift from my teacher. Part of a set."

He nodded sagely. "I see."

"What do you see?" I shook my head, still not believing any of it. "What are you saying? That Kyle was killed with my hammer? Who would do that? I wouldn't do

that! What am I, stupid? Do you think I had anything
to do with it?"

"We're still determining that," he said calmly, and
slipped the bloody hammer carefully back into the
envelope.

Great, they were still determining how stupid I was.
Watch me burst with pride.

"Did you loan your tools to someone recently?"

"No, absolutely not," I said.

"They've been in your possession all along?"

"Yes, they've been in my hotel room since I arrived
yesterday." So I was the only one with access to my
tools. Could somebody lend me a shovel so I could dig a
deeper hole around me?

He started to make a note.

"Wait," I said. "Sorry. I've got my days a little wrong.
I just arrived this morning. Around noon." I shook my
head, a bit dazed. Had it been only ten hours since
I'd checked into the hotel? It felt like I'd been here a
month.

So in the space of a few short hours, someone had
entered my room, stolen my hammer, then lured Kyle
deep into that dark, bleak tenement and killed him in
cold blood without anyone noticing?

And they'd used *my* hammer?

Why?

Was it in incredibly bad taste to feel almost as sorry
for myself as I did for Kyle?

Obviously, I was being set up. Obvious to me, anyway.
Detective Inspector MacLeod didn't seem to be seeing
it my way. No, he was eyeing me with barely concealed
glee, as though he were picturing me inside my very own
jail cell while he received the thanks of a grateful nation
for saving them from a homicidal maniac who looked a
lot like me.

Who would kill Kyle like that? And who would want

to frame me? Of course, the first person who leaped to mind was Minka. She would love to see me framed. But Kyle would never have gone anyplace dark with that woman. He had taste, after all.

So who else was there?

I thought of Perry McDougall. Would he go to all that trouble to implicate me just because I'd waved his paper around earlier? Had I infuriated him so much that he broke into my room to steal my hammer? Was I that nutso?

And then there was Martin, who didn't like me very much at all. Martin had the perfect motive for killing the man, but Helen had already filed for divorce, so it wasn't like she'd go crawling back to Martin if Kyle were out of the picture. But for some men, it wasn't enough that they couldn't have a woman; they didn't want anyone else to have her, either. Still, Helen had sworn that Martin didn't know about her affair with Kyle. Of course, she wasn't the best person to judge whether Martin knew or not.

But then, why would Martin frame me? He was basically a lazy rich boy. I couldn't see him going to all that trouble to break into my room and steal my stuff.

Did Martin know about the Robert Burns book? He was a bookseller. Would Kyle have consulted him? I couldn't imagine him going anywhere near the man whose wife he was pursuing. He wasn't that foolish. Or was I being naive?

I had to figure out the other two people Kyle had confided in. It was more than likely that one of them, or Perry, had killed him.

I couldn't believe it was possible that Kyle had been killed over Robert Burns's illicit connection to the English throne. The story might be considered scandalous to some die-hard Anglophile, but would it really drive someone to murder?

Who in the world was so afraid of something that happened three hundred years ago that they'd actually kill another human being? And why had they taken the time and the risk involved to sneak into my hotel room and set *me* up to take the fall? Whose toes had I stepped on so badly that I'd earned the rage of a cold-blooded killer?

"Do you always travel with a hammer, Ms. Wainwright?"

I flinched as his voice brought me back to my present predicament. "Of course."

"Really?"

His withering sarcasm made me mad, and I had to wrestle with myself to keep my anger from gushing forth like a geyser. I seriously needed a good night's sleep.

But of course I traveled with hammers and other tools of my trade. What if I found a book in need of repair? It was my job to fix it. Was I supposed to feel guilty about it? Just because some evil creep had stolen one of my tools?

But I did feel horribly guilty. And I wasn't even Catholic, so it wasn't like I'd be going to hell or anything. I wasn't Jewish either. From what I'd heard, they had to deal with a lot of guilt. No, I'd been raised in the guilt-free environment of a new-age spiritual commune where we were free to worship any number of gods and goddesses, take your pick. And none of them spouted eternal damnation, so there was never any reason to feel guilty, right? But here I was, riddled with guilt over way too many things. Abraham's death. Kyle's death. Helen's pain. My tools.

Maybe I needed to see an exorcist or something.

"Ms. Wainwright?"

"What? Sorry." Jet lag was turning me into a zombie. "Yes, when I travel on business, I bring my tools with me."

"Including a hammer?"

"Yes. I usually teach a workshop on bookbinding, so I always need my entire set of tools with me."

Didn't everyone? I was willing to bet Detective Inspector MacLeod didn't go anywhere without his claymore or his .45 Magnum or whatever his weapon of choice was.

"And by the entire set, you mean . . ."

I pictured my portable tool set and named off the contents. "I've got my hammer, files, knives, a couple of awls, nippers, brushes, bone folders, some polishing irons, needles and thread, of course, and glue, linen tape, binder clips, rubber bands. Oh, and more tools and supplies for the students."

"Rubber bands?"

"Sometimes the best way to hold a book together is the simplest."

"Ah. And all these tools are in your hotel room?"

I frowned at the incriminating manila envelope still lying conspicuously between us on the desktop. "I thought they were."

He followed my gaze. "Perhaps we should check your room."

"Absolutely. Let's go."

"Please stay seated, Ms. Wainwright. I'll send two of my men to your room to take a look around."

"Oh, right. Okay. Great." Yeah, just great. They'd be looking for more bloody evidence, I supposed. And what if there was some? If someone had sneaked in before, they could probably do it again to plant more evidence and set me up even further. This was so unfair.

There was another knock on the door and I groaned inwardly. Bad things seemed to happen whenever someone knocked at that door.

Derek Stone stuck his head inside the doorway. "You haven't arrested this lady yet, have you, Angus?"

"No, no, just asking a few questions," Angus said, then added reluctantly, "Come in, Commander. We still have some details to hash out."

Derek walked in and closed the door. He looked around at the small space, then leaned his hip against the two-drawer filing cabinet and smirked. "She makes a damn fine suspect, doesn't she?"

"Aye, she does, if you must know," Angus said in a more serious tone than I was comfortable with.

"I was afraid you might think so," Derek said, eyeing MacLeod. "That's why I'm here to spring her."

"Is that so?" Angus sat back in his chair. "We're not quite finished."

"Can't it be wrapped up tomorrow?"

MacLeod folded his muscular arms across his barrel chest. "Questioning can continue tomorrow, but I'll still need to accompany her back to her hotel room tonight."

Derek's eyes narrowed. "For God's sake, why?"

Was he playing dumb? MacLeod seemed to be thinking the same thing but didn't want to say so. I took pity on the cop and said, "My bookbinder's hammer is the murder weapon."

"Oh, brilliant," Derek said, then noticed the envelope on the desk. He glanced at MacLeod as he reached for it. "May I?"

"You might as well, Commander," MacLeod said resignedly, as though he were used to Derek Stone interfering in his cases on a regular basis.

Derek unhooked the envelope's brass fastener and peeked inside, then shook his head at me as he resealed it and put it back on the desk. "You are impossible."

"I didn't do anything," I insisted.

He folded his arms across his chest. "You've sufficiently antagonized someone to the point that they're setting you up to take the fall for murder."

"I've never antagonized anyone."

"If you only knew." He shook his head again.

"This is so unfair."

"Yes, it is." Derek extended his hand to me. "I'm afraid I'm going to have to vouch for her innocence, Angus."

I grabbed hold of his hand and he pulled me up from the chair. Once I was on my feet, I whacked his arm. "You're *afraid*?"

"It's just a manner of speech. Do you want to come with me or not?"

"I do." I looked at MacLeod. "Am I free to go?"

"No, you're not."

"I didn't think so," I said, forlorn.

Derek raised an eyebrow. "What's the holdup?"

"I've told you, her room must be searched."

"Tonight? Is that necessary?"

"Of course it's necessary," MacLeod said, exasperated. "You know very well I can't let her go back to her room and possibly destroy evidence."

"I don't have any evidence to destroy," I said.

"She didn't do it, Angus," Derek said.

MacLeod was unwavering. "I follow the evidence."

"It won't do you any good in her case," Derek said in mock resignation. "She's just not capable of killing anyone. It's too bad, because she's rather a chary sort, don't you think?"

I elbowed him. "Shush."

"Hey." He grabbed his side. "I'm just trying to help."

"You're making it worse," I whispered.

"Me?"

"Just let the man do his job."

Angus eyed us both warily. "Have you thought to take this show on the road?"

"I tell you what, Angus," Derek said companionably. "We'll wait in the hotel bar while your men do their searching. If you find something incriminating, she's all yours. In fact, I'll help you lock her up."

"Help me, will you?" MacLeod said. "You're a fine friend, Derek, but you're a pain in my rear nonetheless."

"You're welcome," Derek said.

As MacLeod opened the door to the hallway, he sighed. "I'm truly not getting rid of you, am I?"

"You know me better than that," Derek said, his amiable grin belying his resolve.

"Come along, then, both of you."

I hustled my butt out the door to freedom.

My hotel room was absent any bloodstained rags or additional bloody weapons or whatever smoking gun MacLeod had hoped to find. He'd called me in the bar where Derek had been sipping Scotch while I'd nursed a cup of tea, trying to stay awake. Derek and I arrived in time to see a rubber-gloved investigator carefully lifting my heavy cloth tool carrier from my open suitcase.

I immediately wondered if they'd gone through my underwear. I couldn't help worrying. Maybe it was a girl thing, but those rubber gloves gave me the heebie-jeebies.

Derek and I squeezed our way farther into the room where Detective Inspector MacLeod, two crime scene guys and the police photographer were working. The first thing I was asked to do was sit down at the desk in the corner and submit to fingerprinting by one of the technicians.

"You may find black residue on some of the surfaces of your furniture," MacLeod explained after I'd washed my hands. "We tried to wipe it off but we might've missed some spots."

"That's okay," I said, knowing that as soon as they left, I'd get out my travel wipes and scrub down everything.

I didn't know what to do with five men cramped inside my little hotel room. It was like a party, only not much fun.

"We assumed this was the bag that holds your tools, Ms. Wainwright," MacLeod said, waving a hand at the investigator who was holding the navy blue cloth bag.

"Yes." Whenever I traveled, I wrapped everything up in the bag I'd made myself out of sailcloth and white grosgrain ribbon. Each tool had its own snug pocket, and the whole thing folded up and tied and fit inside my suitcase.

The investigator placed the tool bag on the queen-size bed.

"Someone has fiddled with it," I said. "The ribbon is tied in a knot and I always tie it in a bow."

"Open it up, Richie," MacLeod said.

Richie carefully spread the cloth out on the green brocade bedspread. Fully opened, the tool bag was two feet long by one foot wide.

"Crap," I muttered.

"What's wrong?" Derek said.

"Three tools are missing," I said, poking my fingers in the empty pockets.

"That's unfortunate," Derek murmured, glancing at MacLeod.

"Yes, isn't it?" MacLeod said. "Can you tell which ones are missing?"

"I can't remember what was in this pocket. One of my knives, I think. Or maybe the polishing iron I brought. No, that's still here."

He reached out and stopped me from pulling the polishing iron out of its compartment.

"Don't touch anything, please," he said. "We'll need to dust the remaining tools for fingerprints."

"Sorry." I grimaced at the thought that I might've destroyed evidence and backed away from the bed. The photographer moved in and snapped a bunch of pictures, then stepped out of the way so that rubber-gloved Richie could move in and fold up the tools. He put them inside another large envelope, then left the room with the photographer and my tools.

"We'll get everything back to you presently," MacLeod said.

"I have a workshop in two days," I said. "Do you think I could have them back by then?"

"It shouldn't be a problem."

"Thank you."

He nodded, then dug in his pocket for a business card and handed it to me. "I'll be around to see you tomorrow, but please call me in the meantime if you think of anything else to tell me."

I slipped the card in my purse. "I can tell you right now that Kyle received a phone call on his cell while we were at the pub. He told the caller he would meet them in five minutes and he took off. And no, he didn't tell me who the caller was."

MacLeod made a note in his pad. "We'll follow up on that. Thank you." He nodded at Derek. "We'll talk tomorrow."

"Of course."

I had a sneaking feeling whom the subject of their conversation would be. Lucky me.

MacLeod reached the door, then turned and pierced me with a look. "I must warn you not to leave the city without informing me."

I licked my very dry lips. "I won't."

"G'night, then," he said, and took off.

"That was pleasant," Derek said, tugging on his jacket. "How about a nightcap?"

I should've said no, but how could I pass up such a charming offer? Besides, I knew that despite the jet lag, I wouldn't be able to fall asleep. "Maybe just one."

We went downstairs to the pub and found it packed
with book people commiserating over Kyle's murder. At
one table, two women talked quietly while dabbing their
eyes with tissues. Over at the bar, several groups were
toasting his memory.

I scouted out a small table at the far side of the room
while Derek went to the bar. He came back with two
healthy shots of Scotch and a small pitcher of water.

He held up his glass and I clinked mine against it. I
took a sip and let the heat trickle down my throat, warm-
ing my insides all the way to my stomach.

"Better?" he asked.

"Not yet," I said, and took another sip, and felt the
warmth slide down my throat. I put my glass down on
the table and sat back. "Getting there."

Derek poured several drops of water into my glass.
I took another sip and savored the subtle change in
flavor.

"Even better," I admitted. "Thanks."

"Good." He sat back in his chair and studied me as he
sipped his Scotch.

"Oh, crap," I said, smacking my hand on the table and
squeezing my eyes shut.

"Now what?"

I shook my head in disbelief. "I completely forgot to
tell him about Perry."

"Perry?"

I glanced around the room, then related an abbrevi-
ated version of the Robert Burns story. I told him that
Kyle had shown the book to three people. The only one
I knew for sure was Perry.

"This man Perry is a prime suspect," he said. "How
could you forget to mention it?"

I rubbed my forehead. "I started to but we were interrupted. Then I dropped the ball. Maybe the sight of
that bloody hammer caused my brain to empty."

He shook his head. "Only you."

"I know."

I pulled MacLeod's business card out of my pocket. "It's late. Maybe I should wait until tomorrow."

Derek checked his wristwatch. "Call him now."

I sighed and dialed the number. When MacLeod answered, I told him everything Kyle had said about Perry. I also remembered to mention the poison-pen letters Kyle had told me about. Unfortunately, he'd thrown them away, but you never knew what might help the investigation. He thanked me and promised we'd talk again tomorrow.

I disconnected the call, then noticed Derek staring at me so intently, I began to squirm. "What is it?"

He smiled. "It occurs to me that you owe me a boon for your freedom."

"I don't owe you a boon."

"Of course you do."

"Hey, what's a boon, anyway?"

"That's for me to decide."

"I don't think so," I said, then blurted, "Maybe you should just go home to your little family."

"My what?"

"You don't have to pretend with me." Now that I'd opened the can of worms, far be it from me to shut up about it. "I saw you outside Heathrow this morning, getting into a Jaguar with a very pretty woman and her small child who looked just like you, Dad."

He looked puzzled, then thoughtful. Then he chuckled. "Oh, that's rich."

He laughed a little more.

"It's not funny."

"No, it's hilarious," he said, and barked out another laugh.

"Oh, stop it," I said grumpily.

He grinned at me. "Where the hell were you? Why didn't you say hello?"

"Oh, and when would I have done that? When you were hugging your wife? Or maybe when you were laying a big fat wet one on her lips? Or maybe when you were cooing at your little baby who, I repeat, looks remarkably like you, God help him?"

"He is the handsome lad, isn't he?" he said with a chuckle.

"Oh, whatever."

He laughed again. "A big fat wet one?"

"I should go now." I took one last sip, then pushed my chair back.

He grabbed my hand to keep me seated. "You silly git, that wasn't my wife and baby."

"I'm a silly git now?" I said, my voice rising. "Git. What does that mean, anyway? Some kind of feeble-brained nutball or something? That's real nice."

I tried to stand but he clutched my arm tightly to hold me down.

"It means you're wrong, love."

"Yeah, yeah. Doesn't matter. It's been a long day. I should—"

"No."

"Yes, really, I've hit my quota of humiliating moments for the day." I managed to stand. "Thanks for vouching for me earlier. I appreciate not having to spend the night in a cold jail cell. Good night. Sweet dreams. Ciao."

He stood, too, and blocked my escape. "You're jealous."

"No, I'm not."

"I'm delighted."

"And I live to delight you." I turned and walked out of the pub.

He caught up and took hold of my arm. "Listen to me, those people are not my—"

"Brooklyn, is that you?"

I turned at the sound of my name. "What? Oh. Hi, Helen."

Ignoring Derek, she threw her arms around me. "I'm so glad the police let you go."

"Well, of course they let me go," I said with a nervous laugh as I pulled away. "What did you think?"

"But I saw you leave with that detective," she said, wringing her hands. "Nobody's seen you for hours. I was so afraid they'd arrested you. I don't know what I would've done if—"

"I'm fine," I said, rubbing her arm consolingly. The woman was turning into a basket case. "Helen, this is Derek Stone. Commander Stone, this is my friend, Helen Chin."

He frowned at me, then turned to Helen and smiled politely. "How do you do?"

"Oh. H-hello, er, nice to meet you, Commander," she said, her eyes wide, clearly intimidated by Derek. She looked back at me. "Please say you're free for breakfast tomorrow morning."

"Okay. Sure."

"I can meet you at the concierge desk at eight or eight thirty."

"Can we make it nine?" I asked, desperate for all the sleep I could get.

"Yes, of course," she said. "Thanks. I'll meet you at the concierge desk at nine."

She cast one last anxious look at Derek, then said good night.

Derek turned to me. "What was that all about?"

"What do you mean?"

"*Commander* Stone? You've never called me that."

"That is your title, isn't it? And it was kind of weird how she reacted, don't you think?"

His eyes narrowed. "Don't."

"Don't what?"

He pulled me to a quiet corner so nobody could over-hear us. "Don't tell me you suspect that tiny woman is capable of bludgeoning a man of Kyle McVee's height and weight."

"Of course I don't suspect Helen, but I'm no more capable of bludgeoning Kyle than she is. So why am I number one on the suspect list?"

"I'm sure you're not."

"I would appreciate your putting a little more enthu-siasm into that."

"I'll talk to Angus."

"Thank you."

"And just to be clear, your friend Helen is not on your imaginary list of murder suspects. Correct?"

"Absolutely." I folded my arms across my chest. "There's no way I would suspect her of murder."

"Honestly?"

I fudged. "Well, I guess anyone is capable of murder under the right circumstances."

"Here we go," he said.

"Okay, no," I whispered. "Of course not. I would never suspect Helen of killing a fly, let alone another human being."

"Then why'd you pull the 'commander' nonsense?"

"I don't know." That wasn't entirely true, so I started over. "I wanted to see her reaction. I'm tired of being the first one accused of murder once again. I know I didn't do it, but that doesn't mean MacLeod will listen to me. So it's in my best interests to figure out who might've done it before the police toss me in the dungeon and throw away the key."

"That won't happen," he said firmly.

"Easy for you to say," I muttered. "Look, Helen thought Kyle was going to marry her. What if she brought up the subject and he laughed in her face? Maybe he'd just broken up with her. Maybe she saw him with me and it pushed her to the edge of insanity and she couldn't take it anymore, so she broke into my room and stole my tools. Or maybe she . . . are you listening to me?"

He was gazing upward, toward heaven, I supposed, as though praying for divine intervention.

"Fine," I said. "I know it's not Helen, but it's somebody out there besides me."

"Yes, but you're grasping at straws, darling."

"It's all I have." I was close to tears, but I refused to lose it in front of him and everyone else in the hotel lobby.

He wrapped his arms around me. "I realize you're upset, love, but don't start looking for murder suspects behind every potted plant. It could get you into trouble, in case you've forgotten what happened last time you tried it."

"I have no idea what you're talking about." I checked my wristwatch. "My goodness, look at the time. It's after midnight. I'm dead on my feet."

"You scare me to death with this dangerous game you're playing."

"Game?" I repeated. "If this is a game, I should be having more fun."

He shook his head, then linked my arm firmly through his. "I'm walking you to your room."

"Not necessary," I demurred, though I was secretly pleased that he'd offered. "I'll be fine."

He tightened his grip on me. "Believe me, it's not you I'm worried about."

Chapter 5

Not surprisingly, I didn't sleep well that night. Sometime around three thirty a.m., I awoke and jumped out of bed, ready to boogie. When I realized what time it was, I groaned and walked to the window, just to make sure the alarm clock wasn't lying. I pushed back the curtains and saw that it was indeed still dark outside, and raining, which fit my mood perfectly. The city seemed to shine in all its wet, fog-shrouded, shadowy glory. The lights from the castle reflecting off the clouds cast an eerie glow over the streets. I worried that I might not be able to enjoy the city as much as I had in the past. So far, the trip was kind of . . . well, to call it a bummer would be putting it mildly.

My eyes slowly focused on the space just outside my window, and I noticed with some alarm that my room was right on the path of the hotel fire escape. Iron stairs ran past my window, and a narrow platform made a perfect little perch for someone to stand on as they jimmied my window open. How damned convenient.

If I hadn't been wide-awake before, I was now.

Shaken, I carefully checked the window locks. They seemed secure enough, but the killer had entered my room by one means or another, and I wasn't going to take any chances. I would demand a new room when I went downstairs for breakfast.

"Now what?" I paced the room, knowing I couldn't go back to sleep. Back at the window, I stared out at the darkness for a few minutes, then suddenly wondered if the killer might be watching me. A little moan escaped my throat and I shoved the curtains closed.

I'd had my reasons for requesting a room on a lower floor, but giving a determined killer a shorter climb wasn't one of them.

But who had broken into my room? So far, the only person I could think of was Perry McDougall, but how would he have gained access? The windows were locked, and besides, I had a hard time picturing him crawling up a fire escape, just to get my hammer. Yes, we'd had our little altercation earlier, but was that enough to use me as a pawn in some weird game of death and revenge?

I knew it wasn't Helen. I'd already decided she had nothing to do with it, even while I'd laid out her possible motives to Derek in the lobby earlier.

But who could've done it? Who hated me so much that they'd risk danger and exposure and arrest to somehow break into my room and steal my stuff in order to frame me for murder?

Minka.

An image of her sneering face caused shudders to vibrate clear down to my bones. Minka hated me enough to do almost anything to destroy me. Unfortunately, that wasn't enough to have her thrown in jail, and sadly, it probably wasn't her anyway. But I recalled with fondness how the San Francisco police had arrested her for a short time while Abraham's murder was being investigated. In the end, though, Minka had been a dead end. Still, it was fun to imagine her living behind bars, forced to hook up with a cell mate named Big Marge.

My shoulders slumped and my eyelids drooped as exhaustion sneaked its way into my system. Just thinking about Minka had sapped every last bit of energy I had.

I crawled back into bed and slept like a dead guy, no offense to Kyle.

The alarm went off four hours later, and this time I had to drag myself out of my warm bed. Stumbling around the room, I tried to figure out what to do first. Instinct led me to the compact coffee butler on the dresser, where I found packets of coffee, decaf, tea and hot chocolate. I knew the powdered coffee would be awful, but hot chocolate sounded yummy. I filled the small pot with water and plugged it in to heat.

Remembering my discovery of the night before, I stared across the room at the curtains. With some trepidation, I peeked outside, then pulled them open and winced at the glare of morning sunlight that poured in. There was frost on the windowsill, but it was no longer raining. The city looked refreshed and alive—and cold. Ordinarily, it would've been a perfect day to sneak out of the hotel and wander for a while, but I was hoping that the book fair committee would arrange some sort of memorial for Kyle. It was the least they could do.

I was halfway through my shower when I remembered that Robin would be here sometime today. I almost wept with happiness. I could really use a good friend by my side.

I finished my shower, then did the hair-and-makeup routine. Twenty minutes later, I was feeling a bit more alert, thanks to the two cups of Cadbury hot chocolate I'd sucked down while getting ready. Ever the optimist, I dressed for brisk outdoor weather in jeans tucked into boots, a turtleneck and my sage-colored down jacket. I slipped a collapsible umbrella into my bag in case the rain returned, then headed downstairs to meet Helen.

It was a few minutes past nine but I didn't see Helen in the lobby yet, so I stopped at the front desk to request a new room.

"May I be of service, ma'am?" the young clerk asked in a charming Scottish accent I could listen to all day long.

When he informed me that the hotel was full, I frowned and explained, "My room was broken into yesterday, so I was hoping there might be something available that's not directly on the fire escape."

"Yer wha . . . ?" he said.

"My room was—"

"Brooken inta?" His eyes widened. "Ach! Om sartin gash! Wuh cana low tha! Wuh canna lehti gon."

"Um, pardon me?" I asked.

"Sa cram!" he cried, pounding his hand on the counter. "Wartha police anya naidem?"

"Um, hmm." I could pick out little phrases here and there but really had no idea what he was saying. I did think his level of excitement and concern was sending the right message, though. On the other hand, he was starting to get strange looks from his fellow clerks.

He grabbed the telephone, then slammed it down. "Wa kana chanty wrassler wuh dit?" He whipped around, looking for someone, then shook his head. "All gie heid bummer."

Bummer. Yes. I caught that word but wondered if it meant something different in Scottish.

He continued muttering as he walked back to an anteroom. I was completely lost on the words, but I got the gist of what he was saying and appreciated his enthusiasm. Despite my problems, there was something sexy and wonderful about a volatile young Scotsman.

I could see him on the phone in the small office behind the desk area. He hung up and walked back.

"I'm sorry to say we have no more available rooms," he said, and I could tell it pained him. "My manager will send security to your room to make sure the locks are in working order, and they've already added an extra guard detail because of the unfortunate death last night."

He spoke with barely a trace of the heavy dialect he'd used only seconds ago. Did he slip into dialect only when he was excited? Interesting.

"My manager has alerted our people to keep an eagle eye on the fire escape as well. That's the best we can do for now, Ms. Wainwright." He placed his hand over his heart. "But I promise you, it won't happen again."

I felt strangely disappointed by his upstanding British accent. Weird. But I also had a feeling he'd stand guard on the fire escape himself, if he had to.

I thanked him for his trouble, then asked, "What's your name?"

"It's Gregory," he said, with just a touch of a lilt in his voice. It sounded like *gray-gree*. He was so cute.

Meanwhile, I was stuck with my same room off the fire escape.

I thought briefly about changing hotels, but that would take me away from my friends and colleagues and the book fair ambience. If the hotel management was serious about fixing my windows and stepping up security, that would have to be good enough. But I'd be sleeping with one eye open from now on.

As I crossed the lobby, I saw a signboard announcing that all book fair activities had been canceled this morning. A memorial service for Kyle McVee would be held at noon in the Triton Room on the conference level.

I still didn't see Helen anywhere in the lobby area. I waited a few more minutes, then took a chance and wandered into the restaurant. The room was a massive, open atrium with a ceiling as high as the hotel itself. There were at least seventy or eighty tables and an enormous breakfast buffet spread along one wall. The room was loud and lively with chatter this morning. Pale yellow walls and floor-to-ceiling windows added to the cheery brightness. Staring at the buffet, I realized I was famished. I walked past rows and rows of people eating and talking, searching for Helen, hoping maybe she'd found a table and was waiting for me.

I stopped when I spied her at the far end of the room, sitting in a comfy booth, snuggled up with someone. And by snuggled up, I mean they were hugging each other as though the world were about to end. Perhaps in Helen's case, that was true.

Except that the guy hugging her was Martin, her ex-husband. I was a few steps away when he opened his eyes and saw me. He huffed in exasperation as he let go of her.

This was going to be awkward.

"What is it?" Helen asked him, then followed his gaze and smiled when she saw me.

I waved weakly.

"Brooklyn, hi!" she said, sliding over in the booth and patting the seat. "I'm so glad you're here. Join us, please."

Join *us*? Oh, no. Her tone bordered on anxious, but I had to be strong. Life was too short to spend a minute of quality time with Martin Warrington.

And Martin wasn't budging.

"Um, I'm sorry, Helen, but I can't," I said. "I was just trying to find you to let you know that I got a call from a client who wants to meet this morning at the, um, the Balmoral. He's a client; did I say that? Anyway, I didn't realize he was coming in today, but then he called and I really should. Um, go. I should go. And, well, I'm sorry."

I needed to learn when to shut up.

I glanced at Martin, whose lips thinned in his version of a satisfied smile. He knew I was lying. Everyone knew I was lying. I was the world's worst liar.

Helen, on the other hand, looked simply crestfallen. "Are you sure?"

I felt like a horrible friend, but Martin's slithery smile cinched it.

"I'm sorry, sweetie," I said softly. "Maybe we can do lunch?"

That earned me an exaggerated eye roll from Martin.

"What?" I asked him, my irritation rising. I couldn't help it. He scraped my last nerve raw.

"I didn't say anything," he said, and gave Helen a look of injured innocence. Didn't I say he was a jackass? I hated that I'd even acknowledged him. And I hated it more that Helen was too nice to tell him to leave.

"Yes, I'll have lunch with you," Helen said, which earned her another eye roll from Martin.

Ignoring him, I looked at my watch. "I've got to run. I'll call your cell later."

I took off at a fast walk. I couldn't help but detest the man. And despite the fact that they'd just been hugging, I knew Helen didn't want to be alone with him. On the other hand, she'd been married to the man, so I supposed she still might've had feelings for him. Didn't mean I had to share those same feelings.

On my way out of the restaurant I was forced to walk past the enormous buffet. I could handle the scrambled eggs and sausage, the grilled tomatoes and mushrooms, even the eggs Benedict. But when I got to the gorgeous display of French toast and caught the aroma of warm maple syrup wafting up from the table, my knees almost collapsed from under me.

I reluctantly passed the coffee station, too, even though I needed caffeine like I needed my next breath. How unfair was it that I couldn't stay and eat? Damn Martin for ruining my breakfast. And Helen's, too, poor girl.

I pouted all the way out of the restaurant and across the lobby. Now what? Room service sounded depressing and slow. I could always walk a half block up to the Royal Mile and go to Starbucks, but talk about depressing. Travel ten thousand miles and eat at a Starbucks?

Just shoot me. I was certain that the next astronauts to land on the moon would find a Starbucks there.

I stood outside by the valet station and wondered which way to go. I knew there were other hotels in the area where I could get breakfast. I flipped a mental coin and headed east. A short block away, I found the Monarch Hotel and ventured inside. The lobby was elegant in a slightly shabby, old-world sort of way, much like an elderly woman who still wore her 1950s-era Chanel suit to entertain her luncheon guests, but her lipstick was a bit smeared and her hair was thinning.

I took the elevator up to the cozy rooftop restaurant. The hostess led me to a small table by a wide bay window, and as I sat down, a waitress hurried over with a pot of coffee. As she poured, I thanked her profusely, pitifully grateful for the caffeine. Then she took my order for French toast, a side of bacon and a glass of orange juice and scurried away. Things were looking up.

As I waited for breakfast to arrive, I pulled out my notebook to study my workshop presentation. But instead of practicing my workshop spiel, I found myself thinking about Kyle. Or more precisely, his killer.

I flipped to a blank page, where I began to list all the possible murder suspects I could come up with. It was silly, really. Derek was right: I should've learned my lesson in San Francisco last month. I had no business sticking my nose in an ongoing police investigation. But I couldn't help myself. It wasn't just about Kyle. Someone had gone to a whole lot of trouble to frame me, so the way I saw it, I was already involved.

And judging from Detective Inspector MacLeod's warning last night, it didn't seem as though the police needed anyone besides me on their suspect list. Ipso fatso, I had no choice but to do their job for them. That was my story, anyway.

The problem was, I could come up with only a few

names—and mine wasn't one of them. I knew I wasn't the killer. And I knew Helen wasn't the killer, either, but I put her name on the list anyway. She was possibly the least likely murder suspect I'd ever met, but she'd insisted that Kyle was going to marry her, so what if he'd turned her down or pissed her off? Who knew how she might've handled it? A woman scorned and all that.

What if Helen had seen Kyle greeting me on the street with a big hug and a kiss? She might've been following him. If she'd been spurned and was jealous and obsessed, seeing me in Kyle's arms would give her plenty of motivation to implicate me in Kyle's death.

I fiddled with my pen as I stared at Helen's name, then crossed her name off the list. It was ridiculous to think she could be a cold-blooded killer. I was better off suspecting that asinine husband of hers, Martin. Now, there was a logical murder suspect if I'd ever met one—and I had.

I wrote his name down, just because it felt good. And because he had the oldest motive in the world for killing Kyle: jealousy, pure and simple.

But why would he implicate me? That was the million-dollar question. Yes, I was sure he despised me, but honestly, we barely knew each other. My only connection to Martin was the book fairs we both attended once or twice a year. And even then, I rarely ran into him. His bookstore specialized in more contemporary works than the books I dealt with. We did have Helen in common, but I hadn't seen her in two years.

No, I believed this killer had to be someone who knew me. And furthermore, I knew in my gut that Kyle's death had something to do with the Robert Burns book.

Now, how could I connect those dots?

I stared at the next name on my list. Minka. Of course, Minka was always on my suspect list. She hated me, and vice versa. I didn't know if she even knew Kyle, but she was always up for throwing me under the bus.

Then there was Perry McDougall. Besides threatening Kyle, he'd threatened me yesterday in the hotel store. Did he storm out of the hotel store and go directly to my hotel room and steal my tools?

Thinking of that scene with Perry, I took a sip of coffee and wallowed in embarrassment. What had I been thinking, throwing a fit like that? I chalked up my reaction to a combination of jet lag, two beers, and my recent bout of melancholy. I felt as though I'd lost control of my life, and Perry showed up to make me feel even worse. Naturally, I opened up a can of whoop-ass on him, as my dad would say.

But was that any reason to frame me for murder?

I sat back in my chair, glanced around the restaurant and thought about Perry. What had turned him into such an angry man? I'd heard he was living off a family trust fund, so he was apparently wealthy. He couldn't use lack of money as an excuse to behave badly.

Well, he could, but he shouldn't. I know money can't buy happiness, but still, shouldn't wealthy people be grateful they weren't living in a cardboard shack?

Maybe he'd been an abused child. That would explain a lot. Or maybe he was dying of something and it pissed him off. But that didn't make sense. He'd been a cranky pants for years. Maybe he had a vindictive wife or a crazy mother-in-law. Whatever the reason, he was one mean sucker.

And if that weren't enough, he'd hired Minka the Dimwit to assist him this week. He had to be tweaked in the head to do a thing like that.

So, to summarize, Perry was a malicious son of a bitch and a bad judge of character. But did that make him a killer?

I took another slug of coffee and pondered my puny suspect list. Kyle had told two others about the history and secrets hidden within the Robert Burns book. Once the book fair began, it would be easier to track down the booksellers and collectors who'd had relationships with Kyle. Maybe there were a few who didn't think he was the darling some of us believed he was.

But again I came back to the real question: How did I fit into the puzzle? Whom had I pissed off so badly? Who wanted to see me hang for murder?

The waitress arrived with my breakfast and I pushed the notebook out of the way, picked up a fork and began to systematically devour the beautiful stack of thick, fluffy French toast sprinkled with powdered sugar and slathered in butter and warm maple syrup.

I took a sip of coffee between bites and stared out the wide bay window at the lovely view of the ancient rooftops and chimneys that seemed to cascade down the steep hill toward the New Town. Billowy clouds drifted across the blue sky. Small puddles of rainwater collected on the rooftops and reflected the sparkling sunlight. I had another urge to get out and walk around the city, as I'd planned to do yesterday before I was so rudely interrupted by darling Kyle.

Unbidden, tears filled my eyes.

"Oh, great," I muttered, and grabbed for a tissue in my purse. I still couldn't believe Kyle was dead. I couldn't wrap my brain around it. What had he done to deserve such a cruel fate? It seemed impossible and unfair that the secrets inside one small book could lead someone to kill another human being. But how else could I explain it? Kyle had told someone about the book and it had cost him his life. I rarely saw him more than once a year, but I missed him terribly now that he was gone.

I sighed, then slowly turned from staring out the window to finish my breakfast—and shrieked.

"Hello, love."

Derek Stone was sitting across from me. He snagged a piece of bacon from my plate, broke off a chunk and popped it into his mouth.

"Where did you come from?" I demanded.

"Cambridge, originally."

"Very funny."

"I thought so." He grinned, reached for my small glass of orange juice and took a sip. Then he looked around. "Nice place."

"I like it." It was lucky I'd already swallowed my coffee or I would've choked when I saw him. "What are you doing here?"

"I might ask the same of you," he said. "There's a perfectly decent restaurant in your hotel and yet you're eating here, all by yourself. Seems a rather desperate move. Are you avoiding someone?"

"Maybe," I said, looked pointedly at him.

"You mean me?" He waved the idea away. "No, I don't believe you. The fact is, I was in the hotel restaurant and saw you talking to your friend Helen. Then you rushed out so quickly, I assumed you were up to some mischief. So I followed you here."

"How clever you are."

"I know." He signaled the waitress for a cup of coffee. She rushed over and filled his cup. As she walked away, he said, "I would've joined you here sooner, but I was intercepted by a former associate downstairs."

"Oh, darn."

"Yes." He picked up his coffee cup and sipped. "When I finally broke free, I was afraid I'd lost you. I was determined to pound on every door of the hotel, but then I remembered your peculiar obsession with food and I came directly here."

"That's a ridiculous story."

He raised an eyebrow. "But it was well told, I think."

"Oh, yes," I said. "You have a theatrical way of spinning a tale."

"Do you think?" He took another sip. "I've always loved drama. I had aspirations of joining the circus at one time."

"As a clown?"

"No, tightrope walker, you see. Drama."

"I can see you wearing stretchy pants."

He studied me. "I think that's a compliment."

"Of course it is." I dredged the last bit of French toast through the syrup and finished it off, then pushed my plate toward him. "More bacon?"

He pondered the plate, then patted his stomach. "Thank you, but no. My girlish figure, you know." He saw my notebook, absently picked it up and started flipping through until he landed on the page with my notes and scratchings.

"That's nothing," I said, reaching to grab it from his hands. "Just doodling."

He whipped the book out of my reach. "Just doodling, you say."

"That's right," I said, maybe a touch too defensively.

He studied the notebook page for a moment, then stared at me so long that I started to fidget.

"What?" I said finally.

His dark blue eyes held mine for another beat before he said, "When will you get it through your lovely head that playing these sorts of games can get you killed?"

Chapter 6

My fists bunched up under the table. "I'm not trying to get myself killed. I'm trying to figure out who set me up."

"That's for the police to handle," he said rigidly, drumming his fingers on my notebook. "If you'd let them do their job—"

"They've done their job," I whispered irritably. The whole restaurant didn't need to know I was a suspicious character, did they? "If Angus MacLeod had his way, I'd be languishing in a jail cell right now. The only reason I'm wandering around a free woman is because of you. And it's not that I'm ungrateful, but that doesn't give me a whole lot of confidence in your pal Angus's ability to be objective."

He paused a beat too long before saying, "Don't be ridiculous."

"That was not convincing," I declared. "Which means you agree with me. This can't be good."

"I'm not agreeing with you," he hedged. "Not exactly."

"My confidence is soaring."

"Now, look, don't worry about Angus. He's simply a stubborn Scotsman." He paused, then said, "Now, that's something to worry about."

"Oh, great."

"I'm teasing you."

"This isn't a good time."

He smiled and reached for my hand. "Don't worry, love. Angus is a reasonable man."

"I'm buoyed by your optimism," I said. Despite his claims, I could tell Derek was worried about how Angus was investigating this murder. In other words, I was screwed.

"Look," I continued, "why should the police go to any trouble trying to figure out who set me up for murder? As far as they're concerned, I'm the perfect suspect. The murder weapon belongs to me and I knew the victim. I was probably one of the last people to see him alive. End of story. Throw her in jail."

"You're being overly dramatic."

I laughed. "Oh, please. You think this is dramatic? This is nothing. Wait'll I get rolling."

He waved his arm. "Check, please!"

"Very funny."

The waitress came running and I handed her my credit card. A few minutes later, we were out on the street. Derek took my hand and we walked back to the hotel, passing pubs and charming shops. One drew my attention and I stopped to stare in the window. I needed a minute to think before I got caught up in the book fair activities back at the hotel, and shopping for tacky souvenirs for my family was a perfect diversion. And better to buy them now before I got locked away in a dungeon somewhere.

I dragged Derek into the store and bought the plaid shot glasses I'd spied through the window. Plaid shot glasses. The perfect gift for my dad and three brothers. While I was in there, I found cute plaid socks for my sisters and Mom. This place was a treasure trove of tartan madness, and I knew my peeps would appreciate my thoughtfulness. Plus, shopping took my mind off the whole pesky, being-railroaded-for-murder thing.

Derek browsed while I paid for my gifts and then we headed back to the Royal Thistle.

"It occurs to me I didn't finish telling you about the woman at the airport," he said.

"Didn't you?" I said, not sure I wanted to know the truth. I braced myself.

"No, I believe we were interrupted."

"Were we?"

He put his arm around me and I realized it was going to be bad news. He was married. I knew it. How stupid could I get—again? I should've pushed him away but I couldn't. I would savor the warmth for a few more minutes, then never see him again.

"Her name is Delia," he said. "She's my brother's wife."

I stopped and stared at him. "You're having an affair with your brother's wife?"

He laughed as he shook his head. "No, you daft woman. She was doing me a favor, coming to Heathrow. I hadn't seen the baby in months, so she picked me up and I took them to lunch."

"Oh." Was my face red? "Did your brother join you?"

"No." He reeled me back to his side and we continued walking arm in arm. "He's a general with the Royal Army, stationed in Afghanistan. He won't be back for six more months."

"Ah." I felt stupid and small for reacting so badly.

"But thank you for reacting so badly," he said.

I drew back. Could he read my mind?

"It makes me think you might care for me," he said.

I stopped again. "Well, of course I care for you," I said crossly. "Are you blind or something?"

He laughed again as he wrapped his arms around me. "There's that sweet disposition I've missed so much."

"Sorry." Maybe I was going nuts, but I really wanted him to kiss me.

And maybe he was psychic, because he reached out and stroked my cheek. "Your eyes make me crazy," he said, brushing a strand of hair away from my face.

"Crazy?" I whispered. "Really?"

"Really." Then he kissed me, right on the street. Well, on the mouth, actually, but we were standing on the street. Oh, hell. The man turned my brain to mush.

But what a mouth he had.

Eventually, we started walking again. He stayed by my side as I stopped at the front desk and asked them to hold my bag of souvenir goodies. Then we crossed the lobby and stepped onto the crowded escalator to go downstairs to the memorial service.

"You don't have to go to this thing," I said, giving him an out but hoping he wouldn't take it. Among other reasons, I wanted Derek to be close by in case Angus MacLeod was in the vicinity.

"I don't mind tagging along for a bit," he said, and wrapped his arm around my waist as we rode down the escalator. At the bottom, he nudged me off.

"I know how to get off an escalator," I mumbled.

"Just being helpful."

"Or not."

He grinned at me. For some perverse reason, that made me smile.

We followed the crowd to the hall where the service was to take place. Several hundred chairs were lined up in rows, facing a podium at the front of the room. The place was filling up fast. He prodded me into the fourth row from the back while he took the aisle seat.

"You're being helpful again," I said.

"Yes, now sit."

Before I could sit, I spotted Royce McVee standing just across the aisle. I knew I had to tell him about the

Robert Burns book. He would probably want it back, since it belonged to his family, but maybe I could convince him to let me keep it for a while. I edged my way to the aisle and called his name.

He turned, saw me, and walked over. "Brooklyn."

"I'm so sorry," I whispered as I gave him a hug.

"Thank you, my dear," he said.

Kyle always said that Royce's sphincter made him the perfect business partner. While Kyle was the front man, the glad hand, the schmoozer, Royce never took his eye off the bottom line. Kyle would say that combination made for the perfect partnership.

But Royce McVee was more than Kyle's business partner. They were cousins. They'd inherited the family business from their fathers, two brothers, both of whom had been knighted for their loyalty to the crown. Kyle was the public face, the upbeat personality who had built up the clientele and made the money Royce counted in the back room. Royce was a nice enough guy but bland. He had pale skin, his hair was thinning and his chin was slightly too small. He was hardly the dynamo his cousin Kyle had been, and I wondered what would happen to the business now that he was top dog. I assumed Royce would inherit everything.

And wasn't that a nice motive for murder?

Royce's eyes were red and his shoulders were more slumped than usual. He appeared awkward and self-conscious as he glanced around the room. "Everyone loved Kyle."

"Yes, they did," I said. "He was one lovable guy."

"Always the life of the party," he said with a tinge of resentment. When he finally met my gaze again, he managed a thin smile. "I should go find the committee members. Perhaps we can speak later."

"Sure." I squeezed his arm in sympathy and he walked away. This was clearly not the time to tell him about the

Robert Burns book after all, but I knew I'd have to do it eventually.

Feeling even more depressed, I took the seat Derek held for me.

"Friend?" Derek asked.

"Kyle's cousin. I suppose he'll inherit everything."

"And you're thinking motive," he whispered.

I frowned. "I didn't say that."

I heard his snort of disbelief but ignored it as I turned to see who was seated nearby. I nodded to a few familiar faces, then noticed Peter and Benny, two bookseller friends, seated behind us. Peter leaned forward and invited me to their private cocktail party later in the week.

"I'd love to," I said, feeling a little more buoyant than before.

"Ooh, and bring that one along," Peter said under his breath as he made eyes at Derek, who paid no attention.

"Pretty," Benny cooed.

"He wouldn't miss it," I said, patting Derek's knee.

They both giggled.

I turned around in time to see Helen walking past us. I called her name and waved.

"Come sit here," I said, then took a quick look around to see if Martin was with her. Happily, he wasn't.

She nodded cautiously to Derek as she slipped past him and sat on my other side. "Thanks. I don't think I could face this by myself."

"Isn't Martin here?" I asked.

She gave me a dour look. "Even if he was, I don't want to sit with him."

"Oh." Well, thank goodness for that.

Peter tapped Helen on the shoulder. "Hey, girl."

Helen squealed and jumped up. She leaned over the

chair and hugged both men, who invited her to the cock-tail party, too.

When she sat back down, she was flushed and happy, but she quickly turned serious and grabbed my hand. "I want to apologize for this morning. It was a fluke. Martin happened to come along and I was still feeling vulnerable from last night, so he consoled me. He can be okay when he wants to be."

"I'm sorry I didn't stay. I just—"

She held up her hand. "Please, I know he's a pain. And he wouldn't take the hint and leave, so I didn't blame you one bit. Are we still on for lunch?"

"Of course." I leaned in closer to her. "So Martin knew about you and Kyle?"

"Oh, God, no." She clutched my arm for emphasis, then whispered, "No one knew about Kyle and me. Please don't say anything to anyone."

"You know I won't. It's just that you said he was consoling you."

Her lips quivered and she blinked back tears. "Because he knew I found the body."

"Ah," I said, not believing for a minute that Martin had merely been consoling her. He was the ultimate manipulator and would probably do anything to get her back in his life. I wondered if maybe Helen was wrong, that maybe Martin *had* known about her affair with Kyle. It would make him the perfect suspect for Kyle's murder. And there wasn't anyone I'd rather see behind bars. Well, except for Minka, but that dream would probably remain unfulfilled forever.

The problem with Martin being a suspect was that I couldn't see him taking the time and trouble to sneak into my hotel room and steal my stuff. Not that he wouldn't enjoy seeing me squirm in front of the police, but Martin was the poster boy for indolence. He simply wasn't the type to get his hands dirty. And climbing up that old fire escape to my room would've been a dirty job.

And for Martin to actually murder someone would mean that blood might spray all over him and those white linen pants he was forever wearing. And what was with those pants, anyway? What was he, the master of the croquet tournament? No guy wore white linen pants every day, did he? I mean, never mind the dirt. What about the wrinkles?

Okay, maybe I was being snotty. I knew this wasn't about white linen pants, because to be honest, I owned a pair or two myself. It was just Martin. I didn't like him, in case that wasn't clear. He was mean and persnickety. Killing someone would mean getting dirty, and I didn't think he had the guts to do it.

I glanced out at the crowded room. "So where is Martin?"

Helen looked around nervously. "He said he'd be here, but I hope he doesn't come. I can't deal with him. Not while everyone's talking about Kyle."

Derek's shoulder was pressed against mine, so I knew he was eavesdropping and I was glad of it. He was the one person who might be able to get me off the suspect list, so I was happy to have him listen in on any conversation that would help the cause.

Winifred Paine walked to the podium to welcome everyone, then began to talk about Kyle. Winnie was the elderly, powerful president of the International Association of Antiquarian Booksellers. I'd known her forever and admired her a lot. She was like the cranky grandmother who sent you to your room, then secretly sneaked cookies up to you.

"He was one of our own," Winnie said, then sniffled and blew her nose with a lacy hankie. "Simply a darling man. A bookseller of sterling reputation and such a gentleman. So full of life. I'm ... oh, dear, I don't know what I am. Devastated. Utterly ... devastated." She swept her arms up to include the throng. "As many of you are, as well."

Winnie Paine was a classy, authoritative woman who ruled the organization with an iron fist. I'd never seen her so overwhelmed with emotion, and watching her fumble her words made my throat swell in sympathy. I must've made some pitiful mewling sound, because Derek held out his handkerchief for me to use. And that was enough to cause my own tears to fall.

It's been said before: Nobody cries alone when I'm in the room. As I dabbed my eyes and blew my nose, Winnie cleared her throat and introduced Reverend Anderson, a local Anglican minister, to say a few words of comfort.

A very tall, scrawny, middle-aged man with thinning hair came to the podium, opened a small book and began to recite prayers. "Most merciful God, whose wisdom is beyond our understanding ..."

I tuned out, as I tended to do when religious people started praying on my behalf. I admit I could get a little impatient with mumbo jumbo church talk. I'd been raised in a commune with lots of all-inclusive, laid-back, cosmically lyrical preaching. But it wasn't just about that. The good Reverend Anderson didn't know Kyle and it was obvious. His generic words weren't personal, and I wanted to hear wonderful words spoken about Kyle by someone who knew him.

But then, maybe I was being unfair. Perhaps his words were soothing to others in the room.

I glanced around, noticing the dark mustard wallpaper and somewhat tacky burgundy candelabra sconces for the first time. I imagined Kyle would have been appalled to know that his memorial service was taking place here in this generic hall. He probably would've preferred to be memorialized at an elegant winery somewhere in the Dordogne Valley, overlooking the vineyards and meandering hillsides dotted with castles and châteaux and old-world villages.

"Amen," said Reverend Anderson.

"Amen," murmured the crowd.

I stared at the backs of all the people and suddenly realized the murderer might be in the room. He had to be here, gloating. He wouldn't miss it. The smug bastard.

The thought made me shudder.

Derek must've noticed, because he took hold of my hand and tried to rub some warmth back into it.

Next, Royce stood up and went to the front of the room. His eulogy was banal, but at least he'd known Kyle and could say something from the heart. His speech was mercifully short, and everyone seemed grateful for that.

I watched Royce as he walked back to his seat. He was a few years older than Kyle, about the same height but a bit pudgy and soft around the middle. I wondered if he might've killed his more attractive, popular cousin. I'd met Royce once or twice when I was dating Kyle but didn't really know him. Which meant he probably didn't hate me enough to steal my hammer and use it as a murder weapon.

Damn, that hammer was a real sticking point.

Winnie returned to the podium, scanned the crowd of three hundred or so and asked, "Would anyone else like to speak?"

She waited a beat, and when no one stood up, she said, "Is Brooklyn Wainwright in the room?"

"Huh?"

Derek was taken aback, too, and frowned at me.

"I didn't do anything," I whispered.

Everyone turned and strained to get a look at me. Was she going to point me out to the cops?

"Brooklyn, dear," Winnie said kindly, "I know you were one of Kyle's special chums. Would you be willing to share some memories with us?"

I groaned inwardly. This felt too much like high school, with me in the role of bad student being culled from the herd for purposes of ridicule. I hated high school.

"Come on, dear," Winnie coaxed.

Derek squeezed my hand. "You can do it, old chum."

"Oh, shut up," I whispered. Sucking in a deep breath and letting it out slowly, I stood and walked down the long aisle to the podium.

I coughed once to clear my throat. "Kyle was, well, more than a friend," I said humbly. "He was—"

A door banged open at the back of the room, and some woman shrieked at the sudden noise. That caused a few people to jump to their feet to see what the commotion was all about.

My view was blocked, so I stood on tiptoe to get a look. No luck. The chattering crowd grew louder as more people stood up to watch whatever was going on.

I left the podium and moved toward the aisle and finally saw what was causing the disturbance.

Minka LaBoeuf.

Why was I not surprised?

We all watched in amazement as she half dragged a sobbing woman down the aisle with her. Minka's face alternated between apprehension at the crowd's disapproval and disgust with her sniveling companion. But I detected a gleam of triumph in her beady eyes.

I didn't recognize the woman with her. She was taller than Minka but wispy, as though a soft breeze would knock her off her feet. She was blond and her face was pale and thin. Her gray raincoat was buttoned up tight and she wore a pink pashmina over her head and around her neck as though she'd been grabbed on her way to church. She looked fragile and frankly terrified, like a lamb being led to slaughter.

Minka, on the other hand, looked like a derelict Goth in frayed, tight black leather pants and matching way-too-tight vest over a purple mock-turtleneck sweater. And too much makeup, as usual. Wait. Were those pants *pleather*? Oh, dear God.

Minka marched right up to me and snarled, "Am-scray."

I held my hand over the microphone and whispered, "Are you nuts? Get out of here. I'm not finished."

Heck, I hadn't even started.

She elbowed me out of the way and leaned into the microphone. "Everybody sit down and shut up. I have an announcement to make."

"Wait a minute," I said.

Minka snapped her fingers. "Serena. Stand over here." She pointed to the other side of the podium.

Before the wispy woman could move, I grabbed Minka's arm and pulled her away from the podium.

"You can wait until I'm through talking," I said.

"Fuck off, *Brookie*." She wrenched her arm away, then tried to push me again, but before she could do it, I caught her hand, twisted it and shoved it away from me.

"Ow! You bitch!" she shrieked. "That hurts."

"Yeah?" I gave her hand another rough twist. "Well, don't call me Brookie."

She yanked her hand away and darted back to the microphone.

I got hold of her slimy pleather vest and hauled her farther away from the podium as three hundred people— some of them potential clients, damn it—attempted to watch every move and hear every word.

"Let go of me!" she wailed. "I have a right to talk!"

"After me," I said through clenched teeth as I clutched her arm tightly. I hadn't even wanted to talk before, but now I was determined not to let Minka push me off the stage. Kyle had been my friend, damn it. Minka didn't have the right to talk about him.

"We take our turns," I said. "It's how civilized society operates."

"Oh, screw you and your civil society." She struggled to get away. "When I'm finished talking, nobody'll care what you have to say."

I still had a tight grip on her arm, so she swung her other arm around and smacked the side of my head.

"Damn it," I said. "I'm sick of you hitting me." I snatched hold of her oily ponytail and pulled until she was bent backward and bellowing like a farm animal. I continued to pull her down until we were both on our knees. She had both arms free to punch and slap me as I jerked and twisted her head every which way.

Without warning, two strong arms pulled me back; at the same time someone else pulled Minka away from me.

"No!" I protested. "Let me kill her, please."

"Easy there, champ," Derek said as he effortlessly hauled me out of harm's way.

"Son of a bitch," I grumbled. "I almost had her."

"Yes, you did," Derek uttered close to my ear as he scooted me farther away. "We're all really proud of you."

"Thanks."

I noticed with some satisfaction that Detective Inspector Angus MacLeod was the one struggling to hold on to Minka. She wasn't going meekly.

The wispy blonde, Serena, stood a few feet away, wide-eyed and trembling.

"Who the hell is she?" I wondered aloud.

"I'm afraid we'll find out soon enough," Derek said as he urged me back toward our seats. I stopped in the middle of the aisle and watched Minka grapple for the microphone despite the detective's grip on her. I should've warned him about the pleather. That stuff made her slippery as a seal.

"Listen to me," Minka yelled, causing feedback to scream back at her. She pointed at the pale blond woman she'd dragged in with her. "This is Serena McVee! She's Kyle's wife. Or I should say, his *widow*."

"What?" I said, and turned to find Helen in the crowd.

"No." Helen gasped, and jumped to her feet. "No, she's—" She stopped, couldn't seem to catch her breath and began to sway. I stood watching as her eyes rolled back in her head and she dropped like a stone.

"You know how I feel about women fainting," Derek said as he paced the floor in front of the settee where Helen lay passed out.

Despite his ambivalence, minutes ago he'd swept Helen into his arms, yelled at Angus to call a doctor, and carried her out of the memorial service into the smaller sitting room down the hall. I'd shut the door and now the two of us stood by as she remained passed out on the couch.

"I seem to remember you had a slight problem with it," I said.

That was putting it mildly. Derek and I had met when Abraham died. Derek had pointed a gun at me and accused me of killing Abraham and stealing a priceless book, and I'd fainted right in front of him. He'd been unmoved, apparently, and had slapped me a few too many times trying to revive me. I hadn't appreciated it. It was the beginning of our beautiful friendship.

"Maybe I should find a washcloth for her forehead," I said.

"She'll come around when she's ready."

"Did she hit her head on anything?"

"No." Derek turned his attention to me. "How are you doing?"

I flexed my fingers and massaged my knuckles. "Great. That's been a long time coming. You should've let me pummel the wicked witch."

He grabbed my hand and examined it. "I would have, but she fights dirty. I was afraid she'd mar your pretty face."

With a sigh, I said, "I don't suppose MacLeod heard what I said out there."

He pursed his lips. "You mean the part where you begged me to let you kill Minka?"

I closed my eyes, nodded. "Yeah, that part."

He chuckled. "I believe everyone in the room heard it."

"Oh, swell."

"If it's any consolation, the bookies had you at four-to-one odds."

"Did you have money on me?"

"Of course, and you held the crowd's sympathies, as well."

"That counts for something."

"Bet your ass," he said, then tugged me closer. "Now tell me where it hurts."

"Everywhere," I whispered.

He kissed my cheek and moved his lips to my ear.

"Much better," I said, sighing.

"Wild women fighting," he murmured in disapproval. "Half the men were drooling over the prospect of watching a real live catfight. I thought I might have to battle some of them, as well."

"My hero." I wrapped my arms loosely around his neck as he ran his lips along my jaw.

"Hey, there y'all are!"

That voice. I knew that voice.

"Oh, Christ," Derek muttered. "I don't believe it."

He pushed away in time for me to be swooped up in a hug so tight, I nearly swooned.

"Oh, sweet Mother of God." I gasped.

"That's right, baby girl," my mother said. "Look out, Scotland, here come the Wainwrights!"

Chapter 7

"Mom, what are you doing here?"

"Came to see you, of course!" She hugged me again and her pretty blond ponytail bobbed with excitement. "Are you surprised?"

"Surprised?" That was an understatement. I'd been expecting Robin, but not in a million years had I expected to see my parents.

"Surprised and happy," I said, glancing from my petite, perky mom to my friend Robin and my tall, thin, handsome dad. "Really happy."

"Good to see you, Jim," Derek said to my dad.

I watched in bewilderment as Dad vigorously shook Derek's hand several different ways, ending with a fist bump. Derek seemed amused as he played along. Me, not so much. Oh, I was glad to see Mom and Dad, but things were just about to get interesting with Derek and—

"We wanted to surprise you!" Mom said. "We were packing for Paris when I got a message from Romlar X saying the northern lights are rocking right now."

"A message?" I said, confused. "Romlar's using e-mail now?"

"Oh, sweetie." She patted my cheek as if I were a

really sharp five-year-old. "Rom's all telepathic, all the time."

"I knew that." Or did I? Romlar X was Mom's astral guide. I thought he lived in another solar system. Who the hell knew how they communicated back and forth?

"We talked it over with Robson and he agreed this would be the best place to go for our anniversary trip," Dad said, pushing his glasses up. "Especially when he heard we'd be surprising you."

"Really?"

Mom nodded. "Robson said you could use a nice surprise or two."

"He has no idea," I murmured.

"Yes, he does," Dad said, eyeing me with concern.

Robson Benedict was the leader of the Fellowship for Spiritual Enlightenment and Higher Artistic Consciousness, the commune where my parents had raised me and my five siblings. Guru Bob, as we called him, was the highly evolved being my parents called teacher, avatar and friend.

Years ago, along with several hundred followers, my folks had followed Guru Bob to the hills of Sonoma County, where they'd bought up several thousand acres of lush fields before the wine country craze drove prices into the stratosphere. A few years ago, our business-savvy commune had incorporated, and now our formerly humble hillside home was a thriving, sophisticated wine-country destination. We'd named our small town Dharma.

"So that's when we contacted our favorite travel maven." Mom reached over and squeezed Robin's arm. "She was able to trade in our Paris reservations for a Scottish Highlands adventure quest."

"A quest. How intriguing." Over my mother's shoulder, I saw Robin grinning like a loon.

"Robin is our spirit guide," Mom said proudly. "So we're off to Kilmartin tomorrow. There's a harmonic energy circle outside of town that might finally prove the existence of the druidic triad."

"Finally." I smiled. Seriously, what else could I do?

"Fingers crossed," she said with excitement. "Then we'll go to Inverlochy to find the faerie hills. And there's a yew tree in Fortingall that's supposed to vibrate if your Vata dosha isn't aligned. I thought your father could use a tune-up."

I glanced at Dad. He shrugged, always happy to go along with Mom. Just like the rest of us.

"Lucky Dad," I said.

"You bet," he said.

"Is anyone else from Dharma joining you on the tour?" I asked them.

"Nope," Robin said. "It was always just me and your folks. I told you I was bringing a whole tour group in order to throw you off the scent. Did it work? Are you really surprised?"

"I'm in utter shock," I said.

"Good," she said, grinning with satisfaction.

"And I wish I could go with you," I said dolefully, wondering what Detective Inspector MacLeod would think if I up and ran off to the Highlands.

"Oh, we knew you'd be busy all week," Mom said, patting my cheek. "We just hope we'll get a chance to see our Pumpkin in action for a day or so! You don't mind, do you?"

Pumpkin. That would be me. The nickname was the result of my unfortunate obsession with Thanksgiving dessert at an early age.

Honestly, just looking at Mom and Dad made me feel better. Let's face it: So far, my time in Scotland hadn't exactly been a vacation. So to see friendly faces? People who actually knew me and loved me and oh, yes, *trusted* me not to be a cold-blooded murderer? Priceless.

"Of course I don't mind." I gave her a fierce hug. "I'm thrilled you're here."

Dad tapped me on the shoulder. "How about some of that for your old man?"

I moved from Mom into Dad's arms while Mom greeted Derek.

"Hello, Rebecca," Derek said warmly.

Mom giggled as she gave him a big hug. Nobody in the world but Derek called my mother Rebecca, and it seemed to delight her. Mom and Derek had experienced a bonding moment last month when they'd found me in the clutches of a killer.

Dad held me at arm's length, studied my face and asked, "How's it going, kiddo?"

I smiled brightly. "Super."

"Whoa, that doesn't sound good," Mom said immediately, her forehead wrinkling as her eyes narrowed. "What's wrong, sweetie?"

"What?" I frowned. "Nothing."

She slapped her hand onto my forehead. "Do you have a fever?" She squinted at me. "Your third eye looks cloudy. Are you constipated?"

"Help," I whimpered.

She tapped the top of my head. "How's your crown chakra? Whistle for me, will you?"

I tried to whistle as Dad turned to Derek. "If there's a disturbance in the force, Becky'll find it."

"Good to know," Derek said.

"I'm fine, Mom." I took hold of her hand, removed it from my head and squeezed it gently.

"I'll be the judge of that," she muttered, turning to rummage through her purse. "I'll need my stick."

Her *stick*? I broke away from her to give Robin a friendly hug.

"Jimmy, did I pack my healing rod?" Mom asked as she piled the contents of her bag on a nearby chair.

"It was on the list," Dad said.

"Why the hell didn't you warn me?" I whispered in Robin's ear. God knows I loved my parents, but a person really did need some preparation time before one of their visits.

"And miss this touching scene?" she said. "Not on your life."

"I'll kill you later."

"You can try," she said. "Cute boots, by the way."

"Thanks. Oh, God, my parents are insane," I moaned softly against her shoulder.

She laughed and hugged me tighter. "I love them."

Robin had practically grown up at my house and had known my family forever. My mom was as close to her as her own mother. Probably closer. She was yin to my yang, madcap Lucy to my down-to-earth Ethel. Since we'd grown up together in the commune, our shared memories were unique, to say the least. There was a bond between us that transcended space and time. If I were in trouble anywhere in the world, Robin would know it.

She knew it now. "What's going on?" she asked quietly.

"I'll fill you in later."

"Okay," she said. "And I want to know where you got that jacket. It's way *très* chic."

"You think? Thanks." I knew she would shriek when I told her I got it at Ross.

"Brooklyn?" a timid voice piped up.

Oops. Helen. I'd forgotten all about her. I rushed over to the couch as she struggled to sit up. She still looked a little woozy.

"How are you feeling?" I asked.

"Just completely embarrassed," she said lightly as

she tried to fluff her hair. "I'll get over it. Is this your family?"

I made the introductions, then explained, "Helen had a little fainting spell a while ago."

"Oh, you poor thing." Mom sat down next to Helen and patted her back. "Can we get you some water?"

"No, I'll be fine," Helen said weakly. "It was just such a shock."

"Of course it was," Mom said sympathetically, although she had no idea what had happened. Or did she? Maybe Romlar X had told her.

"A friend was killed last night," I explained, realizing they would all find out sooner or later anyway.

Mom glared right into my third eye. "I knew it."

Trying to avoid her perceptive gaze, I continued. "Kyle was a good friend of mine and Helen's. There was a memorial service a few minutes ago. It was difficult. Helen fainted."

"Kyle?" Robin said. "Weren't the two of you—"

I cut her off with a warning glance. "We found his body last night."

Helen let out a tiny cry and Mom pulled her into her arms. "Of course you're in pain," she said, rocking her gently. "You lost a good friend."

Tears sprang to my eyes and I was abruptly glad Mom was here. If anyone could deal with Helen's grief, it was my mother. She was the queen of empathy. I wouldn't be surprised to return home in a week and find that Helen had moved in. That was how good Mom was at this shoulder-to-cry-on thing.

"I'll never believe it," Helen whispered.

"What's that, sweetie?" Mom asked Helen. But she was looking at me for the answer. Everyone turned to me.

I gave Robin another look of warning, then said, "Kyle and Helen were in love."

"Oh," Mom cried, wrapping Helen in another hug. "How awful for you."

"But it turns out that Kyle was already married," I continued. "His wife showed up at the memorial service."

"That could get sticky," Dad said.

Derek nodded in agreement but said nothing.

"It could all be a sham," I said lamely. "Minka La-Boeuf was the one who announced the news. It wouldn't surprise me if she was lying."

"Minka?" Mom said. "Your chubby friend who made up those stories about you?"

"She is so *not* my friend," I insisted. I didn't correct the chubby part, so sue me. "But yes, she's the one."

Helen peeked up at me. "You have a real problem with her, don't you?"

I gritted my teeth. "She's a total psychopath."

Helen nodded. "I always thought she was sort of odd."

"Yes, that's a good way to put it," Mom said.

"You're both being way too kind," I said, rubbing my temple where Minka had managed to whack me upside the head, the chubby bitch.

I had to wonder why Minka would go to the trouble of making all this stuff up about Kyle and Serena if it wasn't true. What did she have to gain, either way? And why would that meek woman, Serena, play along with her? Was she an actress? Minka was more than capable of deception, but the other woman had appeared genuinely distraught. I could only conclude that she really was Kyle's wife. I still didn't want to believe it, mainly because she didn't look like she was a whole lot of fun. Kyle would've needed someone full of life and fun like him.

Wouldn't he?

Oh, how would I know? I didn't know him anymore.

And that hurt. I no longer had the right to judge what Kyle needed in a relationship. Obviously, he hadn't needed me. If he had, he never would've cheated on me.

But had Kyle needed Helen? Had they planned to marry? Maybe Kyle had been trying to get a divorce from this Serena person. Helen seemed so sure of him and their shared love. But if he was married, how had she gotten that impression? She'd been genuinely shocked to hear he had a wife. Now wasn't the time or place to ask Helen just how certain she was about Kyle's feelings, but I'd find a time later to pursue the question.

Derek glanced at his watch, and I realized I'd been staring into space ever since Minka's name was mentioned.

I shook myself out of my thoughts and turned to Robin. "What are your plans? I have to give a presentation in two hours and I need a little prep time. But I'll be free around four."

I explained that I was giving a seminar on book fraud and two bookbinding classes at the book fair this week.

"Can we sit in on your workshop this afternoon?" Mom asked.

I laughed. "You didn't travel over six thousand miles to sit in a stuffy conference room with me, did you?"

"Of course we did," she said with a grin.

"Suit yourself, but the subject matter's pretty dry."

"You'll make it sing," she predicted.

"Why don't we blow this place for a while," Dad said, shoving his hands in his pockets. "Take a look around town. We'll be back in time to see you in action."

"Great idea," I said. I could tell he was antsy. Dad thrived in the outdoors. He loved working in the vineyards back home, any time of year. Raised to join the corporate banking world of his wealthy father, Dad had rebelled and gone off to follow the Grateful Dead. Then, thanks to the Fellowship, he'd morphed again into a happy, successful farmer. He would have a grand time tramping through the Highlands.

"Helen, do you want to come with us?" Mom asked gently. "Some fresh air might do you good."

"I'd love to," Helen said excitedly, then grimaced and looked at me. "But we're having lunch."

I laughed. "We can always catch up later. Mom's right about the fresh air."

Relieved, she turned to Mom. "I'd love to go with you. Thanks so much."

Mom had worked her magic again. Maybe she truly did have an enchanted stick somewhere in her purse. If she did, I guess I could've used a shot at it myself. On second thought, I was going to let that go.

"I must run off to a meeting now, but I'd like to take you all to dinner tonight," Derek said out of the blue.

"Really?" I said, pleased by his offer.

"Yes, really," he said, aiming an intimate smile at me. Was I blushing?

"Oh, Derek!" Mom said after a quick exchange of looks with Dad. "We'd love that."

"But we'll take you," Dad said, getting an early start on the manly tradition of fighting over the bill.

"No, you're in my territory and I insist," Derek said with a firm smile. "You'll be my guests."

Dad knew when to capitulate. "That's very generous. Thanks, Derek."

Helen started to stand and Mom helped her up.

"Thank you," Helen whispered. "I hate feeling so weak."

Mom tucked Helen's arm through hers. "You should try to get your ojas replenished while you're here. I understand there's an excellent panchakarma clinic in the Grassmarket."

Helen raised an eyebrow in my direction and I stepped in to translate for Mom.

"Ojas," I said. "It's Sanskrit. Basically, it's the body's essential energy, or fluid of life, both physical and spiritual. So this panchakarma clinic will clean you out physically and set you right spiritually through enemas, some therapeutic purging and bloodletting. The usual stuff."

Her eyes widened.

"Don't frighten her," Mom admonished.

"Me? I'm not the one who— Never mind," I said when Mom gave me the raised-eyebrow look.

She patted Helen's arm. "When you get to be my age, you'll find out it's better to relieve psychic cramping than live with it."

"Hear, hear," Dad chimed.

The door opened. "I hate to interrupt."

I turned to see the burly presence of Detective Inspector Angus MacLeod standing in the doorway. Oh, great. Was I about to be arrested in front of my family and friends? What would my mother do if that happened? Would she threaten MacLeod with an ayurvedic cleansing? Talk about your international incidents.

"Hello, Angus," Derek said, moving to stand beside me. It wasn't a good sign.

"Hello, Detective Inspector," I said, wondering if there was some shorter version of his title I could use, since we were getting to be such close, personal friends.

He glanced around the room until he spied Helen. "Are you all right, miss? The hotel is trying to locate a doctor."

Helen shook her head. "Please, I'm fine. I don't need a doctor."

"If you're sure, I'll let the front desk know."

"Thank you," Helen said.

MacLeod signaled to an officer outside the door to call the front desk. Then he turned and handed me my canvas tool bag. "We're finished with these. Please put them in a safe place, Ms. Wainwright."

"I will. Thank you for returning them so quickly."

"You're welcome. Now, I had a few more questions."

I quickly swept my arm out toward my parents. "Let me first introduce my parents, Mr. and Mrs. Wainwright, and this is my friend Robin Tully."

"How do you do?" he said, tipping his head slightly to my parents. He turned to Robin and said, "How do you . . ."

His mouth hung open but he was no longer capable of speech. I'd seen it happen before. Some men found Robin, who was gorgeous and petite and fun-loving and stylish, utterly captivating. Apparently, MacLeod was one of them.

"I do just fine," Robin said in a sultry voice.

I stopped my eyes from rolling back in my head at her obvious come-on, because this was a new and welcome development. Maybe MacLeod wouldn't be so quick to arrest me if he suspected it would displease the fair Robin. Ooh, maybe he'd get so busy with Robin he'd forget about arresting me altogether.

Hey, we all have dreams.

I didn't know if she read my mind or not, but Robin turned her charm to full strength and aimed it right at MacLeod. "I was just on my way out to explore your beautiful city, Detective Inspector."

He slowly salvaged his senses. "I'd be pleased if you'd allow me to act as your guide."

"How lovely," Robin purred. I swear, she purred.

"Didn't you have questions for me?" I asked.

MacLeod didn't tear his gaze away from Robin as he said, "They can wait."

"Isn't that sweet?" Robin murmured.

"Sweeter than pumpkin pie," I said with a grin. "You kids go enjoy yourselves."

*   *   *

Left alone in the lobby, I headed for the front desk to retrieve Kyle's book from the hotel safe. As I stepped forward to speak to the clerk, Royce McVee stormed up to the desk.

"I'll be checking out directly," he said, sliding his credit card toward the clerk. "Please prepare my bill."

The clerk grabbed the credit card and started typing on the keyboard in front of him.

"Royce?" I said. "You're not leaving, are you?"

He jolted. "Good heavens, Brooklyn. Didn't see you there."

"Are you all right?"

He fussed with his collar, huffing and puffing. There was a light sheen of perspiration on his ruddy forehead. "No, nothing's all right. I'm leaving. With Kyle gone, I don't know what to do with myself. My clerks can handle the booth and the book fair particulars but I . . . I need to go."

"But the police are still investigating."

Clearly insulted, he darted a look at the clerk before whispering to me, "What are you insinuating?"

"Nothing," I said, waving my hands in protest. "Just thought you might want to take an interest in their findings."

"They know where to reach me." He tapped his foot, then exhaled heavily and shook his head. "I'm no good at this. I don't have Kyle's facility for superficial small talk. Never did. I have nothing to say to these people. I want to get home."

"I don't blame you," I said. "Is Kyle's wife going with you?"

His eyes flared and he clenched his jaw. "That lying tart is not my cousin's wife."

I blinked. "Really? Are you sure?"

"I've never seen her before in my life," he said in a

quietly furious tone. "And if she thinks she's getting one iota of McVee Partners Limited, she's got another think coming."

I winced. "But don't you suppose—"

"The woman just appears out of nowhere with this claim of—" He stopped, blew out another breath, shook his head, then laid his hand on my shoulder. "I beg your pardon, Brooklyn. Forgive me for going off. I'm simply upset about Kyle. Pay no attention to my ravings."

"Royce, maybe you should talk to the police. If you think Serena is a—"

He shook his head vigorously. "No, no, no, I can't go to the police."

"But if you think there's something fishy about this woman Serena, if you think she might be after Kyle's money, you should tell the police."

He huffed again. "Why would they believe me? They think I'm after the same thing."

"They do?"

"Kyle and I each held a fifty percent interest in the company," he whispered. "Even these Scottish detectives have enough brains to follow the money."

And all this time I thought I was the number one suspect. It was good to know that Royce thought he held that distinction instead.

"But if you leave town, don't you think the police will assume the worst?"

"Bugger," he muttered. His bushy eyebrows furrowed as he worried over that possibility.

The clerk walked to the printer, then returned to the counter. "Your statement, sir," he said, sliding the bill across the marble surface. "I hope you found everything to your satisfaction."

"I've decided to stay," Royce said with a determined nod as he pushed the papers back.

"Uh." The clerk looked slightly panicked and began typing even faster on his keyboard. "Yes, sir."

Royce shook his finger at me. "If that woman is staying, then so am I." His chin jutted out and he stood inches taller. It appeared as if he'd just discovered his backbone. Or maybe he'd just readjusted the stick up his butt.

"I'm glad you're staying," I said, "and I'm glad I ran into you. I have a book that belongs to you. I was just about to retrieve it from the hotel safe."

"A book? For me?"

"It's a book of poetry by Robert Burns." I explained how Kyle had wanted me to study and authenticate it. I assumed he knew the secret history since the book was part of his family's legacy.

After listening for a few moments, Royce waved his hand impatiently. "Yes, yes, I know the book you're speaking of. Kyle was quite exclamatory about it, but I simply can't bother with it right now. Would you mind holding on to it, Brooklyn? I'll obtain it from you eventually, but ... please, I haven't the wherewithal to deal with anything else just yet."

"I'm sorry."

He shook his head and fluttered his hands. "It's not your fault, my dear. I don't understand books, nor do I care to. Except for their monetary value, of course. Perhaps I should've been a banker, as Kyle always said." He laughed without humor. "I don't belong here. I should probably go home, just as I'd planned, but that woman ... well, I've said enough."

"I'll let you go then," I said, then remembered one more thing. "I wonder if I can have your permission to use the book in my workshop tomorrow?"

"I don't see why not," he said with a slight shrug. "You don't plan to rip it apart or some such thing, do you?"

I chuckled. "Absolutely not."

"Then you have my blessing."

Given the events of the last twenty-four hours, I had to admit I was relieved to find that the Burns book was still securely tucked away inside the hotel safe. Retrieving it, I hurried to my room, where I opened a bottle of water and sat at the desk to study my workshop notes, adjusting parts of it to accommodate the new addition. *Love Poems to a Flaxen'd Quean.*

I pulled my magnifying glass out of my tool pack and carefully checked the smooth fore-edge for telltale signs of mismatched paper. I checked the squares, that place inside the cover where the pastedowns met the leather turn-ins, for odd glue markings that might indicate twenty-first- rather than eighteenth-century binding. Then I leafed through the text block, spread the signatures and flicked the open threads with my thumbnail. I also studied the title page, looking for signs of forgery. I couldn't find anything suspicious.

This book was a genuine Cathcart; I knew it in my heart and could feel it in my hands as I ran my fingers over the elaborately gilded cover and raised bands of the spine. It was exquisite, right down to Cathcart's clever inset flyleaf with the thin band of gold leaf running under the edge where paper met leather. The book was small, maybe six inches by four, and one inch thick. It could be tucked into a pocket. A dear bitty thing, as Abraham, my old mentor, would've said. He tended to be gruff except when it came to books.

I studied the sentiment and signature on the white flyleaf page across from the title. Had Robert Burns truly signed it? I could go to the library and find examples of his signature, but actual confirmation would have to be done by someone with far more expertise than I had.

As I packed my briefcase with books and notes and tools, a tingle of excitement tickled my shoulders. Yes, I was a book geek. I couldn't help it. I knew the Burns book would get everyone in the workshop psyched up and asking questions and spouting theories that would create lots of buzz throughout the book fair. And at the risk of sounding like a crass capitalist, buzz meant business. I did love a good buzz.

The conference room designated for my presentation was surprisingly comfortable and inviting, with dark paneled walls and warm beige carpeting. Brown glazed art deco–style lamps hung from the ceiling, and matching sconces decorated the walls.

I'd expected the workshop to be attended by both book lovers and professional buyers curious about the problem of forgery inherent in the new-age world of fine-book collecting. I just hadn't expected a standing-room-only crowd.

I picked out Mom and Dad and Robin in one of the back rows and waved to them. Robin caught my eye, then turned her gaze toward the side wall. I followed her direction and was disconcerted by the presence of Angus MacLeod standing next to Derek. I looked back at Robin, who wore a smug grin. Rats. I would have to wait a full hour to find out what that grin meant.

I tried to ignore the cop as I showed examples of books that had been passed off as rare and antiquarian. My methods for proving fraud occasionally brought laughs and some groans. Many rare-book purchases are now transacted online, so it's easier than ever to defraud an unsuspecting buyer. Occasionally it was as simple as retouching a photograph of a book, but the most common method of fraud was when the seller glued an aged facsimile of a copyright page over the existing page to give the illusion that the book was decades older than it was.

I held up a sturdy, clothbound copy of Steinbeck's *Of Mice and Men* and told everyone they could come up after the workshop was over and study it.

"This was the subject of a criminal case I testified in, and when the case was over, I was able to buy the book."

I opened it and held up the front inside cover for the group. "If you study it up close, you'll notice extra little globs of glue along the boards."

I spread the covers open so that a gap appeared between the spine and the sewn and glued signatures. As I continued to bend back the covers, I heard a few gasps in the audience at my treatment of the book.

"It's okay," I said, giving them all a wide smile. "I'm a professional."

Some chuckles erupted, fortunately. In a book-loving crowd, breaking the spine of a book could get you drawn and quartered.

"Okay, you'll notice when you look through this gap that the signatures are sewn unevenly." I wandered up the center aisle, pointing out the defects as I spoke. "It's amazing that the defrauders actually went to the trouble to take the book apart and sew the fake pages in with the other pages, but didn't bother to even them out or check that the shade and thickness of the paper were anywhere similar to the original. Conceptually, I suppose they were pretty clever. But in reality, they needed a more professional bookbinder to carry it off. I don't mean to brag, but I would've done a far better job."

That line always got a laugh.

Finally, I brought out what I hoped would be the pièce de résistance, the Robert Burns poetry book. For a brief moment, I recalled the excitement in Kyle's eyes when he'd first shown me the book. Maybe I shouldn't have included it in my talk this afternoon, but I had a feeling Kyle would've approved and enjoyed it. Then I smiled for the audience and explained that this was the type of book that might create quite a stir in the bookselling community. The book itself was exceptional, and the story behind it was sensational.

"Now, it's undoubtedly an original Cathcart binding and very rare," I said. "But here's how a criminal—oh, let's call him an overenthusiastic businessman—might boost his income. First of all, *Love Poems to a Flaxen'd Quean* is thought to contain poems written by Robert Burns, but never before seen anywhere in Great Britain."

A murmur rumbled through the crowd and I knew I had them.

"So you might be willing to spend more to get your hands on this book, right?" I asked.

Several in the crowd nodded eagerly.

"And what better way to pull a fast one on a Scottish book lover than to combine never-before-seen poems from a beloved poet with a compelling legend that includes star-crossed lovers, a secret baby and a powerful monarchy bent on destroying the evidence of their love? And by evidence, I mean this very book."

The murmuring grew to comments and gasps and a few laughs as people got into the story. I looked over the crowd and spotted a frown on the detective inspector's face while Derek was giving me his piercing, narrow-eyed look.

Was he reacting to the crowd or to my story? I hesitated, but then plunged ahead. "The question is, is the story true? Or did the seller, looking for a way to jack up the price, spin an alluring tale of a king's daughter giving birth to a child of the Scottish—"

"Stop!"

The crowd turned to see who had yelled, but Perry

McDougall was already stalking toward me, his fisted hand raised up in angry protest.

Before anyone could stop him, before I even had a chance to react, he grabbed the book from me and shouted, "You'll not besmirch the monarchy, ye Yankee bitch!"

Chapter 8

Without a thought to my personal safety, I snatched the book back from Perry and ran for the door—and crashed straight into the substantial chest of Angus MacLeod. He threw his arms around me instinctively, a protective gesture against Perry, who lurched to a stop right behind me.

"Give me the book," Perry demanded.

"No," I shouted back, my fervor muffled somewhat by MacLeod's wool jacket.

"You haven't the right to—"

"Enough!" MacLeod bellowed, and the entire room fell silent. The man had a way of controlling a crowd; I'll give him that. With a snap of his fingers, he gestured to one of his men to take hold of Perry, who struggled briefly but then walked away, all dignified and huffy, with the cops following close behind him. Only then did MacLeod let me loose. But not for long.

"You'll come with me now, Miss Wainwright."

"When do we get to see the fake book?" a lady piped up in the front row.

I tried to shake off the adrenaline rush as I composed myself and turned to the audience. "I'll try to post information on the bulletin board with the time and place I'll be showing the books I discussed today. Thank you all for coming."

The room burst into enthusiastic applause and I wanted to take my bows, but MacLeod had other ideas. His meaty hand clutched my arm as he led me out of the room.

"I'll be here all week," I cried, waving to my people.

"You sound like a stand-up comic in Vegas," Robin said heatedly as she sidled up beside me. "'I'll be here all week?' What was that all about?"

"Hey, I was a hit."

"You almost *were* hit," Robin hissed. "Your parents are going bananas."

I whirled around and saw Mom beaming at Derek, who seemed to be distracting both Mom and Dad with a story of his own. I would thank him later. "Mom looks fine. Everything's fine. I've got the book. That's all that matters."

"I'll be the judge of what matters, Ms. Wainwright," MacLeod grumbled.

"Hey," Robin defended, "she's the one who was attacked."

The detective beamed at Robin, but didn't let go of my elbow.

"Where are we going, anyway?" I asked, but Mac-Leod didn't seem inclined to answer.

So I went along quietly, studying the Burns book as we walked. It looked so small and defenseless for having caused so many problems.

"That's all that matters to you," Robin said, shaking her head in resignation. "You really are mental."

"I had to save the book," I said as I tucked it inside my jacket pocket. That was what my mentor taught me: Books were sacred.

"I know," she said, conceding the point. She was well aware of my philosophy. I'd been binding books since I was eight years old, and she'd been my best friend the whole time.

"I thought the workshop went well," I said as Mac-Leod continued down the hall with all of us in his wake.

Robin laughed. "The audience won't forget it anytime soon."

"That's a good thing, right?"

"Depends on your definition of *good*."

"Memorable?"

"Most definitely."

"We'll go in here," MacLeod said gruffly, after checking that the conference room was empty.

"We're right behind you, honey," Dad said staunchly. A child of the sixties, Dad still had issues with "the Man" and wasn't about to let his little pumpkin be led off to some airless interrogation room to be brutalized by the police. Not if he had anything to say about it.

"Thanks, Dad." I waved to him over my shoulder, noting that Mom and Derek were right behind Dad. Two policemen followed in their wake. Oh, boy, the gang was all here.

"We're staying with her," Robin said to MacLeod. A look passed between them. He considered her for a long moment, then nodded.

I raised an eyebrow at Robin and she gave me a minute nod. Something was definitely going on between those two. Fascinating. I itched to know what had happened but knew I'd have to wait to hear the whole story later. If I wasn't carted off to jail first, that is.

I hadn't had much of a chance to tell Robin anything about the murder, but she seemed to have some awareness that I was in trouble. Yes, we were close, but I didn't think she could read my mind. Had MacLeod told her anything? That seemed like a breach of something, not that I cared if Robin knew. But still, didn't he have a code of ethics to follow?

The small room was set up with a podium up front

and about fifty chairs arranged in rows. MacLeod suggested I take an aisle seat and he turned a chair around to face me. Then he pulled a small notebook and pen from his jacket pocket.

Dad, Mom and Robin sat two rows back, within listening range. The two officers stood near the door and Derek prowled the perimeter of the small room, making me more nervous than I already was.

"So, were you besmirching the monarchy, Miss Wainwright?" Angus MacLeod asked right off the bat. His tone was light, but I wasn't fooled. That question put an end to any thought of presumed innocence.

"Absolutely not," I said stoutly. "I was giving a book-fraud workshop. This book provided a perfect example of a mythology that could be built up in order to swindle a potential buyer. It had nothing to do with the monarchy, for goodness' sake."

"Do you know Perry McDougall, the man who attacked you?"

"Yes."

He waited, but I didn't say anything more. Hey, I watched *Law & Order*. I knew how to play the game.

He sighed. "And how do you know Mr. McDougall?"

"Oh, Perry's been attending the European book festivals for years. He's got an antiquarian bookstore in Glasgow, and he has an online presence, as well. He's considered an expert when it comes to books on Celtic history, British and Scottish history, World War Two, guns, all sorts of things."

"Did he have a particular grudge against you?"

"Not really," I said, but it was the bad liar in me talking. Everyone in the room knew it.

"Okay," I said, before anyone else could snort in disbelief. "We had a little run-in the other day, but nothing to get all freaked out about."

"So what would you say freaked him out, then?"

I pulled the Robert Burns out of my pocket. "It has something to do with this book."

"That seems clear," MacLeod said, eyeing the book. "Is it yours?"

"No."

He nodded. "May I see it, please?"

I gave him the Burns and was pleased to see him handle it gingerly. He opened it, stared at the signature page, then looked at me through wide eyes.

"Is it what I think it is?"

I knew how he felt. I must've had the same look of astonishment when Kyle first showed it to me.

"It hasn't been authenticated," I said, hedging.

He frowned. "Is it your job to verify an author's signature?"

"Not usually," I admitted. "But I'm often hired to authenticate the book itself. Its age, provenance, history, the bookbinder who made it and usually the bindery it came from. But none of that information can actually prove that Robert Burns signed it. For that, we'll need handwriting expertise, ink testing, and more historical data."

"You'd test the ink?" MacLeod said. "Wouldn't that destroy it?"

"Not necessarily," I said, getting into the topic. "Still, it would have to be done with extreme care, and I wouldn't want to be the one to do it."

MacLeod's fingers moved slowly over the page but avoided the signature itself. I was glad I didn't have to tell him not to touch it. I didn't want to antagonize him more than I already had.

"So this book is in your possession in order for you to authenticate it?"

"Yes."

He turned the book over in his hands. "It's obviously quite valuable. Who entrusted you with it?"

I swallowed hard. "Kyle McVee."

He sighed.

I rushed to add, "I told you I ran into Kyle yesterday afternoon. That's when he gave me the book and asked me to study it."

"And hours later, he was brutally murdered."

I bit my lip as my stomach took a dip. "Yes."

"Over a *book*?"

He made it sound like an insult to books everywhere. I folded my arms across my chest, lifted my chin and said, "Maybe."

"Why didn't you mention the book when we questioned you last night?"

My mother shot to her feet. "I object!"

I gasped.

MacLeod was clearly taken aback. "What?"

Derek snorted with laughter.

I managed a chuckle. "Mom, it's okay."

"Sorry," Mom muttered, waving away her outburst as she sat again. "Wrong number."

"Oh, God," Robin whispered, then covered her face with both hands, but I could see her shoulders were shaking with laughter.

MacLeod stared at me in disbelief. Hey, it wasn't my fault my mother lived in a parallel universe.

The "wrong number" reference came from Mom's belief that everyone had a sort of tape recorder inside their brains that played the everyday phrases people used. According to Mom, each phrase on this imaginary tape recorder was numbered, and, at appropriate times, our brains pushed a button to allow us to say something appropriate. It took very little conscious thought to say, "How are you?" or, "Fine, thanks," "I'm sorry for your loss," "You're not wearing that," "Because I'm the mother," and so on.

Apparently, "I object!" was also one of Mom's catch-phrases. And why not? She was a *Law & Order* junkie, too. Not to mention she had six kids. That gave her plenty to object to on any given day.

So Mom was apologizing for playing the wrong number on her "tape recorder." In essence, it all had to do with cosmic consciousness and being present in the moment, but I wasn't about to go there with MacLeod.

I blew out a breath. "I tried to tell you about the book, but we kept being interrupted and I forgot to bring it up again."

MacLeod thumbed through his notes, then tapped a page with his pen. "Ah, I do remember you starting to tell me something, when my investigator came to the door."

"That was it." My stomach twitched at the memory of the investigator walking in with my bloody hammer.

MacLeod put down his notebook and picked up the Robert Burns again. Resting his elbows on his knees, he studied the book some more. Then, almost under his breath, he said, "I dinna ken why anyone would murder someone over a bleedin' book."

Was that another book insult? I told myself not to pursue it, but when was the last time I listened to my own good advice? "People have killed for much less than a rare, priceless book, Detective Inspector."

Oh, why didn't I just shut up and stop provoking him? I glanced at Derek, whose firmly set jaw indicated he was wondering the same thing.

But MacLeod just nodded and said absently, "Yes, of course they have." Still holding the book, he said, "Excuse my ignorance, but what did you mean in your lecture when you talked about mythology as it pertains to a book?"

I settled back in my chair, finally comfortable with a question. "A less than scrupulous bookseller will occasionally take a book's history and provenance and embellish it in hopes of stirring up interest and raising the price of the book."

"So they lie to get a better price."

"Basically, yes," I said, though my terminology sounded classier. "They don't see it that way, of course. Anyway, that's why I included this book in my fraud workshop. It's got a truly bizarre and exciting mythology to go with it."

"Something about star-crossed lovers and a secret baby?"

So MacLeod had actually been paying attention to my workshop talk. It made me smile. "Yes, something about that."

"What else?"

"It's just a theory," I said hesitantly, moving back into my discomfort zone.

"It's obvious that something you said set McDougall off," he said. "So let's hear the whole story."

I could've lied. I was getting better at it. I peeked at Derek's frown and realized that, no, I wasn't. Fine.

I took a deep breath and said, "This book is supposed to contain love poems by Robert Burns never before seen anywhere else, poems dedicated to an English princess. In theory, one of King George the Third's daughters, Augusta Sophia, came to Scotland and had an affair with the poet Robert Burns. She went back to England and soon gave birth to a son. That young son took his place in the line of English succession and was never acknowledged to be the child of Robert Burns. But he was, according to some, and the proof is in the extremely graphic, never-before-seen poems in this book."

I sat back, feeling a little dizzy with all that I'd divulged in one breath.

There was stunned silence for a few brief seconds; then Robin whispered, "Cool."

MacLeod burst into laughter. "You're pulling my leg, Miss Wainwright."

Not the reaction I'd expected, but it was better than a poke in the eye, as Dad would say.

"No, I'm not," I said. "That's exactly what Kyle told me. Now, whether it's true or not, I can't say. I'm not an expert in British and Scottish history. But Perry is, so that's why Kyle asked him about the history behind the book. Perry went ballistic, and the next thing Kyle knew, someone was trying to kill him. And they succeeded."

MacLeod shook his head. "So you think Perry Mc-Dougall killed Kyle McVee."

I opened my mouth but quickly shut it. Who was I to accuse someone of murder?

"Miss Wainwright?" he coaxed.

"Kyle said he talked to three people about the book. Perry was one of them."

"You were another."

I grimaced. "Maybe. I guess so."

"Who is the third person?"

"I don't know. Kyle rushed off before he could tell me."

"Bummer," Mom said.

"Indeed." MacLeod checked his notes. "So when you began besmirching the monarchy during the workshop, were you goading Mr. McDougall?"

"I wasn't besmirching anybody, and no, I wasn't goading Perry."

His eyes narrowed. "Honestly?"

"I wasn't besmirching anybody," I repeated impatiently. "I was just making a point about slightly improper bookselling practices. I wasn't going to reveal the whole King George connection to the workshop participants."

"You were skirting a bit close, though."

Jeez, whatever. "Maybe. I didn't think so."

"I've got to go with the Man on this one, sweetie," Mom admitted.

"Mom! Not helpful."

She pointed to the middle of her forehead, to her third eye. "Justice is blind and the truth hurts, Pumpkin."

Huh? I caught Derek grinning and I glared at him.

"Okay." I waved my hands in defeat. "I just didn't think it would be that big a deal. I mean, the Scots aren't all that enamored of the British monarchy, are they?"

"To most Scots," MacLeod surmised, "it would be more of a killing offense to besmirch the memory of the beloved poet Rabbie Burns than the English monarchy."

"I know, right?" I said, grinning, but the grin was not returned and I groaned inwardly. It would help if I remembered whom I was talking to, namely, a cop who might want to drag me off to jail. Nice.

With some reluctance, I said, "Okay, I suppose I might've gotten an eensy bit too close to the real story, and that must've upset Perry."

"You think so?"

I exhaled resignedly. "Okay, it definitely maybe did."

He tipped his head, accepting my answer, however much I'd tried to obfuscate it.

"But," I added quickly, "the only reason I mentioned the Burns book in the workshop was that it was a perfect example of a story that could be exploited in order to raise the price of the book."

Dad gave me two thumbs-up, as though I'd made a wickedly smart move in a game of checkers. Dad's standards were overly generous where his kids were concerned.

"Yes, so you've said," MacLeod said.

"Well, it's true."

"That's all well and good for the purposes of your

presentation," MacLeod said philosophically, shutting his notebook and sitting back in his chair. "But who's to say your words didn't inflame a killer? You might want to consider that, and perhaps think before you speak next time."

I bristled at first, hearing only his insult—which was so unfair. I often thought before I spoke. Then a chill speared my shoulder blades at the thought that at this very minute, Kyle's killer might be roaming the book fair, looking for me.

It took another beat before the meaning behind his words hit me. He thought the killer was still out there. "Wait. Does this mean I'm no longer a suspect?"

"No." He shoved his notebook in his pocket and handed me the Burns.

"Uh, no, I'm no longer a suspect?" I asked hesitantly. "Or no, I'm still a suspect?"

He smiled indulgently. "You own the murder weapon and you have no alibi, Miss Wainwright. What do you think?"

My shoulders slumped. "Right."

"You're free to go for now," he said, then stood and held out his hand to help me up. "But don't leave town."

"I think that went well," Mom said as we walked down the hall to the escalators. Dad and Derek were trailing behind, deep in conversation.

"He thinks I'm capable of murder, Mom."

"Oh, no," she said, waving her hand to dismiss my fears. "His sixth chakra was practically glowing indigo, which means he's highly intuitive and clear-sighted."

"Well, that's something."

"And in combination with his rather stunning Martial essence, he'll make a passionate lover for some lucky woman." Mom winked at Robin, who made a strange gargling sound.

"Do you need a Heimlich?" I asked her.

"Stop looking at me," Robin said between gasps.

I grinned and turned back to Mom. "I'm happy for that lucky woman, whoever she may be. But the fact remains, he still thinks I'm guilty."

"No, he doesn't," Mom said with perky assuredness. "He let you go, didn't he?"

"He knows where to find me," I muttered, stepping onto the escalator. When we reached the lobby, Mom and Robin went to the pub, Derek left to take care of dinner reservations and Dad went off to talk to the concierge to get directions for their trip tomorrow. I headed for the front desk to put the Burns book back in the hotel safe.

As I crossed the lobby to join Mom and Robin in the pub, I saw Perry talking to three other men near the entrance to the shopping arcade. So I guessed the police hadn't detained him, either. He didn't see me, and I planned to keep it that way.

Mom and Robin had already grabbed a table and ordered our beers, so I sat down and filled them in on some of the details about the murder, such as why I was the prime suspect. When I mentioned the bloody hammer, Mom shrank in horror.

"Honey, you're attracting some awfully bad juju lately," she said in a worried voice. "I recommend a spleen wash PDQ."

"Mom," I started, just as the waitress brought our beers. I guzzled mine down as Mom studied me.

"Or maybe you should get a cat," she said finally.

"Cats fix bad juju?"

"No," she said with a smile. "But they make such sweet companions."

I glanced sideways at Robin, who looked as baffled as I felt. I took another sip of beer. "Thanks for the suggestions, Mom, but that's a big 'no way' on the spleen wash."

"You say that now, but it's obvious that your chi is stagnating, and nothing clears that up like a good old-fashioned spleen wash followed by a granola enema."

"Ouch," Robin said. "Granola?"

"It's a finely ground blend of oats, crisp rice and sesame seeds infused with mineral oil," Mom assured us.

It was a miracle I didn't choke on my beer. "I'll get back to you on that."

She shrugged. "Or you can always get a cat."

Chapter 9

The next morning I dressed in jeans, boots and a forest green turtleneck sweater, then went downstairs to meet Mom, Dad and their stalwart spirit guide, Robin, in the hotel restaurant. I slid into the booth next to Mom and gratefully accepted a cup of coffee from the passing waitress.

As I poured cream into my coffee, I said, "Wasn't that a great dinner last night?"

"Oh, yes," Mom said. "Derek is the perfect host, isn't he?"

"He was too generous," Dad said.

I took a sip of coffee. "So, are you all packed up and ready to go?"

No one responded. Robin wouldn't make eye contact with me. Dad busily stirred honey into his tea. That was when I knew something was wrong. Dad hated tea.

"What is it?" I asked. "What's wrong? What's going on?"

"I knew she'd make a fuss," Mom said with a flustered wave of her hands.

"What fuss? Who's making a fuss? What aren't you telling me?"

"We're not going anywhere, sweetie," Mom said defiantly. "And that's final."

Dad reached across Mom and patted my hand. "How

can we leave you when you're going through such trauma?"

Alarmed, I turned to Robin, who said simply, "They want to stay."

"But . . . but what about the druidic triad?" I asked. "And the vibrating yew tree thingie? Dad?"

"We'll get there sometime," he said. "But right now, you need us more than my dosha needs an alignment."

"Are you sure, Dad? Because you look a little bent."

He chuckled. "Now, see, Becky? There's her sense of humor coming back." Dad wrapped his arm around Mom because she looked about ready to cry. That couldn't be good.

"Mom, I'm thrilled that you want to stay," I said quickly, and really hoped I sounded sincere. "But I won't be able to spend much time with you. I've got the book fair."

"We can amuse ourselves," she said with a sniffle. "We'll have our own minitour around Edinburgh."

"I'll take care of all the details," Robin said.

"Thanks, sweetie," Mom said, then looked at me. "We just want to stay close by in case you need us. In case they put you in . . . in . . . oh, God, we won't let you go to jail."

"I'm sure that won't happen," I said, not so sure of anything. I gave her a hug before she started wailing. "But thanks, Mom. I'm happy you're staying."

"I love you," she whispered as she dabbed her eyes with her napkin.

"I love you, too."

She composed herself as the waitress brought her a bowl of fruit and rushed off. Mom speared a chunk of pineapple, then said thoughtfully, "You should schedule a high colonic while you're here. You know how travel affects your nama-rupa equilibrium."

"Mom, please, not before breakfast." According to

the most basic tenets of Buddhism, nama-rupa was the coexistence of mind and matter. Both contained combinations of elements and sensations. I could go on and on, but seriously, before breakfast? I needed food first.

Mom pointed her fork at me. "It might bring you to moksha; I'm just saying."

"Come back, Mom," I said, teasing her. Some believed moksha was comparable to nirvana, or ultimate peace. I was all for that, but didn't really think I'd attain it with a high colonic.

"I could go with you," Robin said, winking at me. "I'm always up for getting hosed."

"I'm having the waffles," Dad said helpfully, passing me the menu.

Over breakfast, Mom and Robin planned their little tour of Edinburgh sites. Mom said she'd heard from a woman in the elevator that there was an energy convergence circle halfway up the back side of Arthur's Seat, Edinburgh's highest peak, that was rippling with powerful soul medicine. Robin suggested that maybe after their tour of the Palace of Holyroodhouse, they go on a hike up the mountain to find it.

Dad and Mom were both up for the trip.

Then Robin announced that she knew of a shaman out near Rosslyn Chapel who conducted drum circles and occasionally manifested as a crow. Mom started twittering with excitement.

I gave Robin a grateful smile. I hated seeing tears threatening to gush forth from Mom's eyes. She might be loony, but she was mine.

Once breakfast was over and they'd taken off for the palace tour, I hit the book fair. It was barely ten o'clock, but the great assembly hall was already crowded with people wandering up and down the aisles, checking out some eight hundred booths of booksellers, art gallery owners and vendors hocking ephemera, engravings, posters and maps. Some sellers earnestly discussed their wares, while others bartered and kibitzed with the passing crowd. Many in the mass of people were serious buyers, others just book lovers hoping to see something beautiful, unique or odd.

I stopped at one counter to admire a beautiful copy of *Sense and Sensibility*. The navy blue leather cover was inlaid with an exquisite miniature painting of the author framed by rows of tiny pearls. I checked the price. Eight thousand dollars.

"A real bargain," the bookseller said, tongue in cheek.

I laughed. "I don't know how, but I'm going to pass."

He chuckled good-naturedly, and I took the opportunity to ask if he knew anyone who had been close to Kyle.

"I'm just looking for people to commiserate with," I said, which was true, sort of.

He pointed out two booksellers I should talk to, so I thanked him and headed their way. The two older men owned Fair Haven Books in Dublin, and I was pretty certain they were innocent of murder, but I asked them a few questions anyway. The first man, Duncan, didn't know Kyle, but the other one, Jack, told me that he and Kyle were old friends and that he had, indeed, discussed the Burns poetry book with Kyle. He was enthusiastic and, given his own knowledge of British history, believed it was entirely possible that the story behind the book was true. He'd told Kyle he couldn't wait to see it.

"I was deeply saddened by the news of his passing," Jack said.

"Thank you," I said. Walking away, I felt even more depressed than before. So Jack was the third person Kyle had talked to, if I was included in that number. I would let Angus know, and he'd probably want to question the Irishman, but I knew there was no way Jack had

anything to do with Kyle's death. First, because he was
rather frail, but also because he was excited about the
book, not angry like Perry was. Jack wouldn't want to
stifle the book being introduced to the public.

As I wandered the aisles, I had the uncomfortable
thought that Kyle might've shared the book's history
with Jack and Perry only in order to titillate them in
hopes of raising the selling price. I hoped it wasn't true.
I hated to think that his death was caused by his own
greed.

I decided to let go of my immediate worries over
Kyle's personal motives and his death, as well as the attack by Perry McDougall, not to mention possible jail
time or the fact that my parents were staying for the
whole week, and simply enjoy the book fair.

I passed a booth featuring original French movie posters from the fifties and decided on the spot I had to have
one. I spent twenty minutes trying to choose which of
them would look more fabulous on my living room wall
back home. I narrowed it down to either a tormented
Doris Day starring in *Piège à Minuit* (*Midnight Lace*), or
an almost whimsical poster for a horror movie, *La Nuit
de Tous les Mystères*, or *House on Haunted Hill*, starring
Vincent Price. This one featured a scary skeleton grabbing at a lady's flimsy negligee.

In the end, the decision was easy. The randy skeleton
won the day. I grimaced at the price tag of four hundred
dollars but happily paid it when the wily owner offered
to ship it back to San Francisco for free. It occurred to
me when the transaction was completed that my recent
inheritance of Abraham's six million dollars hadn't sunk
into my brain yet. I might not have balked so much at
the price if I'd remembered.

It was occasionally startling to realize I could buy almost anything I wanted now. I'd never been much of
a shopaholic, much to Robin's exasperation. She was a

shopping connoisseur and made no secret of her desire to drastically improve my wardrobe, while I really didn't see the need.

I turned at the last booth and headed down the next aisle. I was approaching a stall that sold beautiful sheets of Asian book cloth when I spotted Helen a few booths away. She was talking animatedly to someone I couldn't see. I walked toward them, then abruptly stopped. The other woman was Serena, Kyle's wife, the wispy woman Minka had dragged into the memorial service yesterday.

The two of them bonding seemed so wrong in so many ways that I wanted to turn around and run. But Serena was just the person I needed to talk to, so I steeled myself and walked over to them.

"Oh, Brooklyn," Helen said, waving me closer. "Have you met Serena McVee, Kyle's wife?"

"No," I said, holding out my hand to shake hers. "Hi."

"How do you do?" she said in her softly chirpy British voice. Her eyes were wide and friendly, but how could I trust them? I still couldn't believe Kyle had been married. She dabbed her nose with a tissue and I remembered my manners.

"I'm sorry for your loss," I said, then thought, *What a totally lame thing to say*. I sounded like a cop.

She didn't seem to notice as she thanked me. "You've all been so very kind."

"I didn't know Kyle was married," I said, and immediately wanted to slap myself for saying something so idiotic and thoughtless. But again, Serena didn't seem to take offense.

"I didn't know many of Kyle's friends," she explained. "We came from two different worlds, and I suppose we simply continued to keep those two worlds apart. I'm embarrassed to admit I only just met his cousin Royce earlier today."

"You just met Royce," I repeated. "That's, um, nice. And comforting," I added.

"Oh, he's wonderful, isn't he? So supportive. So kind."

Royce? Were we talking about the same uptight, chinless businessman?

Serena giggled. "I'm sure he must've thought I was a madwoman, coming at him from out of the blue."

You have no idea, I thought, but kept my mouth shut.

"You see," she continued, "Kyle and I have been in love since we were teenagers, but I'd never met his family."

"Since you were teenagers?" I repeated again. I couldn't help it. I didn't know what else to say. Royce's furious words were still fresh in my mind.

She smiled bashfully. "Young and foolish, I suppose. But the feelings never went away."

Okay, that was weird. I'd practically lived with Kyle for those brief months back when we were dating. We would go out and see friends all the time. We'd had cocktails with Royce more than once. What the hell had Kyle been doing with me if he'd had a wife all that time?

I managed to swallow a shriek to ask, "So you and Kyle have been married since your teens?"

"Married? Oh, no, no, no," she said quickly. "We only married last year. But we've known each other, were pledged to each other, for . . . goodness, it must be more than ten years."

"I see." Well, that was something. At least he hadn't been married to someone else while he was cheating on me. But "pledged" to each other? Good grief, I'd always known Kyle was a cad, but this was ridiculous.

If it was true. Royce's angry words continued to swirl around my brain, gathering strength.

I coughed to clear my dry throat. "So you said you've never met Kyle's family before?"

"He wanted our love to be ours alone." She smiled sweetly. I hated to admit it, but she seemed naive and innocent, not the lying tart Royce had insisted she was.

"This weekend was to be my coming out, so to speak." She began to tear up and blotted her eyes with the tissue. "I can't believe he's gone."

"Neither can I," Helen said, gripping Serena's arm. "It's so awful."

"But it's been wonderful meeting so many people who loved Kyle," Serena said.

"Yes, we all loved Kyle a lot," I said, then bit my lip as Helen shot me a dirty look.

"It's almost made this trip worthwhile," Serena continued. "If only . . . if only . . ." She gasped, tried to catch her breath, then dissolved into tears.

Helen hugged her close. "It's okay," she whispered, then met my gaze and shook her head in pity. "Poor thing."

I gave her a look of complete disbelief. I couldn't help it. Helen was too sweet for her own good. And Kyle had betrayed her in the worst way. Yes, he'd betrayed Serena, too, but I was more concerned about Helen.

And frankly, I was a little concerned about myself, too. Had Kyle really known this woman since high school? Had he pined for her all that time? Even while we were dating? Maybe I was deluding myself, but I couldn't believe it. Okay, Serena was pretty, yes, but in a vapid, pasty-faced way. Not Kyle's type at all.

But as I stared at Serena, I had to question whether I really knew anything about Kyle's type of woman. He'd been a cheater, a player. How could I claim to know him at all?

Oh, hell, of course I knew him. Yes, he was a player. Yes, he was dangerous to a woman's heart. No, I couldn't claim to know his every thought and reason for doing what he did. But I was still willing to swear on a stack of Bibles that he never would have fallen for this insipid woman.

And that was my final answer.

"Let's get you something to eat," Helen said, still rubbing Serena's back.

"I would love that," she said. "You're so thoughtful, Helen."

"Brooklyn, can you join us?" Helen asked.

"Uh, no," I said quickly. "Thank you. You enjoy your lunch. I've got some research to do before my workshop."

"Maybe we can have a drink later," Helen said in a hopeful tone.

"Absolutely," I said. "Leave a message for me. Nice meeting you, Serena."

"You, too."

I took deep breaths and tried to think good thoughts as I walked away. I considered exploring more of the book fair, but meeting Serena had sucked the joy out of the day. And speaking of joy sucking, I suddenly realized I might run into Minka if I stayed here much longer.

I rubbed my arms as goose bumps broke out. Just thinking about Minka made me uneasy. What if I saw her here? I'd deliberately avoided walking near Perry McDougall's booth, where I thought she would be working, but now it occurred to me that she could be anywhere.

That was when I remembered there was something I needed to take care of. Something that would take my mind off Serena and the possibility that Kyle had been married to her all this time.

I walked a little faster and exited the wide doors

of the book fair pavilion and entered the hotel lobby, where I stopped at the front desk to pick up the Robert Burns. With nothing on my schedule until a cocktail party later that afternoon, I went to my room and spent forty-five minutes checking online sources in hopes of verifying Kyle's story and finding a connection between Robert Burns and Princess Augusta Sophia.

I found very little online and began to wonder if Kyle or someone in his family had made up the whole story. I preferred to think someone had lied to Kyle rather than deal with the possibility that my old pal had blatantly lied to me.

Of course, if he'd truly been involved with Serena for all those years, "blatant liar" was the nicest thing I could think to call him. But with Royce's insistence that Serena was the liar, I would hold my judgment until I had further proof.

I pulled out my paperback book of Robert Burns poetry and looked through the index of poems. I laid it next to the Cathcart edition and compared the two lists. There were several poems in the Cathcart that weren't in the paperback, but that didn't mean anything. Different editions of any poet's works often omitted some and included others. But when I checked the questionable poem titles online, I found no references for them. It was just as Kyle had said.

I searched for more information on Princess Augusta Sophia and found that she'd led an extremely sheltered life, never marrying or having any children. So where were the husband and baby Kyle had mentioned? There was one Web site that suggested she gave birth to an illegitimate son sometime before 1800. But that same site called her by a different middle name, so I certainly had to question its credibility.

Added to that, there was the niggling little fact that

Robert Burns had died in 1796. So a child of his would've definitely been born well before 1800.

"Duh," I said. Sitting back in my chair, I tapped my fingers on the desk. At this point, I wasn't even sure what I was looking for or why it mattered anymore. Well, except for the fact that if it were true, it would literally change history. Did it matter? Did I care?

I did. It would be one last tip of the hat to my old friend Kyle to prove the story true. It might allow him to rest in peace, if only in my own mind. And I could rub that in Perry's face, which was always a plus. Yankee bitch, my butt. He had no idea what a bitch this Yankee could be.

That thought made me smile.

Figuring a visit by a royal princess would've been all over the newspapers of that day, I started a search for Edinburgh papers in business in the late seventeen hundreds. That led me to the National Library of Scotland Web site, where they'd digitized every newspaper in the country from 1600 to the present. The problem was, the information had to be accessed in person.

"Oh, great," I murmured. But I checked the library location just in case, and as luck would have it, the main library was just a few blocks from the hotel. Looking out my window, I decided it was a perfect day for a walk.

I locked up my computer, grabbed my purse and warm jacket and went downstairs to return the book to the safe. I stopped at the concierge to get directions, and he was nice enough to insist on calling the library to verify that, as a book fair presenter, I could obtain a reader's ticket immediately. It was like a temporary pass, which I would need if I wanted to use their computer system. I thanked the concierge and took off for the National Library.

Outside, I breathed in the clear air of the ancient city. I had a moment of guilt, knowing I should be inside, meeting booksellers and talking up my business, but the thought of running into Minka or Serena or Perry made my stomach churn. I loved books and I loved my work, but I seriously needed a break.

The haunting sound of bagpipes drifted up a narrow alley, and just for a moment I felt transported to another time. I took another deep breath. Intellectually, I knew the man in the kilt was playing the pipes for the benefit of tourists, who would throw coins in the box he'd placed on the sidewalk, but it didn't matter as the wail of the pipes moved me to tears.

Yes, I seriously needed a break.

The wind was brisk as I turned the corner at George IV Bridge. I zipped up my jacket and shoved my hands in my pockets and walked until I found the big square building that housed the National Library of Scotland.

At the front desk, I showed my passport to the assistant librarian and filled out the necessary forms; then the librarian issued me a short-term ticket and a password. I followed her directions to the North Reading Room and logged on to one of the available computers.

After an hour of searching through their database of local newspapers, I knew plenty about the royal family of King George III but next to nothing about a possible liaison between Robert Burns and Princess Augusta Sophia. And my shoulders were beginning to ache from hunching in front of the computer screen.

There were vague indications that the family might've traveled to Scotland, but there was no mention of the princess specifically. And even if she had been allowed to visit the rough northern capital of Scotland, Queen Charlotte, her mother, was reported to have protected her six daughters fiercely—and not in a happy, friendly mama-kitty kind of way.

Evidently, Kyle was right about that.

The girls had been sheltered, of course, but this was

ridiculous. The queen had assigned them all to be her ladies-in-waiting. They were rarely allowed to attend dances.

I tried to imagine a spirited Augusta Sophia sneaking off to do some quality flirting with the darling bad-boy poet of Scotland. But it wasn't working. As much as I'd have liked to make it true, it just didn't fly for me.

I rubbed my eyes and sat back. I'd always figured being a princess would be a kick in the pants, but for poor Augusta Sophia it sounded like drudgery. What kind of a life had she led if all she'd done was tote and lift for her pushy mother, never partying, never marrying or having kids?

And to top it off, her dad, old King George III, had gone mad. That couldn't have made for much merriment at the family dinner table.

On the other hand, the king and queen managed to give birth to fifteen children, so it wasn't like they didn't have their own good times. Too bad their daughters hadn't been allowed to have their own fun.

I cross-checked King George's other five daughters but nothing really clicked. The others were either married or too old or too young. No, if the story were true, it would've been all about Augusta Sophia. But some articles reported that Augusta Sophia had worked for her mother until the queen died. The princess was in her fifties by then.

Could she secretly have given birth to a child out of wedlock? Without the knowledge of the people? Why not? She was royalty. Back then, they probably could've gotten away with anything.

Maybe it was just me and my Yankee-bitch sensibilities, but I really liked the idea of the princess escaping the palace for one wild fling before being consigned to work as her mother's glorified servant for the rest of her life.

I sighed, knowing I'd spent too much time chasing this wild goose. I stood up and stretched my muscles, glanced at the twelve or fourteen people scattered around the North Reading Room, and asked myself what I was doing here. It was almost one o'clock and I was starting to get hungry. That was no big surprise. I was always hungry.

But there was one more hunch I wanted to follow before I gave up.

If Kyle had been telling me the truth about his relationship to the bookbinder William Cathcart, then maybe I could trust that he'd thought he was telling the truth about Robert Burns and the princess, too. Even if it turned out to be untrue. But if he was lying about Cathcart being his ancestor, then I would know it was time to let Kyle go.

I ran a search on William Cathcart and found that his bindery had been operating during Robert Burns's time in Edinburgh. Interesting, but it still didn't answer any questions.

I began a genealogical search for any McVees living in Edinburgh around the time of William Cathcart. It turned out the city was crawling with McVees.

"Hmm," I said, and began to work backward from Kyle and Royce. I found a link a few generations back to an Edinburgh McVee named Thomas. Thomas's ancestors could be traced back to the late seventeen hundreds, to a Douglas McVee who ran a paper mill.

Paper and bindings. A perfect marriage there.

I gave up on the McVee line and moved to Cathcart, working forward to see if any of his daughters or granddaughters might've married a McVee. I felt a tingle and realized I was excited to think I might actually find a link.

I boiled it down to a few possibilities. Either Margaret or Doreen Cathcart could've married Russell or John

McVee. The computer showed a marriage certificate that was so faded I couldn't actually read the names. But there was a reference to the actual document in the genealogy stacks.

I wrote down the coordinates, grabbed my things and wandered off in search of the stacks. I found a bracket on the wall listing the different rooms, with arrows pointing the way. I realized at that moment that the arrow pointing to the ladies' room was most appealing.

Minutes later, refreshed and hands cleaned, I found the tall, heavy door leading to the genealogy room and entered. The door closed with a dull thud and I looked around. The room was dark, huge, high-ceilinged and deserted. Rows of waist-high map cabinets ran lengthwise across the room, the same type of cabinets I'd seen used for blueprints and ledgers. I had a similar, smaller cabinet in my workshop to hold the wide sheets of marbled paper I used for end sheets.

Curious, I approached the nearest cabinet and opened the wide, shallow top drawer. It held five or six three-foot-long, thin, aged ledgers. I counted the cabinets in the room and did the math. There had to be thousands of ledgers in here. I pulled one out and laid it on top of the cabinet, then carefully opened it. There were hundreds of rows of names entered in old-fashioned handwriting. Names and dates, as well as some charts with lines indicating family trees. Some connected to more names and dates. One family listing began in the year 1477.

I stared at the faded handwriting, fascinated. Then I shook myself. I was wasting time. I knew where I needed to go for a look at the Cathcart marriage certificate: the stacks. I stared at the narrow aisles of tall bookshelves that climbed to the ceiling and stretched all the way to the back wall. The room was like a warehouse. Here and there in some of the aisles were industrial-type ladders on wheels, used for reaching the highest shelves.

There had to be thousands of ledgers and journals in those shelves too. Maybe millions. Good grief.

I looked around. The room was still empty of people, and I wondered briefly if I should've asked for a special pass to come in here. At the same time I felt excitement. I could geek out for hours in this room, poring through the fascinating family histories contained in these books.

But I didn't have hours of time to waste. I checked my watch. I'd give myself a half hour to find the certificate; then I was going to go back to my hotel room for a late lunch and a nap.

And wasn't I the party girl?

I checked my coordinates and found the shelf I needed, but there were easily a hundred thin ledgers on that shelf.

"Got to start somewhere," I murmured, and went looking for a library ladder. It was on wheels but heavy and unyielding. After dragging it over to my section, I grabbed the flimsy railing and climbed seven steps up until I could reach the top shelf.

These narrow back aisles were claustrophobic and musty, and the shelves were so high that not much light illuminated the area. Moldering leather ledgers and journals were crammed into rows and rows of high, wooden bookshelves. I sneezed as I pulled one dusty old book out and read through pages and pages of names.

I swore mildly when I found nothing about Cathcart and McVee. At this rate, I had little hope of finding my happy couple. I pushed the ledger back in and pulled another one out.

That was when I heard a distant, quiet thud. It sounded as if the room's heavy wooden door had closed. If that was a librarian, I was willing to admit I could use some help.

"Hello?" I called, but there was no answer. I took a

deep breath and let it out. The creaks and groans from the bookshelves shifting and settling were making me jumpy.

"Meow."

"Holy—" My heart stuttered in my chest and I grabbed hold of the railing to keep from falling. I looked down and saw a fluffy, tiger-striped cat staring up at me.

A cat?

I slowly let out a breath and tried to get a grip. The cat jumped on the first step, then hopped up to the next step. Then he stopped and stared at me again.

"Well, come on up if you want," I said, and moved over on the platform as the cat bounded up. As I thumbed through the next ledger, the cat wound its way around and between my legs.

I leaned over to pet the cat and earned a soft purr as it stretched its neck for maximum scratching benefits. "You're awfully friendly, aren't you? Not in a cloying, puppy-dog way, of course. No, you're very elegant. You remind me of my friend Splinters, back home. He's an Abyssinian. Are you? I think you might be."

The cat said nothing but seemed happy to stick around, despite the foolish human trying to carry on a conversation. It dawned on me that I was glad to be right here in this strange room with a friendly kitty instead of at the book fair, where I would've spent all my time and energy avoiding Minka and Perry.

When I got back to the hotel, I was going to track down Helen and see if she wanted to meet for that drink. Then I would ask her what in the world she was thinking, hanging out with her dead lover's wife, Serena.

As I turned the ledger page and scanned down the list of names, my mind casually wandered off in Derek's direction. I wondered where he'd gone off to this morning. We hadn't made plans to meet, but I assumed I'd run into him at some point today. I realized he'd never told me what he was doing in Edinburgh, besides keeping me out of jail.

And there was the kissing.

That thought caused my stomach to tilt, and I must've jolted, because the ladder began to sway and the cat meowed in complaint. I clutched the ladder's railing again to keep myself steady.

Good grief, the man was dangerous to my health in more ways than one. His tall good looks and all-seeing, all-knowing eyes, his quirky smile and sardonic wit could overpower my puny will at times. If I hadn't seen him at Heathrow with the woman and her baby, I probably would've jumped into bed with him while we were here. But now I was hesitant, even knowing the woman was just his sister-in-law. That shock had gone a long way toward reminding me that I needed to think before I jumped.

After all, I wasn't exactly the best judge when it came to choosing boyfriends, as I'd been reminded so many times by my family members. But hey, they always liked the guys I dated, so maybe it was a genetic thing.

Seriously, Derek Stone was just a bad choice for a boyfriend. Not that I'd ever call him a boy. Anyway, besides the fact that he lived six thousand miles away from me, the man carried a gun.

So even if I were to get involved with Derek this week—and yes, by getting involved, we were talking sex—eventually we would drift apart and I'd forget all about him and his thighs of steel.

"Whoa." Okay, the genealogy search was no longer providing the distraction I required. Shaking off all thoughts of Derek and, you know, his thighs of steel, I tried to concentrate on the job at hand.

A scuffing noise from the next aisle over surprised me, and I wobbled on the step, causing the cat to meow again loudly.

"Hello?" I called.

Nothing.

I blew out a breath and gazed up and down the aisle. My imagination was going a little crazy, I supposed. It was easy to get spooked back here in these constricted spaces, surrounded by the ghosts of history.

The cat settled itself across my feet as I pulled another ledger out, opened the page and stared at the marriage certificate of Doreen Cathcart and Russell McVee.

"Holy mackerel," I said. "Kitty, look what I found."

The cat made mewing noises, as if he were just as happy as I was. I figured he was just humoring me.

I gazed at the faded legal paper and thought of Kyle. So at least part of his story was true. Maybe if I did more research, I could find out the truth about Robert Burns and the princess. But I couldn't do anything else today.

I pressed the book back into place on the shelf. "Come on, kitty. It's time to—"

Without warning, the bookshelf began to tremble.

"What the—"

An earthquake? For real?

A few books from the highest shelf tumbled down on top of me.

"Crap!" I covered my head with my hand to keep from getting hit, but it was impossible. The bookshelf was rocking so hard, I needed to keep both hands on the ladder railing.

The cat howled and leapt ten feet to the ground, then ran down the narrow aisle and disappeared.

The shaking grew even more violent, and hundreds of books slid out and down, battering me, their sharp leather edges scraping my skin.

"Ack!" The massive bookshelf banged against the ladder, throwing me back and forth like a sailor on a storm-tossed sea. I held on to the insubstantial railing and tried to climb down, but books were everywhere. I

tripped over one and lost my footing, fell hard on my ass
and slid the rest of the way down to the floor, bumping
my backbone against each ladder step as books continued to fall and hit me.

I landed on the ground and stared up at the heavy
wood bookshelf as it leaned precariously over me.
My throat closed up. I was in serious danger of being
crushed. I scrambled to my knees, then tried to stand,
but I kept slipping on books. As panic set in, I scurried
down the narrow aisle on my knees. Finally, I pushed
myself up to run but slid on another damn book. As I
fell, I felt my ankle twist painfully.

The bookshelf groaned as it sprang free from whatever bolts had held it in place. I watched it careen and
bounce against the bookshelf across the aisle from it.
It made an awkward half spiral and I screamed as it
crashed to the floor inches away from me.

The silence was sudden. Seconds later, I heard the
heavy door slam shut and knew there hadn't been an
earthquake.

Chapter 10

I tried to stand but shards of pain shot up my leg and I moaned.

"Okay, that hurts," I admitted under my breath. Had I really twisted my ankle? It didn't matter. I didn't expect emergency medical help to show up anytime soon, so I had to get myself out of there.

Just for a moment, I lay on the floor and tried to pull myself together, afraid to move too quickly. I stared at the bottom edge of another bookshelf, one that was still standing, and saw that it was bolted to the floor. Checking the seam between the two shelves, I couldn't see any brackets holding them together. I guessed they didn't have earthquake problems in Scotland. If this were California, there would be brackets upon brackets to hold everything in place in case of a temblor.

"Meow."

"Hi, kitty," I whispered.

"Meow," the cat said more loudly, as though he might be complaining about the mess I'd made.

"I know." I gritted my teeth and pulled myself to my knees. The cat bumped his head against my thigh as if that would help me get up.

Finally, I managed to stand, and the fact that my legs were still working was such a relief, I almost cried. I found my purse and jacket among the piles of ledgers and, with the cat bounding over books to lead the way, slowly made it out of the stacks.

My ankle throbbed but I could walk. Sort of. Slowly. It hurt but it was manageable. I slung my purse across my chest and hopped on my good foot over to one of the low cabinets, then stopped to get myself situated.

At that moment, the door opened and two women walked in and glanced around. They both wore badges attached to their jacket lapels, so I assumed they were librarians.

"I swear I heard something crash in here," the taller one said. She wore her hair pulled back in a severe bun and she scowled as she surveyed the area.

"Maybe it was upstairs," said the other woman, a short, older woman with curly gray hair. "They've painters working in the offices." At that moment, she noticed me. "Oh, hello."

"Hello." I clutched a nearby drawer pull to keep myself upright. My ankle throbbed and I was getting a headache. "The crash you heard was one of the bookshelves in back. It came unhinged and fell to the floor. The books are scattered everywhere. It's a real mess."

The taller woman rushed across the room to inspect the damage. "Good heavens, it's chaos. Have you ever seen such a disaster?"

"How in the world did this happen?" the shorter one asked as she patted her chest in distress.

"I have no idea," I said, fairly certain they wouldn't believe me if I told them someone was trying to kill me. "But I fell off the ladder and the bookshelf almost landed on top of me."

"Goodness, you could've been killed." She took a moment to consider me. "You don't look at all well, miss. Do you need assistance?"

I was so grateful, I almost wept. "No, thank you. I just want to get back to my hotel and rest."

The taller librarian's eyes narrowed. "Why are you in here? You're not allowed to use this room without a special certificate."

"Ah," I said, unable to keep the sarcasm out of my voice. "That explains it, then."

She sniffed in annoyance.

"Shirleen, the girl is injured," the nice librarian said.

Shirleen pursed her lips in displeasure. "She shouldn't be in here. Will you look at this horrible disarray? I'm going to have to report this upstairs."

She stomped off. I couldn't do anything about the mess, and my head was pounding in earnest now. "I'm sorry, but I need to leave."

"Of course, dear. Let me help you out." The nice woman took hold of my elbow and walked me to the door. As soon as she opened it, the cat flew out and down the hall.

She jumped back. "Good grief, was that a cat?"

"I didn't see anything," I said, not willing to get the cat in trouble, too. "Thank you for your help. You're very kind."

I limped down the hall to the street entrance, where the cat sat waiting patiently. I opened the door and walked outside and the cat followed. On the sidewalk, the cat looked up at me and meowed once, then took off running.

"Thanks, kitty," I said, and smiled as the cat disappeared down an alley. "Adios, amigo."

The wind had died down and the sun felt wonderful on my back. It was a beautiful day for a walk, or a slow shuffle, in my case. The fact that I could put pressure on my foot told me I hadn't broken anything. It was just sore and bruised, along with the rest of me. Frankly, my butt ached more than my ankle. I couldn't wait to get back to the hotel and take a couple of aspirin and a long, hot bath.

As I limped across the George IV Bridge street at the High Road, a black taxi screeched to a stop. I jumped to the sidewalk to avoid being hit and landed on my bad foot.

"Gaaaahh!" I cried.

A man stepped out from the backseat and grabbed hold of me. "Ah, now that's a shame, isn't it? Let me help you, miss."

He was really good-looking, with closely cropped dark reddish hair, and was nicely dressed in black wool trousers and a black turtleneck sweater. Normally I would've been more polite, but I was tired and in pain and just wanted to get back to the hotel.

"I'm fine," I said. "The cab startled me." I started to leave, but he held my arm.

"There, now, miss," he crooned. "You must be more careful."

I smiled. "Yes, I'll be careful. Thanks." If the cab hadn't spooked me, I wouldn't have to be so careful. I pulled my arm away, but he wouldn't let me go.

I no longer cared how cute he was. I was getting mad. "I don't have time for—"

"You'll make time," he said, and shoved something hard against my back.

A gun?

I froze. I couldn't breathe.

"There, now, I think we understand each other. Let me help you to the cab."

"No way," I said, knowing that if I got in, I might never be seen again.

"Get in the cab or I'll—"

"I'll scream."

"It'll do you no good."

I screamed anyway, as loud as I could.

"Jesus, that's not necessary," he said, wincing.

I kept screaming as the back door swung open and another man yanked me into the backseat next to him. The gunman jumped in after me, and the driver peeled off around the corner.

If I weren't so scared to death I'd be totally pissed off. I was already in pain, and now I was being kidnapped? Who were these guys? I glanced at the two sitting on either side of me. They looked like nice guys who enjoyed a whisky at the pub once or twice a week, not hired gunmen.

"I don't have any money," I said. Not on me, anyway.

The good-looking guy next to me frowned. "We don't want your money."

"What do you want? Where are you taking me? I need to get back to my hotel. People are waiting for me. And there were witnesses. Somebody had to have seen me and they'll—"

"Darlin', please," the driver said, meeting my gaze through his rearview mirror. "We're just wanting your word that ye'll not be making a mackedy of our Robbie."

"A *mackedy*?" I repeated. "What's a mackedy?"

"It's what we're stopping you from doing," the third guy said firmly.

The driver turned and glared at me. "Ye'll not be mocking our beloved hero."

"Oh." *Mockery*, he'd said. Not *mackedy*. So much for a common language.

"I would never mock your hero," I protested.

Frowning, the gunman eyed me. "The society looks askance at such disrespect."

"You have a society?"

"Aye, the Robert Burns Society," the third man said, beaming. "We're Freemasons, sworn to uphold the dignity and good name of our own best man."

"Aye, Rabbie Burns," the gunman said, nodding.

"Miss, are ye familiar with the sights of our fair town?" the driver asked.

"I beg your pardon?"

He pointed out the window. "If ye'll look between the two hills, you'll catch a glimpse of the engineering marvel that is the Forth Bridge."

"Crosses the Firth of Forth," the gunman elucidated, then leaned back to give me a better view out the window.

"Can you see it now?" he asked.

"A beautiful sight, that," the driver said proudly.

"Um, yeah." I stared out the window to my right. "It's beautiful." And it was. Dramatic and impressive. On my last visit to Edinburgh I'd taken a tour of the city, during which I'd learned firsthand that Scotsmen were fiercely proud and knowledgeable of their history and heritage—and their bridge. The tour guide had positively gushed as he explained that the Forth Bridge was one of the world's first major steel bridges. Its unique cantilever design was considered a miracle of modern technology back in the 1890s.

But what in hell did that have to do with me and these men and this cab? What was I doing here? I furtively checked my watch. I'd been on the road with these would-be kidnappers for less than ten minutes and still had no idea what they wanted from me.

The cute gunman noticed me looking at my watch and tapped the driver's shoulder. "We should get her back."

"Aye," the driver said.

"But we'll need your word on this matter, miss," the third man said.

"Okay," I said hesitantly. I was willing to agree to almost anything, but God only knew what he was going to insist upon. They all seemed a little nutty, as though I'd stumbled upon a Freemasons' mad tea party.

The gunman held up his finger. "First, this notion that our Rabbie might've loved a royal Sassenach bitch?"

The third man glared at the gunman, then said pointedly, "You'll pardon Tommy's French."

The gunman, Tommy, grimaced. "Ach, pardon my French, miss. But it's daft."

"Makes no sense a'tall," said the third man, shaking his head.

The driver nodded. "Aye, Rabbie was a great lover, but he would've drawn the line at a snooty English royal."

"Och, aye, he was a lover, he was," Tommy agreed, chuckling. "He loved many a lass."

The third man laughed. "Aye, that's our boy Rabbie."

The laughter stopped abruptly as the driver wrenched the wheel. The cab lurched to the side of the road and stopped. The two men beside me tensed up, and I started to panic as the driver maneuvered himself around to face me.

"Understand, miss," he said. "Robert Burns was a Freemason, a well-known dissenter who supported both the French resistance and your own American Revolution. He was a Scottish nationalist and a harsh critic of the Church of England. He never would've consorted with the auld enemy, and that goes double for the royal family. This you must believe."

"All right," I said, talking slowly as I nodded. "I see your point. I don't know what I was thinking. I'm not very familiar with the history of your country, so I appreciate your patience with me." I would've said anything at that moment to get back to the hotel. But the more I thought about it, the more it seemed that the legend of Robert Burns and the princess was too good to be true.

"Do you mean it, miss?" the driver said.

"Absolutely," I said. "And I want to apologize for upsetting you. I didn't realize that what I was saying might be so offensive."

"Ah, see there?" said the third man, slapping the back of the driver's seat. "She didn't realize what she was saying."

"I didn't," I said promptly. "I swear. I'm so glad you've enlightened me. And now that I know the truth, please believe I'll never again say anything contradictory to the facts."

"There's a fine lass," Tommy said, patting my knee fondly.

"Thank you," I said, determined to make eye contact with each of them. "I really appreciate knowing the truth."

The driver breathed a sigh of relief. "We'll thank you as well, then. We didn't know what else to do when we heard you were spinning tales but try to appeal to your higher principles."

By kidnapping me? I thought, but resisted saying it, instead asking, "How did you hear about me?"

"Anonymous phone call," the driver said with a shrug. He settled back behind the wheel and started the car, leaving me to wonder who had made that anonymous phone call. It could've been anyone attending my workshop, but my money was on Perry McDougall.

We drove the five miles back to the Royal Mile in silence. When they reached the drive in front of my hotel, Tommy turned and faced me.

"We'll come in with you and spring for a pint to celebrate."

"Oh, no!" *Dear God, just let me go in peace*, I thought. But I squeezed out a smile and said, "I would love to, but

I injured my ankle earlier and should probably soak it in Epsom salts."

"You're injured, miss?" the third man said.

"It's probably nothing serious, but I should take care of it."

"Are you sure it's not serious?" Tommy said. "Harry's a doctor."

I gaped at the third man.

"Aye, I am," Harry said, then glared at his partner. "Did Tommy push you too hard?"

Good grief, thoughtful kidnappers. Only in Scotland. And a doctor among them? I was truly going mad.

"Uh, no, it happened earlier today," I said, waving a hand in dismissal. "It'll be fine tomorrow."

"If you're sure."

"Walk her to the door, Harry," the driver prompted.

"Aye." Harry the doctor whipped out of the car and held his hand out for me. I had no choice but to allow him to help me. My ankle throbbed and my back was stiff. I swayed once before steadying myself.

"There, see?" I said, giving Harry my best smile. "I'm fine."

"If you're sure."

"Absolutely."

"We'll take a rain check then," the driver said as we passed by his open window.

"Perfect," I said.

Harry dug into his pocket and pulled out a business card. "You'll call if you have any problems while you're in town."

I glanced at the card and I prayed my eyes didn't bug out of my head. HARRISON MCFARLAND, MD. It was true, then. One of the men who'd kidnapped me was a doctor. Maybe Tommy the gunman was a lawyer.

"Are you sure you'll be all right?"

I stared at him. "Absolutely. Thanks."

"Go inside and rest, miss. You've had a day."

"Thanks for making it more interesting." I waved good-bye to my new Freemason friends and hobbled to the door.

The first person I saw when I entered the lobby was Derek Stone, and I almost wept with relief. And hunger. Dear God, I was hungry to the point of starvation.

He saw me and sauntered over. "Where did you run off to?"

"Ah, where to begin?" I said. "But first, I need food. Do you want to come with me?"

He threaded my arm through his. "While it's always entertaining to watch you consume food, I must run an errand first. I was hoping you'd come with me."

I rubbed my stomach.

He smirked but took hold of my arm and we walked back outside. "I believe this short detour will be worth your while, and I promise to feed you afterward."

"I hate to remind you, but when we last spent quality time together, I ended up hiding in a closet and finding another dead body."

He leaned in close. "Are you too much of a coward to give it another try?"

"Coward?" I said, insulted and excited all at once. "Lead the way, Jack."

A black Bentley limousine pulled up. The driver hopped out and opened the door for us. When we were ensconced in the backseat and the driver made his way out to the Royal Mile, I turned to Derek. "Where are we going?"

"To the palace."

"What?"

Within minutes we'd left the High Street behind and I could see rugged Arthur's Seat rising up to stand sentry over the Palace of Holyroodhouse. Then, within moments, we were actually driving onto the stately grounds of the palace.

Wow.

I turned to Derek. "What are we doing here?"

"Just picking something up," he said cryptically.

The driver opened the door and Derek led me to a side entrance away from the public tour area. Before I could get over my shock, we were met at the door by an older woman in a slim blue dress. She escorted us to an elegantly appointed sitting room, where a well-dressed man in his early forties was waiting.

"Ah, Mr. Stone," the man said. "Here you are, right on time."

"Hello, Jones," Derek said. "This is Brooklyn Wainwright, the book restoration expert I was telling you about."

"Lovely," he said with a slight nod.

"Brooklyn," Derek continued, "this is Phillip Pickering-Jones, personal secretary to the royal highnesses."

The royal highnesses?

"Nice to meet you, Mr. Pickering-Jones."

"Delighted," he said, extending his hand to shake mine. "And just 'Jones' is fine. His Highness is quite delighted at the thought of your doing the work. He asks only that you ship the parcel back within a month, in time for the young lady's birthday."

His Highness?

Were we talking about the prince? Like, the real freaking prince? Was it the cute one? Or the other cute one? Or the much older, not-so-cute one? Did it matter? I looked from Jones to Derek. "What am I working on?"

"Ah, you haven't informed her, then?" Jones asked Derek.

"No," Derek said with a slight smile. "I thought you might do that."

"With pleasure, sir." He walked to a small, elegant pale green desk set against the wall under a portrait of some distinguished lord of something or other. He picked up a brown-paper-wrapped parcel and handed it to me.

"It's a favorite childhood book belonging to a dear friend of His Highness," Jones explained. "Now tattered and torn, as you'll see. We would be most appreciative if you would work your magic to transform it into a gift of beauty for his lady friend's birthday."

I took the parcel and found the seal. "May I?"

He nodded regally. "Of course."

I unwrapped the package. It was a leather-bound version of what I assumed was a British children's book I'd never heard of: *A Flat Iron for a Farthing*, by Juliana Horatia Ewing. I turned it over in my hand. It was fraying at the edges and torn through to the boards in spots. My brain went into bookbinder mode, cataloging the book itself and the work required: original green leather binding so faded it appeared light gray. Title embossed in gold on spine. Faded. Masking tape residue on front hinge. I resisted shivering in disgust.

The front and back boards had come loose from the spine. The paper was thick and in decent condition, with only a bit of insect damage and foxing on several pages. The signatures had begun to unravel from the tapes. It would need new tapes, new flyleaves and a complete new binding.

"It's charming," I said, and it was, despite its disrepair—and the masking tape. Ugh. I opened the book to the title page and noted its printing date: 1910. "Do you know what type of binding His, er, Highness would prefer?"

"Leather, of course," Jones said, waving his hand theatrically.

"Of course."

"Something elegant and pretty, perhaps somewhat close to the original green."

"Sounds perfect."

I turned the book over and studied the back board. Forest green morocco would be pretty. "Would he prefer gilding or heat stamping? Raised cord spine?"

He gave me a deferential nod. "I was told that the details were to be handled at your discretion, Miss Wainwright."

"And you'll need it back within a month?"

"Yes, miss."

I nodded. "I can do that."

"Excellent." He bowed. "Thank you, miss."

"Thank you," I said. "It'll be my pleasure."

He handed me a small white shopping bag with the royal crest imprinted on it in black, and explained that inside the bag was a card with instructions as well as a preaddressed overnight mailing packet for my convenience.

Then he walked with us back along the wide gallery, allowing us a brief glance at the library and identifying the subjects of a number of different paintings. He stopped to allow us to admire a huge set of Sèvres urns that were particular favorites of Queen Victoria. Farther along, he proudly pointed out the impressive silver tea service on display that had been a gift from Lord Wellington.

When he bade us farewell at the limousine, I didn't know whether to curtsy or bow, so I just shook hands with him.

Once inside the car, I turned to Derek. "Oh, my God, I'm working for His Highness. Whichever highness it is, it totally rocks. You rock. Thank you."

I kissed him, then sat back. "Wow, this is so cool. I really—"

"Come here." He drew me back into his arms and proceeded to finish the kiss properly. Before my eyebrows singed and I turned into a yearning puddle of need, the chauffeur had stopped the car.

"That's a short drive," I mumbled.

"You're welcome," Derek said.

Once inside, we made tracks straight to the restaurant, where the hostess led the way to a corner booth. I scooted in on one side and met Derek in the middle. He ordered a cup of coffee and I went with the ploughman's platter and a pint of pale ale.

"Platter's enough for two," the waitress said as she wrote the order.

"Yes, we'll have two plates," Derek said with a smile.

The waitress returned his smile, looked at me and patted her heart, then walked away.

I grinned, then remembered he'd asked for two plates. "I thought you already ate."

"I did," he said. "And no, I'm not going to take your food."

"I'd like to see you try."

"I'd rather keep my skin intact."

The waitress delivered his coffee and my beer. He took a sip and whispered, "I asked for two plates because I didn't want our waitress to fret about your eating issues."

"I have no eating issues."

"I know that, but she doesn't."

"Oh, I get it. You were being thoughtful."

"Yes, I was."

"That's such a gift." I smiled and leaned back against the cushioned booth. I was exhausted and achy. I needed a nap and a massage, not necessarily in that order. But I had my royal assignment, and that made me feel all rosy inside.

"Thank you again," I said.

"You're more than welcome," he said. "I know you'll do a good job."

"Well, of course I will, but . . ."

He was staring.

"What's wrong?" I asked.

He moved closer and brushed my bangs off my forehead. "You've got a bump and a bruise."

"I do?" Before I could touch my forehead, he pulled my hand away.

"It looks painful."

"Now that you mention it, I do have a slight headache." I'd forgotten all about it, thanks to the distraction of our little errand to the Palace of Holyroodhouse.

He stared at my palm. "And you've scraped your hand." Without warning, he kissed my wrist. I almost moaned as my system went to code red. My arm tingled, my heart raced and all the breath in my body got caught in my throat. With my luck, these were the first symptoms of a heart attack.

I eased my hand away and reached for the beer. "I had a little mishap at the library."

"Define *mishap*."

I sighed. "I think someone was trying to kill me."

"Do tell," he said calmly, but his eyes were narrowed and his mouth was a thin, grim line.

I took off my jacket and laid it on the seat, then told him the whole story about the genealogy room and the bookshelf falling on me.

"And you didn't see anyone?" he asked when I'd finished. "Hear anyone?"

"Not really. I heard the door open and shut once, and I heard some scuffing sound, but I brushed it off. The shelves were wood, so they made lots of settling, groaning noises. I chalked the other noises up to that. I never saw anyone."

"And this bookshelf just toppled? Aren't they bracketed together or bolted to the floor?"

"As a matter of fact, I checked while I was lying flat on my face, and yes, the shelves were bolted to the floor but not to one another."

He shook his head, concern etched on his face. "You're lucky you only turned your ankle."

"Lucky seems to be my middle name."

"So you were on your way back from the library when I saw you?" he asked.

Before I could respond, the waitress brought my ploughman's platter. And okay, yes, it probably was big enough for two, but I knew I would have no problem finishing the whole thing. I made myself a sandwich from two thick slices of bread, some fresh ham, two chunks of cheese, a tomato slice and various condiments.

After savoring a few luscious bites, I finally lost the debate with myself and related the whole story of my improbable kidnappers.

Derek listened with outward patience, then said adamantly, "Let me see the business card."

"I don't think so."

"Did those men frighten you?"

I pursed my lips, considering whether to answer or not, but finally relented. "Yes, they did at first. I was terrified. But after a few minutes of driving around and talking, they seemed more like my three brothers than any thugs I've ever seen. They were cute, too."

Derek frowned and I waved that statement away. "Never mind. Anyway, I realized they just needed to talk."

"By dragging you off the street and kidnapping you?"

"Well, when you put it like that . . ." I dabbed my mouth with my napkin. "But I was never in any danger."

"You didn't know that," he said.

"I admit I experienced a minute or two of terror."

"May I see the card, please?"

"I don't want to press charges," I insisted, spreading mayonnaise on another slice of bread. "They made their point and I appreciated it."

"Fine," he said, holding out his hand. "But if I need a doctor, I want to know who not to call."

"Good point." I would probably regret it, but I pulled the card out of my pocket and handed it to him.

He rubbed his thumb against the grain. "Good quality," he mused.

"I thought the same thing."

"Yes, you would," he said absently. "An MD with the Royal College of Surgeons. What's a surgeon doing terrorizing young ladies on the streets of Edinburgh?"

"Just making his case, I guess."

He put the card in his pocket. "I'll hold on to this."

I waved my fork at him. "If I find out you sicced the police on them, I'll be very put out with you."

He folded his arms across his chest. "I'll have to live with that."

I took a bite of pickle, then shook my head. "Can't trust anyone."

"It's a sad truth," he said, moving close to wrap his arm around my shoulder. I closed my eyes and leaned against him for a long moment. I could've stayed there all day, but he'd pulled his cell phone out with his free hand.

"Finish your lunch," he murmured, then pressed a button on the phone. I wasn't surprised when he greeted Angus MacLeod, told him about my library mishap, and asked him to meet us right away.

"Don't you dare tell him about the Freemasons," I warned when he ended the call.

"They're the least of your worries, darling."

"Perry McDougall has an alibi," MacLeod said. "He's been working in his booth at the fair all day."

So Perry wasn't my library attacker.

My shoulders fell. "Are you sure?"

MacLeod had arrived only minutes ago to interview

me in Derek's elegant penthouse suite. That's right, Derek had rented the *penthouse suite*. The man had quite the expense account. Of course, since he owned his own security company, it probably wasn't a problem convincing the boss he needed all this space.

I wondered if the Bentley limo we'd driven in was his company's car or provided by the palace. It wouldn't surprise me to find out it was his own car. He really was a conspicuous consumer.

But the suite was the most private place he could think of in which to have a conversation with MacLeod, so I was grateful he'd offered. Before MacLeod arrived, Derek had poured me a beer from the well-stocked minibar, then forced me to sit back on the luxurious white sectional sofa while he slipped off my boot and checked my ankle.

"It's slightly swollen, but not broken," he reported, patting my ankle gently. "Just a bit twisted, I suspect."

Was he talking about me or my ankle?

He grinned, having read my mind. "You're more than a bit twisted."

"And you're so cute." I'd said it to be sarcastic, but it came out in a breathy whisper. Good grief.

"Rest," he said, and leaned in and kissed my forehead. Then he tucked a plush, soft afghan around me, and it must've taken only seconds before I passed out. At MacLeod's arrival, I awoke feeling groggy and disoriented.

Always the delightful guest, that was me.

Before getting into the library attack, I told MacLeod about my discussion with Jack from Dublin earlier that day at the Fair Haven booth. "He was one of the people Kyle consulted about the book, but he couldn't have killed him."

"And why not?" MacLeod asked, humoring me.

"He's shorter than me, and thinner," I explained. "And I'd guess he was in his late sixties. I doubt he'd have the strength to bludgeon someone of Kyle's size. And besides, he was excited to be getting a look at the book. Why would he kill Kyle?"

As MacLeod wrote out his notes, something else occurred to me. "Did you ever find out who called Kyle's cell phone?"

Angus and Derek exchanged looks, something they did a lot when I was around. Derek merely lifted one eyebrow, and Angus sighed. "The call was made from a disposable cell," he admitted. "Untraceable."

"Damn it," I muttered. Whoever owned that phone was probably Kyle's killer.

"My sentiments exactly," Angus said, then requested a full report on the library fiasco. When I was finished, he flipped his notepad to another page. "As far as your suspicion that Perry McDougall followed you to the library, my men interviewed a number of vendors near McDougall's booth, as well as one of his employees."

"Yes?" I said.

He sat across from me in a soft, buttercream leather chair, with his legs crossed in the manly style of one ankle propped on his other knee. "Everyone swore McDougall has been there all day. His alibi is ironclad."

I wondered about that. "Was Minka LaBoeuf one of the employees interviewed? Because she would lie at the drop of a hat."

He checked his notes and I saw his eyebrows lift. I took that to mean he'd found Minka's name.

"I can't reveal the names of witnesses," he said gruffly. "But why would you accuse this person of lying?"

"She hates me," I said gloomily. "If she knew it would screw me up, she'd lie without batting an eye."

I stood and started to pace, but my ankle was still a little tender, so I leaned against the wall. "I'm not making it up. Somebody tried to kill me at the library."

"I believe you, Miss Wainwright," MacLeod said, and

gave Derek a meaningful look. "After we spoke, I went by the library and saw the damage done. Someone went to great lengths to try to hurt her, with little regard for public property, I might add."

Derek hissed out a breath and his jaw clenched.

Scowling, I turned to the picture window and stared out at the breathtaking view of Princes Street Gardens and the New City beyond. I wanted to enjoy the spectacular sight, but I was too furious to think straight. I couldn't believe they were taking Minka's word that Perry was innocent. It burned my butt to think that my fate might be in the hands, once again, of that deceitful, conniving Minka LaBitch.

Chapter 11

I left Derek's suite shortly after MacLeod took off.

Mom and Dad had decided to go to the Witchery restaurant for a romantic anniversary meal, and Derek had some business dinner thing to attend, so I blew off my scheduled cocktail party to hang out with Robin and catch up on all the news.

"Angus kissed you?" I asked as I laid out my clothes for the evening.

"Yes," Robin said. "We'd walked about a block from the hotel and he stopped and apologized. I asked him why and he goes, 'Because I'm going to do this.' And then he kissed me."

"Wow. I've got goose bumps."

"I know," Robin said. "So then he says he took one look at me and felt like he'd been struck by lightning, and if I didn't marry him, he'd spend the rest of his days tracking me down until I relented."

"Wow," I said again. "Good lines."

"I know."

"I need a shower."

"I need a drink."

While I took a shower to wash off the day's craziness, Robin popped open a half bottle of red wine from the minibar and poured us each a glass. After the shower,

I felt wide-awake and about two hundred times better than before. More relaxed and less achy. The wine might've helped a little, too.

What was I thinking? Of course the wine helped.

We decided to get out and explore Edinburgh. About time, too. I loved this city and hadn't had a single minute to enjoy it.

I pulled on a clean pair of jeans and a pink long-sleeved knit top; then Robin filled me in on the news from home while I blew my hair dry. The big news from Dharma, our hometown, was that another store was about to open on Shakespeare Lane, the town's main drag. Well, "main drag" was a bit of an overstatement. Shakespeare Lane, or "the Lane," as we locals called it, was a quaint, narrow two-lane street of charming shops, cafés and restaurants.

Barely two blocks long, the Lane had become something of a wine country mecca, thanks to the small luxury hotel and spa that capped one end of the street. It also helped that two world-class restaurants had moved in over the past year. Our commune's excellent winery now had a tasting room on the Lane. There were clothing shops, a baby store, an antique shop. My sister China owned Warped, a high-end yarn and weaving shop next door to the town bookstore.

"Who's opening the new shop?" I asked after I turned off the hair dryer and grabbed my brush.

"Annie."

Startled, I dropped the hair dryer and the brush flew out of my hand. I scrambled to catch the hair dryer, but it was attached to the wall by a curly cord, so it just bounced up and down instead of crashing to the floor.

Robin stood in the doorway, laughing at me. "I knew that would get your attention."

Annie, or Anandalla, as her mother had named her, was Abraham's long-lost daughter. The week before

Abraham died, Annie showed up to meet the father she'd never known. Then he died and left me his entire estate, along with a boatload of guilt I'd been dealing with ever since. Once paternity was established, I asked the lawyers to change the title deed to Abraham's home in the hills from my sole ownership to joint tenancy with Annie.

Annie moved to Dharma and the community took her under its wing, especially my mother. Annie was quickly becoming the third sister I'd never known I needed.

As I slipped on my walking boots, I frowned at Robin. "Wonder why Mom didn't say anything about it."

Robin shook her head. "She's too worried about you to think of anything else."

"Yeah, I guess she gets distracted."

"Your mom? Really?" She smiled. "You think so?"

"No, of course not. What was I thinking?" I grinned. "So what kind of store is it?"

"Kitchen stuff."

I thought about that as I finished my wine and grabbed my gloves from the drawer. "Not a bad idea. We don't have anything like that in the area."

"Yeah, and did you know she cooks?"

"I had no idea."

"She's going to give cooking classes and mix it up with wine pairings from the winery."

"Smart." I wrapped my ankle with an elastic bandage Derek had given me, then slipped on my sturdy boots. Most of the pain was gone, but I didn't want to take any chances of twisting it again on the cobblestone sidewalks. I zipped up my fleece hoodie, then checked that the windows were still secured before grabbing my purse and jacket and leading the way out the door. "I've only been gone a few days. Why didn't I hear about this before?"

"You've been involved with this trip for weeks. Guess it didn't register."

"So how do you know so much about it?"

"Hey, it's my town, too. I do get up there every so often."

"Especially recently," I said, studying her. "You've been talking to Austin."

"No," she said a little too quickly. "Well, of course. I mean, no more than usual, which is rarely."

"Liar," I said, grinning.

"I'm rubber, you're glue."

"And you're so mature."

"Just don't be blabbing to him about Angus," she said darkly.

"Hey, a little competition might do him some good."

My brother Austin had been Robin's secret crush since we were in fifth grade. I'd seen them together at Mom and Dad's anniversary party and they looked perfect. I just hoped Austin didn't blow it. Because if he broke Robin's heart, whether he was my brother or not, I would have to kill him. And that would play hell with my karma.

As we turned the corner to the elevator banks, Robin changed the subject. "I stopped by your place before I left town and talked to Suzie and Vinnie."

My neighbors had been indispensable to me when Abraham's killer made a shambles of my studio and apartment. Suzie and Vinnie were wood artists, specializing in redwood burl. Burl was a growth or deformation of a trunk or root of a tree. I hadn't known this, of course, until Vinnie had taken a long night and two bottles of wine to tell me all about it. Anyway, depending on the tree, the hunk of burl could be huge, weighing hundreds of pounds. The girls worked only on trees that had fallen by nature's hand, as they liked to put it. They billed themselves as the all-natural chain-saw-wielding lesbian artists, and it seemed to be paying off for them.

"How are they doing?"

She smiled. "They insisted on feeding me, so I totally get your devotion to them."

"Aren't they great?" Suzie and Vinnie didn't cook, so they were always eating out and always bringing me their leftovers. They knew I would eat anything. Really, anything. Apparently, I had been malnourished as a child.

"Yeah, they are," she said, grinning. "I'm supposed to tell you that Pookie's fine but Splinters hurt his front leg and had to get four stitches."

"Poor Splinters! What happened?" Pookie and Splinters were the girls' beloved cats. I was proud to be their designated cat sitter, a fact that had brought Robin to near fits of laughter when she first heard. Not that it was my fault, but despite my love of animals, I'd never been very good with pets. I hadn't mentioned that to Suzie and Vinnie, and I didn't want them finding out the hard way.

Robin grimaced. "He lost the battle trying to take down the vacuum cleaner."

"Ouch, I thought Splinters was the smart cat."

"I guess not. And Suzie said you received some certified letter from France."

"It's probably my contract," I said. "I'm scheduled to teach another class at Lyon this summer."

Lyon, France, was considered by many to be the heart and soul of bookbinding and all things book related. The city had an entire museum dedicated to book art, and the Institut d'Histoire du Livre in Lyon was a top school for advanced study in book history, conservation and restoration. It was the same place I'd last spent any time with Helen.

"Cool," Robin said as we rode the elevator down. "You'll get to see Ariel and Pascal again."

Years ago, Ariel Hodges had come to Sonoma to work with Abraham on some big book restoration projects, and we all became her surrogate family. Then she moved to Lyon to run the institute, where she met Pascal, a curator at the Musée de l'Imprimerie, the printing museum.

"I can't wait," I said. "Maybe you should plan a trip while I'm there."

"I'll do it," Robin said. "I suppose Pascal is still as sexy and annoyingly French as ever."

"I imagine so." I laughed. Pascal was totally hot but completely in love with our friend Ariel, which naturally made him even more adorable in our eyes.

We walked outside and I breathed in the crisp, clean Scottish air and admired the odd shadows of the Old Town rooftops as the sun set behind the castle. Was it silly to think that air and light were different depending on the part of the world you were in? If so, call me silly, but the northern lights and the arctic air that passed over Scotland seemed to transform me. Everything was different here. I loved San Francisco, but as I took in the sights and sounds and views from the top of the Royal Mile, I knew I could be happy living here for the next few years.

As we passed St. Giles' Cathedral, Robin pointed across the street at Mary King's Close. "Isn't that where you found Kyle's body?"

At the unwelcome memory, I felt a chill and tugged my jacket tighter. "Yeah. In one of the tenement rooms."

"Ugh."

"Yeah."

"Whoa." She stopped to stare at a store window filled with every kind of tartan pattern imaginable. It was dizzying.

"Looks like *Brigadoon* on acid," Robin muttered.

I snickered. Not that either of us had ever dropped acid before. Looking at this place now, I was assured we never would.

Dozens of people passed us on the street, their conversations rising and falling around us like music. There was something spectacular about a rolling Scottish burr. And speaking of rolling, the sidewalks were a little uneven, so we had to watch our step or that was what we would be doing. The cold wind kept pushing at us, as if determined to drive us back to the hotel.

We continued walking, but stopped again to look at another wondrous storefront filled with lace items: doll clothes, a wedding gown, a little girl's starched, high-collared dress that looked horribly uncomfortable, napkins and doilies and petticoats and curtains and all sorts of table runners strewn like crepe-paper ribbons across the ceiling.

"God, that's bizarre," Robin said, but she couldn't look away. The store window was practically hypnotic.

"Come on, sweetie, let's keep walking," I said, nudging her out of her stupor.

She blinked and nodded. "Thanks."

"That was close," I muttered, knowing that if Robin actually went into one of these stores, she'd leave with her credit card sizzling.

Back to her old self, she said, "Would you mind if I take your mom and dad on a ghost tour this week?"

"Oh, they'd love it. You should do it."

"But you won't be joining us."

I shuddered. "No way."

"I could contact a different tour than the one you used."

"I don't even want to think about it." I would never be able to take a ghost tour again without half expecting Kyle to be one of the ghosts.

We stopped at a corner and Robin looked around. "Where are we going, by the way?"

"Dinner. There's a good restaurant another block or two from here."

"Great." She shoved her hands in her pockets as we maneuvered along the cobblestone sidewalk. Robin's heels were wobbling over the ancient stones, and she looked almost drunk as she walked. "I was reading about Deacon Brodie's Tavern. It's supposed to be good."

"Sort of touristy," I said. "It's back toward the castle a few blocks."

She turned to look up the street. "Do you want to go there?"

I shook my head and winced. "I made the mistake of reading about it. Brodie was this upstanding citizen—a deacon, as you might've figured—who took up burglary at night. So they hanged him—or maybe he escaped. Since this is Scotland, the legends go both ways, depending on the day of the week. But he was supposedly Robert Louis Stevenson's inspiration for *Dr. Jekyll and Mr. Hyde.*"

"You know way too much history for someone who never liked high school."

"It's a curse."

"Maybe I'll take your parents there tomorrow."

"Don't tell them about the icky Mr. Hyde part."

"I think they might like that aspect."

I chuckled. "You're probably right."

We passed through the long shadow of the Tron Kirk spire and crossed the High Street.

I'd heard that many people in Scotland considered Glasgow, not Edinburgh, to be the garden spot to visit, because Edinburgh was rife with counterculture, drugs, AIDS and crime. But the public perception outside Britain was that Edinburgh was the jewel in the crown of the British Isles. In that regard, it reminded me a lot of San Francisco, and maybe that was why I loved it so much. It was the scruffiness around the edges that appealed to me, as well as the fact that, to my mind, the view from every direction was picture-perfect.

I pointed out a cheery, wide-windowed pub with flower-pots hanging from the tops of each of the tall columns. "That's where we're going."

"The Mitre. Looks nice, but what about that place?" She pointed to another pub two doors down.

"Do you really want to eat at a place called Clever Dick's?"

"Depends," she said with a grin.

Do I know how to pick a best friend or what?

"I'm stuffed," Robin groaned as we walked out of the Mitre. "Let's walk for a while."

"You didn't have to order dessert," I said, as we walked east along the Royal Mile, in the opposite direction of the hotel. It was cold, but the air felt good. The sky was studded with stars and the sidewalks were crowded with people out looking for a good time.

"It's not every day you get to eat spotted dick."

"You can say that again," I said, as we passed the aged, turreted Tolbooth. It had been a wretched prison in the sixteenth century, with public hangings and all that fun stuff, but now it was a museum, with its ten-foot-high fancy clock hanging five stories up above the street. "And I guess you could say the same for tatties and neeps."

"Oh, my God, don't remind me. That waitress was trying to terrify me on purpose."

I laughed at the memory of Robin's expression when the waitress suggested tatties and neeps on the side, then gave her a break and explained that it was the local name for potatoes and parsnips. We figured she did that to all the tourists. At the end of the meal, Robin asked for the recipe and the chef himself came out to recite it, basically mashed root veggies with a touch of this and that—and tarragon, the secret ingredient.

When Robin invited him to move to San Francisco to cook for her, I knew it was time to leave.

"Look, puppets!" Robin cried, and hurried over to a storefront display of numerous stringed puppets in intricate costumes, all standing and ready to perform. There was a bagpiper, a ballerina, a golfer, three soldiers, all in different uniforms, a harlequin clown and a pirate. Their oversize faces were carved from wood and their cheeks were splotched with bits of red paint—to make them appear happy and healthy, I supposed.

"Kind of creepy, huh?" I said, struggling to keep a steady foot on the wily cobblestones after having shared a bottle of wine with Robin.

"I think they're pretty," Robin said.

"Oh, sure, until they come alive in the middle of the night and try to kill you."

She frowned. "I hate when that happens."

"Should we start back?"

"Do you want to walk up to the castle?" Robin asked as we headed west. "I still need to walk off dinner."

"Sure." It was a beautiful night, cold but not unbearable, and I didn't want to go back to the hotel just yet.

"We can stop at a few pubs for a nightcap or two," she added.

"That's why I love you," I said, weaving our arms together and pulling us to a stop at the red light.

"Well, we are in Scotland, after all," Robin said. "Home of the best pubs in the world, filled with hardy, handsome hunks in kilts who drink Scotch all night and play rugby all day. That takes balls, you know. Big ones, made of leather."

"And we're back to our theme of the night," I said with a laugh, then shivered from a cold waft of air that swept up South Bridge.

Robin continued singing the praises of hunky Scotsmen, but I tuned out as a sudden stinging awareness told me that someone was watching us. I'd felt that same eerie sensation once before, in San Francisco after Abraham was murdered. I'd brushed it off then, to my detriment. Now, after another murder and a day of near misses, I wasn't quite ready to dismiss it.

I glanced around but couldn't see anything out of the ordinary. People walked the streets, going from here to there, minding their own business. A group of college boys whooped it up outside a record store across the street. None of them cast a menacing scowl my way.

But there were shadows and dark alleyways everywhere along the Royal Mile. Was someone hiding, waiting, planning?

Beside me, Robin was humming and swaying to some internal groove, daydreaming of men in kilts, oblivious to any danger lurking nearby.

So okay, maybe it was my imagination. Let's face it, I was slightly tanked and still on edge from the attack at the library earlier. And these narrow, cobbled streets of Old Town naturally conjured up ghosts and spirits and evildoers where there was really nothing, nothing but the whispers and sighs of the soft winds that wafted up the myriad lanes and passageways leading to the High Street.

Uh-oh. I was waxing poetic, and that was never a good sign. I shivered again, grabbed my gloves and put them on, then rubbed my hands together to warm up.

When the light turned green, I breathed a sigh of relief and stepped off the curb. A black car came screeching toward me.

"No!" Robin screamed, and yanked my arm. I fell backward and landed right on my ass. Again. Pain shot up my spine and I groaned as I lay back on the sidewalk.

The car roared away down North Bridge toward the New Town and disappeared. He never even slowed down.

"Damn, that hurt," I muttered, staring up at the sky,

trying to figure out why this kind of thing kept happening to me.

"Brooklyn?" Robin called out. Seconds later, her face appeared in my line of vision. "Are you okay? Did you see that? The guy didn't even stop. Are you hurt? Can you talk? Oh, my God, please say something."

"I'll live," I managed to say. But my butt was going to be bruised.

I heard footsteps running toward me. "Are ye all right, miss?"

I tried to focus as another pair of eyes stared down at me.

"Tommy?"

"Aye, it's me," said my cute, would-be kidnapper from this afternoon. "And the slightest bit too late coming, I see."

"Excuse me, but who're you?" Robin demanded, then looked back at me. "Who is he?"

"Long story," I muttered.

"Are ye all right then, love?" Tommy repeated.

"Have you been following us?"

He ignored my question as he crouched down and slipped his warm hand behind my neck. "Let me help you up, miss."

"We haven't met," Robin interrupted, holding out her hand to the handsome gunman.

Tommy, always polite, pulled his hand out from under my neck and stood to shake Robin's. That was okay; my head barely bounced more than once on the hard cobbled surface.

"Tommy, meet Robin," I said, waving in the air to introduce them. "Robin, Tommy." It was about all I could manage between moans, what with my head reverberating from hitting the pavement.

"Pleasure to meet you, Robin," he said with enthusiasm, then remembered his duty and knelt down on one knee, attentive once more. "Did you happen to get a good look at the car, miss?"

"My name's Brooklyn, by the way."

He smiled and took my hand in his. "'Tis a lovely name."

"Thanks," I said.

"The car, dear," he reminded me gently. "Did you see it?"

"It was big and black, with tinted windows. Looked like a Mercedes."

"No particular markings?"

"You mean, besides the creep driving it?" Robin pointed out, fiercely protective.

I had to think. Focus. I'd been in this position before, unfortunately. I should've been getting better at it. "No. In fact, it was conspicuously free of markings. I don't think there was a front license plate. It was very plain, dark, almost somber. Then I fell, so I didn't see a back license plate when it took off."

"Okay, that's good."

Good? How was that good?

A dim lightbulb in my brain flickered on. "It was like one of the cars they use at the hotel to chauffeur people around." Like the one Kyle had described when he was almost run down. My shoulders bunched up as I shivered. "I'm cold."

"Can we get you up off the walk, then?" he asked, again wedging his hand under my neck to support my head.

"Um, ow, not just yet," I said, trying not to groan as my lower back sent a spasm of pain up my spine.

"Jeez, Brooklyn," Robin said, leaning over me. "Should we call an ambulance?"

"No, I just need a minute." And a pillow. And an aspirin. Or twenty.

"Take your time, Brooklyn, love."

"Robin," I said feebly, trying to make conversation, "Tommy was one of the men I was telling you about in the cab this afternoon."

"Ah, you're a Freemason," she said, and demurely touched his shoulder. "I'd love to discuss some of your secret handshakes sometime. I find them oddly arousing."

Ah, jeez. Was there anyone she wouldn't flirt with?

Tommy whipped his head around to assure himself that no one had overheard her utter the name of the esoteric society. Then he frowned down at me. "Did you tell her, then?"

"She's my friend," I explained, giving Robin a warning glance. "She won't say a word."

"I swear I won't," Robin said, holding up her gloved hand in promise. "Although I don't see why we can't—"

Heavy footsteps pounded across the intersection.

"Oh, look, it's Derek," Robin announced gaily.

I groaned again. Of course it was Derek. Didn't he always show up when I looked my absolute worst? I wondered idly if the cobblestones couldn't just swallow me whole.

"What the hell happened?" Derek said, and quickly knelt down on my other side and grabbed my hand. "Are you hurt, darling?"

I smiled. It was hard not to when looking at Derek. "I'll be fine, just a little tumble."

"I'm handling things here," Tommy said gruffly as he moved to kneel on my other side.

Derek cast a suspicious glower at Tommy, then looked at me. "Who is this guy?"

"A car almost ran her down, mate," Tommy said, his tone defensive. "Damn good thing I was here to take care of matters."

"Derek, meet Tommy," I said, fluttering my hand in the air again. "Tommy, Derek."

"Pleasure," Tommy muttered.

I stared up at Derek. "What are you doing here?"

He continued eyeing Tommy as he said, "I got a phone call."

"A phone call?" I was confused for a second; then it sank in. "You had me followed?"

"Of course I had you followed," he said, also striking a defensive chord. "Someone already tried once to—"

More footsteps approached and Robin laughed. "It's Angus! Whoa, he's wearing a kilt."

"A kilt?" I said, and struggled to sit up and see him.

"I think my heart just stopped," Robin said, pounding her chest as she watched Angus's kilt swing in the wind. "Medic!"

"You're partial to a man in a kilt then, darling?" Tommy asked as he stood and brushed the sidewalk grit off his pants.

"What's not to like?" Robin said, her voice breathy.

"Are you after wondering what a man wears underneath?" Tommy asked, grinning.

"Who the hell is this guy?" Derek asked me.

Oh, sweet baby James. What next? I fell back against the cobblestones, closed my eyes and prayed for divine intervention. And that aspirin.

"Figures it would be her," some woman whined as she stopped to watch the activity. "What a drama queen."

I stiffened in revulsion.

Shit. All this and *Minka*, too?

I finally forced myself to stand. My lower back ached, but I managed to keep from complaining as long as Derek kept his arm securely around me the entire two blocks back to the hotel.

Tommy refused to leave the party despite Derek's best attempts to get rid of him, so we were quite the jolly crowd as we pulled several small tables together in the hotel pub, where I'd insisted we go for a nightcap, rather than heading straight to my room. For all I knew, I'd be attacked again. Best to be prepared. And I figured a wee dram was as good a remedy as a couple of ibuprofen any day.

When I realized that Minka and her new best friend, Serena, were still hanging with our group, I stared Minka down until she bared her teeth at me like a deranged hyena and flounced off to find her own damn table. Serena's gaze lingered on Angus, Derek and Tommy, clearly the three best-looking men in the place. Her bottom lip formed a pout as Minka beckoned her away and she reluctantly followed after her new BFF.

For the life of me, I couldn't figure out that relationship. And I still didn't know if Serena really had been married to Kyle or if it was just some twisted scheme of Minka's. I made a mental note to track down Kyle's cousin Royce tomorrow and see if he'd learned anything new.

We all sat down and ordered drinks. Angus and Tommy bookended Robin, who flirted outrageously with both men, neither of whom seemed to mind that they were competing for the attentions of the same woman. In fact, they seemed rather chummy for two guys who'd just met a few minutes ago out on the street.

As I watched the barmaid pass out the drink orders, I cautiously stretched my spine. The old-fashioned captain's chair was comfortable enough, but I didn't think I'd be able to sit too long. God, it was hell getting old. And come on, I wasn't even thirty-three. Pitiful. I took a slug of the single-malt Scotch to ease my pain.

Derek turned to Angus. "Your man was good enough to call me when Brooklyn was injured, but I never did get a chance to thank him for his work."

Angus's eyebrows dipped in surprise, and he jerked his thumb in Tommy's direction. "You're drinking with him as we speak."

Derek did a double take and I choked on a laugh, which led to a minor coughing fit.

"Will you be needing a Heimlich?" Derek asked, one eyebrow raised in mock concern as he watched me make a fool of myself.

"No, but thanks," I said when I got my breath back. "But let me get this straight. You hired Tommy *the kidnapper* to follow me?"

Tommy's ears perked up, but Robin said something and his attention was diverted.

Derek was indignant. "Angus, I asked you to find a responsible private investigator. This is the same man who abducted Brooklyn this afternoon at gunpoint."

"He's usually quite responsible," Angus said, then cocked his head. "And he doesn't carry a gun, do you, Tommy?"

Tommy struggled to look away from Robin. "A gun? Me? I'm a lover, not a fighter. I don't own a gun."

"But you put a gun to my back," I said in protest. "You forced me into the cab."

"Och, I wouldna." He pulled out a small, cylindrical cigar case and waved it for everyone to see. "I prefer to rely on my charms, but occasionally I employ my traveling humidor."

I frowned, then grumbled, "Felt like a gun, anyway."

Robin slapped Tommy's knee. "You scared her half to death."

"I'm sorry, love," he said, his hands splayed in apology. "But all's well that ends well, right?".

Derek gave Angus a pained look.

Angus shrugged. "The man does good work on the whole."

It turned out that Tommy, the very man who'd snatched me off the street that afternoon, was a respected private eye who regularly worked in conjunction with the police department. In the end, Derek took the news rather philosophically, but I was still miffed that someone in law enforcement would seize me off the street and scare the crap out of me like that.

But yeah, all was well that ended well, I thought, after another two more healthy sips of Scotch. Thanks to that ride in the cab, I was pretty well convinced that Robert Burns and the English princess weren't the secret lovers Kyle had sworn they were. If Kyle had manipulated me, I hated to admit it wouldn't have been the first time.

As far as the unknown poems in the book were concerned, I would need to talk to an expert in that area. Not tonight, though. I was well on my way to being toasty-roasty and ready for beddie.

Uh-oh, waxing poetic again.

Robin leaned across Angus to whisper to me, "What's with the cow bitch?" She jutted her chin in Minka's direction.

I leaned my elbow on Angus's convenient thigh—he didn't seem to mind at all—and shook my finger at Robin. "Do you remember what I told you about her?"

"Yeah, she's the beeyotch who stabbed you," she hissed, referring to an incident in my past when Minka had tried to injure me as a means of getting me out of the way so she could move in on my boyfriend at the time. She'd been dogging me ever since.

"Yeah, and did you see how she tried to sit with us?" I said, suddenly feeling as if I'd been transported back to high school, to the times when we used to gossip and giggle with our pals.

"I saw it, my friend," Robin said. "She's, like, such a loser." She grinned and added in a more hushed voice, "It's because we've got the cute guys at our table."

"You betcha." I glanced at the three interesting men and was impressed despite myself. And maybe I had regressed to high school, because I suddenly felt like I might pass out. Whether it was from the Scotch, my aches and pains, or the men, I couldn't say, but I had to take a few fortifying breaths to get myself back on track. Passing out would be tacky and a bad way to end a really fun day. Well, fun except for a murder attempt or two.

"Three cutie-patooties," Robin said, slurring her words. So it wasn't just me. She took a quick peek at the other table and rolled her eyes. "Minka keeps laughing too loud, then looking right at this table. It's like she's dying for attention."

"That's exactly what she wants," I said. "Just don't make eye contact."

"Okay." But Robin couldn't help casting another glance Minka's way, then flinched when the evil woman held up her claw and raked the air as she glared daggers back at Robin.

"Gah," Robin said, staring wide-eyed at me. "Me scared."

"I warned you," I said, draining my glass. "Never underestimate the fearsome power of the cow bitch."

Chapter 12

As Tommy called the waitress over for a second round of drinks, I happened to make eye contact with Derek.

Without a word, he stood, held his hand out and helped me up.

The speakers in the pub were blaring vintage U2, so I waved to everyone and said loudly to Robin, "Good night."

She pouted. "Does this mean I have to leave, too?"

"Absolutely not," I said. As if she would. "I'm just beat, and I have a class to teach tomorrow afternoon, so I'd better hit the sack."

"I'll walk you up," Derek said, as though anyone doubted his intentions.

"Thank you," I murmured. I weaved my way around the tables scattered throughout the dark pub and Derek followed closely, his hand touching the small of my back.

Little sparks were igniting inside me, and I was pretty sure it was due to him. I wondered what was about to happen and had to take some deep breaths as we left the pub—and ran right into Mom and Dad.

"Hey, sweets, you look pretty," Dad said, and kissed my cheek.

"She always looks pretty," Mom said, kissing my other cheek. "She's beautiful, isn't she, Derek?"

Oooh, boy. Exactly how much wine had they consumed during their anniversary dinner?

"She's devastating," Derek said, his voice so deep my toes tingled.

Mom's eyes widened and she elbowed Derek. "Oh, woof, you sexy beast."

I gasped.

"How was your dinner?" Derek asked, a broad grin on his face.

"Hey, that place is a gas!" Dad said. "We had a Jordan cabernet tonight that blew me away."

"Good, I'm glad it worked out."

"Um, how many bottles did you go through?" I asked cautiously.

"Two, but who's counting?"

"And a groovy little after-dinner drink," Mom added. "What's it called, Jim-Jim?"

Jim-Jim? So not a good sign.

"Drambuie, Louie," Dad said, wiggling his eyebrows at her.

"Yumbo," she said in as sultry a voice as anyone could muster while saying *yumbo*.

"Oh, my God." This was just too much to take.

Mom laid her head on my shoulder. "I love you, sweetie."

"I love you, too, Mom," I said, frowning at Derek, who was taking way too much pleasure in my parents' state.

Mom turned to face me and gripped my shoulders. "Now listen, sugar bean: I want you to come with us to Rosslyn Chapel tomorrow. All those ancient Templar vibes will help boost your auric field."

Trying to get past the shock of being called *sugar bean*, I finally managed to stutter, "I-I'm not sure I—"

"Either that," she continued as if I hadn't said a word, "or we take advantage of the two-for-one irrigation special at the green spa. My treat!" She turned to Derek and confided, "I always say, an impacted colon is one bummed-out pooper shooter." Then she turned back to me. "Whaddaya say, hmm?"

Derek sputtered with laughter.

"Rosslyn Chapel it is," I said brightly.

"Dandy!" she said.

"Cool!" Dad said. "See you in the morning, kiddo." Then he grabbed Mom and nudged her toward the pub. "Come on, baby, what say you and me liven up the place with a little conga line?"

"Ooh, conga!" Mom cried, and swung her arms in the air as she danced her way into the pub.

"Oh, dear God," I whispered.

"They're plastered," Derek said with a laugh.

"Sometimes it's hard to tell," I muttered.

The next morning, I awoke feeling refreshed and happy.

And alone.

Okay, not so happy. I stared at the ceiling and thought back to the evening before. My life might've been notably different this morning, I suppose, if we hadn't run into my parents.

Talk about a buzz kill. The way I saw it, one minute Derek and I were insanely hot to jump each other, and the next minute, well, he was howling with laughter and I was mortified and searching the lobby for a potted plant to hide behind.

He assured me in the elevator that my parents were the loveliest and most honest people he'd ever met, but let's face it, my mother had uttered the phrase *pooper shooter*, and nothing would ever be the same again.

I understood my mother's need to maintain regularity while she traveled, but for God's sake, did she have to bring up the subject in front of the man I might've awakened next to this morning? I dare anyone to feel sexy with those two words lingering in the air.

Still, Derek's kiss at the door to my hotel room managed to curl my toes and heat up my insides so completely that I wouldn't have been surprised to see sparks fly out of my ears.

He pressed his forehead against mine, stared soulfully into my eyes, and smiled. I smiled back and was about to drag him inside my room, when his smile turned to a grin and he chuckled. Then he guffawed, and seconds later he was leaning against the wall, holding his stomach, laughing and begging for mercy.

So much for the famous unruffled calm of the British secret agent.

"Pooper shooter!" He gasped. "Christ on a cross, she's priceless!"

That was when I thanked him for the good time and called it a night.

As I rolled out of bed, I felt a small twinge in my lower back, probably from landing smack-dab on my ass more than once yesterday. I did some slow stretches, bringing my knees up, then bending right, left, then over. They seemed to help. The hot shower helped, too.

My sore ankle barely even registered on the pain-o-meter, so that was something to be thankful for.

I popped two ibuprofen and drank my cup of hot chocolate as I dressed. Frankly, I was ecstatic to feel only a slight throbbing in my head, considering the half bottle of wine and Scotch nightcap I'd consumed the evening before. Okay, maybe it was a little more than half a bottle of wine, but the hangover gods must've taken pity on me anyway. I sent a silent prayer of thanks to the astral plane, where I figured most hangover gods hung out during the day.

My luck ran out when I stepped into the elevator and saw the only other passenger inside: Martin Warrington,

Helen's estranged husband. For once, he was alone, without Helen to hide behind.

"Hello, Martin," I said, unable to be completely rude and ignore him.

"Brooklyn," he said. "I'm glad I ran into you."

"You're kidding, right?" I made a face. I guess I could be a little rude, after all.

"No." He smiled contritely. "I've been meaning to track you down and force you to listen to me."

"Why?"

"Because I need to apologize."

"Apologize?" I said. "For what?"

"For being a consummate clod, of course." He took a deep breath and exhaled. "This isn't easy to admit, but when Helen and I first got together, I was jealous of all her friends and I acted like a complete ass."

"Well," I started, but didn't know what to say next. I couldn't dispute his words, because they were true, and frankly, I was still suspicious of his motives.

He chuckled. He had to know what I was thinking. "I screwed up," he said. "I admit it. But I'm trying to make up for lost time. I love Helen, and I've spent these last few days realizing how unhappy I made her, and I hate myself for it. I just want her to be happy."

"I want that, too," I said cautiously.

He smiled and it seemed sincere, not the least bit reptilian or smug. "You're a good friend of hers and your opinion matters to her, so I'm hoping it's not too late for us to be friends."

"That might be asking a lot," I said, but I tried to smile as I said it.

He grinned, relaxing a bit more. "I completely understand. Perhaps we can start over as semifriendly acquaintances, then."

He held out his hand, and after a moment of consideration, I shook it, then said, "I'm not sure Helen cares what I think of you, Martin."

"She cares," he said. "A lot."

"Okay, then here's the deal. If you do anything to make her unhappy, all bets are off."

"I love her," he said simply. "I don't want her to be unhappy."

We stood in silence. To fill the void, I asked, "I guess this means you two aren't filing for divorce?"

He smiled tightly. "She told you about the divorce?"

"She mentioned it."

He exhaled heavily again. "Let's just say I'm determined to change her mind."

I studied him for a moment, then nodded. "Well, good luck with it."

He laughed. "Thanks, I'll need it."

That might've been the first time I ever heard Martin laugh. A small miracle.

Bemused, I walked away from the elevator. That was weird, I thought. But good, I guess. I'd actually seen a glimmer of the nice guy Helen had always said he could be.

I walked into the restaurant and found my parents and Robin eating fresh fruit and oatmeal.

"What's with the oatmeal?" I asked Robin as I sat. She never ate oatmeal, and I was in the mood for French toast and bacon.

"It's good for me," she mumbled.

"Since when?"

"Since your mother swears by it."

I frowned at Mom. "You do?"

She nodded resolutely. "Robin needs more fiber."

Robin smiled weakly. "I seem to be experiencing psychic energy interference."

Glancing back at Mom, I said, "That's not another euphemism for the colon thing, is it?"

She pressed her hands together in a prayer pose. "All is connected," she said, evading the question. Which I guess meant, yeah, it all came back to the colon thing.

I turned back to Robin. "Are you sure you don't just have a hangover?"

She yawned. "Probably. I was up kind of late."

I sighed. "Okay, I'll have the oatmeal."

"Solidarity," Robin whispered, and held out her fist to bump mine.

"Tomorrow, we're starting a juice fast," Mom said. "Then we'll join the screaming prayer circle that meets at sunrise on the Salisbury Crags. Are you in?"

I coughed. "Sunrise?"

"Absolutely," Mom said. "That's when the core fire of enlightenment is most rampant."

"But that's, like, in the morning."

"Exactly."

"No, thanks."

"Your father will be there."

"Really?" I turned to him. "Dad, are you going on a juice fast?"

"Sure," Dad said, spearing a thick piece of bacon. "If cabernet is considered juice, I'm there."

They didn't seem to be suffering any lingering effects from the alcohol they'd consumed last night. Maybe there was something to the whole colon thing, after all.

I shivered as I remembered Mom's statement from the night before. On second thought, I was going to forget I ever had that thought.

After breakfast, as we waited for the valet to bring the minivan around, a taxicab pulled up and Helen climbed out of the back, carrying three Jaeger shopping bags. She paid the driver, then rushed over to Mom and gave her a big hug.

"I feel like I haven't seen you in days," she said, then laughed. "It's crazy how life can change in a day."

"It's so funny you should say so," I said as I pulled her away from the family and walked with her toward the wide sliding doors of the hotel. "Because I rode down in the elevator with Martin a little while ago."

Her smile wobbled. "Oh, dear. Should I apologize?"

I frowned, then shook my head and chuckled. "No, strangely enough, he took care of that."

"What do you mean?"

"He apologized to me," I said.

Her eyes widened. "That's weird."

"I know." I laughed. "But he did. He was actually nice about it, said he's determined to talk you out of the divorce and make your relationship work. And he wants us to try to be friends."

She tensed up. "He mentioned the divorce?"

"Just that he wants to change your mind about it."

"And what did you say?"

"I wished him luck." I frowned. "What's wrong?"

"Nothing." She breathed again. "I'm just surprised he approached you."

"It couldn't be avoided. We were stuck in the elevator together."

She smiled. "At least he made the effort."

I studied her. "Helen, are you going to go back to him?"

"I don't know," she said, waving her hands in frustration. "I'm so confused. He's been on his best behavior. I should go find him." She checked her watch. "Phooey. I think he just started a two-hour meeting."

"If you've got two hours to kill, why don't you come with us to Rosslyn Chapel?"

"Is that where you're all going?"

"Yes."

"It sounds like fun," she said hesitantly.

"Fun and educational."

She laughed. "I'd love to. I'll give my bags to the bellman."

"I'll go with you."

We checked her shopping bags and walked across the lobby. I hesitated, then finally asked what I'd wanted to know for days. "So, Helen, what about the thing with Kyle?"

"For goodness' sake, Brooklyn, he was married." She shook her head in distress. "What was I thinking? My feelings for him were obviously one-sided."

"It's not your fault," I said lamely, having been there, done that. "He was an adorable cad."

"I suppose so, but I completely deluded myself."

"You thought he was in love with you."

"Yes, and how pathetic does that sound?" she said, clutching my arm as we walked over to the valet station. "I've had to do some serious soul-searching in the past day or so. Was I really in love or was Kyle just the excuse I needed to leave Martin? Was I looking for another guy to take care of me? Am I that helpless? What do I really want? Martin and I had a good relationship in the beginning. Do I want to throw that away?"

"That's a lot of questions."

"I don't know what to do."

"Give yourself a break. You don't have to do anything right this minute."

She pursed her lips in thought, then nodded in agreement. "You're right. I'm just going to enjoy the ride for now."

"Great."

"It feels good to talk to you about this. I've been so conflicted."

"I'm always here for you," I said, hugging her. Not that I could help much, because let's face it, I was the last woman on earth to be writing the advice-to-the-lovelorn column. Never seemed to stop me, though.

The minivan had finally arrived from the parking garage and Robin was already at the wheel. Mom had the front passenger seat, so Helen and I climbed in the back with Dad.

"Helen's coming with us," I said, stating the obvious.

"Wonderful," Mom said.

"Super," Dad said, sliding over. "Buckle up, everyone."

"The concierge gave me directions for a scenic route, so let's hope we don't get lost." With that warning, Robin drove south out of the city down a busy two-lane highway. After a few miles, suburbia turned to rural farmland, with mown fields and low hedges. In one field, six large haystacks were piled in a neat row.

"It looks like a van Gogh painting," Mom said with a sigh. "I want to get a picture of that on the way home."

After twenty minutes, Robin turned onto a slightly hilly, residential street and followed it until the road ended in a wide, well-paved parking lot. As she pulled into a space, the car lurched forward and she pumped the brakes a few times.

"Everything okay?" Mom asked.

"I'm just not used to the brakes," Robin said with a shrug. "British cars take some getting used to."

I looked around at the smoothly paved surfaces and shiny brick wall surrounding a new visitors' center. "They've upgraded this whole area."

Robin nodded. "I'll say. It used to be a dirt lot."

Hollywood crews had invaded Rosslyn Chapel a few years back to film one of the climactic scenes in *The Da Vinci Code*. I'd heard that the producers had paid Rosslyn Chapel a potful of money to upgrade the place. It was a good thing, since the book and film had been responsible for bringing thousands of thundering hordes of tourists to the small, fragile chapel, disrupting the neighborhood and challenging the Rosslyn estate to take drastic measures before the church was completely destroyed.

A semipermanent canopy and scaffolding covered the ancient roof and sides, protecting the chapel from the rain that seeped into the walls and softened the stone.

We stopped to buy tickets at the clean, modern visitors' center, noted the addition of a small but fully stocked café, then walked across the grounds to the chapel.

As we stepped inside the dark church, my first thought was how impossible it would be to describe Rosslyn Chapel in just a few words. Enigmatic, charming and otherworldly were several that came to mind, but they weren't enough.

Even though I'd visited before, it was still a shock to realize how small it was, only thirty-five feet across and maybe twice that in length. It was also darker than expected, and so incredibly ornate; with carvings on every surface of every wall and ceiling, it was almost overwhelming.

Every inch of carved stonework seemed to hold some esoteric meaning. There were symbols from every biblical lesson, every saint, every sin, every virtue. The vast and complex story of creation was carved into one wall. The history of Scotland was represented, including a small sculpture of Robert the Bruce and his well-known heart. One prominent pillar showed angels playing every musical instrument imaginable. Mythological creatures ran amok. Even Scandinavian dragons dwelled at the base of one pillar, with vines streaming from their mouths.

Signs and symbols of the Knights Templar and the Freemasons who'd built the structure were everywhere.

It was said that the only reason Rosslyn Chapel was spared by Cromwell during Britain's own civil war was that Cromwell was a Freemason.

Mom walked around, staring up at the ceiling with its thousands of small carved flowers and stars. When she bumped into one of the pillars, I hurried over and put my arm through hers.

"Mom, why don't we explore together for a while?"

"Oh, that would be fun," she said, patting my arm. "This place rocks. I'm getting all sorts of supreme vibes, aren't you?"

"Oh, yeah, I feel the power." I actually did. You couldn't help but feel the energy of the place.

I took her into the Lady Chapel that ran along one end of the church and pointed out a green man carved on the end of a protruding arch that jutted from the ceiling near the altar of Saint Andrew.

"What in the world?" She moved in as close as she could get and stared at the strange, ancient pagan fertility symbol whose round face was always shown surrounded by leaves. Green men could be found all over Rosslyn Chapel, carved on the walls, the ceiling, the pillars, and hidden among the seven deadly sins.

One school of thought claimed that the little green man symbolized man's capacity for great goodness versus his corresponding facility for evil— whatever that meant. Some said the story of Robin Hood had its origins in the green man legend. The eerie thing was, green men had been found carved in the old stone walls of churches and abbeys all over Britain, depicted as demon, trickster, or lord of the forest. His true meaning remained a primordial mystery.

Surrounded by all the symbols of freemasonry in the pillars and the walls, I felt my thoughts begin to run wild. It occurred to me as I stood staring at a carving of an angel playing bagpipes that there might be some deeper significance to the Robert Burns poems than an illicit love affair and a secret baby.

What if the story of Rabbie and the princess was true? What if the royal family had known about the baby being Robert Burns's child all along? What if they had not only refused to allow the upstart, rabble-rousing Freemason Scotsman to be an acknowledged link in the royal lineage, but also decided to do something about it? Burns had been ill ever since he'd left Edinburgh and died prematurely at the age of thirty-seven.

What if his death had been less than natural? What if he'd been murdered?

"What if you're hallucinating?" I muttered as I shook my head to clear away the murderous thoughts. "Jeezo, Wainwright, chill out."

I loved a conspiracy theory as much as the next girl, but that was ridiculous. In my defense, it probably wasn't the first time someone had suffered acute delirium inside Rosslyn Chapel.

"What'd you say, honey?" Mom asked.

"Nothing." I smiled gaily, causing her to frown.

"What's this?" I asked quickly, pointing to the arch above us. It seemed to distract her as she checked her brochure.

"The *danse macabre*," she explained. "See the little skeletons walking next to their earthly bodies? They're supposed to represent death's supremacy over mankind."

"Cheery," I said.

"I know." She mused, "I wouldn't be surprised to find out these old Freemason dudes were once Deadheads."

It was useless to point out that the chapel had been built over six hundred years ago, while the Grateful Dead and their Deadhead followers had come into being only forty or so years ago, not the other way around. Mom had a whole different way of dealing with that pesky space-time continuum thing.

And who was to say she wasn't right? I thought, staring at the perky little carved skeletons. In my current state, I wouldn't have been surprised to see them pop out of the wall and start grooving to "Iko Iko."

And now that I thought about it, that carving of the last prince of Orkney, William St. Clair, over in the corner near the entrance to the baptistry, bore a striking resemblance to Jerry Garcia.

Oh, good. More hallucinating.

We caught up with Dad downstairs in the sacristy, an austere space with none of the ornate carvings found in the main church. Here, six feet below ground level, was where a number of tombs of the Rosslyn barons and Orkney princes were located. If there were any ghosts in Rosslyn Chapel, I figured they slept here at night.

"Who's ready for lunch?" Dad said, not a moment too soon.

We all blinked like baby possums as we stepped outside into the glaring sunshine. After wandering around the lovely grounds for another twenty minutes, we decided to buy sandwiches and tea and water for Dad in the café and eat in the car.

On the drive back, I sat with Robin in the front seat while Mom and Dad started a songfest in back. Dad wanted to start with sixties hits, but Mom insisted on Scottish tunes. She began to sing "Loch Lomond" and we all joined in.

On the chorus, my father's tenor voice filled the car and made my eyes sting with pride.

"Oh! Ye'll take the high road, and I'll take the low road,
   And I'll be in Scotland afore ye,

But me and my true love will never meet again,
On the bonnie, bonnie banks of Loch Lomond."

Mom kissed him on the cheek and I saw that her eyes were damp, too.

"Second verse is yours, Helen," Dad said jovially.

"But I don't know the words."

So they just sang the chorus a few more times, and Helen laughed a lot, making me smile. I figured Mom and Dad had started the singing to coax her out of her shell, and it was working. She seemed to be her old self again, relaxed and upbeat. Maybe she and Martin would work things out, after all. I hoped not, but that was just me. I would give him the benefit of the doubt if it made her happy.

I turned to face the front window and sighed. Not with happiness, exactly, but I felt good. I thought about Derek and wondered what he was doing today, wondered what might happen tonight if . . . well, hmm. I'd let the possibilities percolate for a while. Otherwise, I'd be a basket case by the time I saw him next.

I sighed. It felt great to get away from thoughts of killers and falling bookshelves, not to mention one very recent hit-and-run attempt. Cold prickled my arms at the thought of that black car zooming straight at me. I stiffened, causing my back to cramp up, so I slowly stretched from side to side to ease the lower back pain. I was way too young to feel this old.

The backseat group continued their chatter, so I turned to Robin to talk. "How's it going?"

She gripped the steering wheel with a look of grim determination. "Great."

"Something wrong with the steering?" I asked.

"It's the brakes," she said. "They're weak."

"Can you downshift?" I asked.

"It's an automatic."

She took the next curve too fast and Mom grabbed hold of the back of my seat.

"Slow down there, Parnelli," Dad said with a chuckle.

"Sorry," Robin said, but her jaw was tight and her lips were thin as she held on to the wheel.

We hit a stretch of straight road that ran through flat green fields, and Robin pumped the brakes a few times.

"Nothing," she muttered, then tried the hand brake.

"Nothing?" I asked.

She shook her head.

"Crap."

Dad caught the vibe and moved forward, wedging himself between the two front seats. "What's up?"

"Brakes are fried," Robin explained.

I realized we were heading for a sharp curve to the right, then straight ahead into a more populated area. "Turn off the engine," I suggested.

"Can't," Dad told me. "The steering will lock up if you do."

"Crap again."

"Get off the road, now," Dad said firmly, pointing to the wide field to our left.

Robin's head whipped around frantically. "But it's—"

"Now," he directed, still pointing as if he could guide her along. "You can do it. Ease over the shoulder and keep going, toward those haystacks."

"Everything okay?" Mom asked.

"Brakes," Dad explained calmly. "We're going into that field. Now."

"Sounds like a plan," Mom said, keeping upbeat as she pulled Dad back. "Seat belt on, Jimmy."

Robin jerked the wheel off to the left and the minivan bumped and bucked like a wild horse over the low rows of hedges lining the highway.

The seemingly smooth field was full of ruts and

mounds, and we were bounced and thrown like a dinghy on a raging sea.

"Oof," Dad said when his head hit the car's ceiling.

"Oh, dear." Mom's voice trembled.

Helen screamed.

My already aching back was wrenched from side to side; then my head struck the headliner hard and I saw stars.

"Damn it!" Robin swore as she hit one last deep pothole.

The car slammed into a haystack with a jarring thud followed by a deafening explosion.

Chapter 13

News flash: Air bags are a lot louder and messier than advertised.

I can also report that, contrary to popular belief, a haystack is not the fluffy, puffy fun time it appears to be in the comics. Considering the alternative, though, I had to admit it was a relatively soft landing. Not soft enough to keep the air bags from deploying, however. White powder went everywhere, and my ears were ringing from the blast of the release mechanism.

I pushed open the car door and hay fell on my head as I stumbled from the car. I leaned against the door and shook the hay out of my hair, then noticed white powder all over my hands and arms. As I brushed the air bag residue away, I glanced back at the highway and sighed in relief. Robin had managed to avoid careening through a traffic circle surrounded by shops and houses by a mere few hundred yards or so.

"Everyone accounted for?" Dad asked as he helped Mom out of the car.

"Uhh," Helen groaned.

"Helen, are you okay?" Mom said.

"I'm okay." But she rubbed her temple where her head had probably hit the side window.

"That was quite a ride," Mom said, and staggered

around the car to envelop Robin in a hug. "You did a good job, honey."

"We could've died," Helen said, patting Robin's arm. "You saved us."

Robin sank down on the ground, holding her forehead. "I think I hit my head on the steering wheel."

I walked to the other side of the car as Mom knelt down next to Robin and flicked bits of powder from her hair. "Must've been before the air bag blew up."

"I guess."

An older man walked toward us from the barn that stood several field lengths away. He wore worn blue overalls, a flannel shirt and work boots.

"Are you all right?" he shouted from yards away.

"We're fine." Dad waved. "Just a little banged up. We lost our brakes."

"I've called the constable. Wasn't sure if there were injuries."

"Just to your haystack," I said in apology, assuming he owned these fields.

Closer now, he waved a hand and chuckled. "Och, don't you be worrying about such a thing."

We heard a siren in the distance.

"That'll be our police now," he said. "Hope you're not bank robbers making a getaway."

We laughed dutifully as the siren stopped.

"I'd better show them over here," the farmer said, and took off, jogging back to the barn.

"Are we going to be arrested?" Robin asked, then buried her head in her arms.

"Of course not," I said firmly.

Dad rubbed Robin's shoulder as we watched the farmer lead two policemen on the long trek across the field.

"You've had some trouble," the taller cop said.

"Our brakes gave out," Dad said.

"Our driver saved our lives," Helen said staunchly, "and probably the lives of any number of bystanders, by driving off the highway."

The shorter cop, a skinny youngster who still had pimples, took notes, while the tall cop knelt down next to the rear driver's-side tire and poked at the ground. I moved closer to see what he was looking at and caught a glimpse of some drops of liquid seeping into the ground.

"Looks like brake fluid," he said to his partner. Then he gripped the rim of the fender and handily slid himself under the car, somehow avoiding the slimy puddle of brake fluid altogether. How did he do that? Must've been a guy-and-car thing.

A few seconds later, he glided out, hopped up and brushed a few flecks of grit off his perfectly pressed black trousers. "Brake line's been cut clean through."

"What the hell?" Dad said.

"Does that happen through normal wear and tear on the car?" I asked, already knowing the answer.

The tall cop looked at me warily. "No, ma'am. That happens through mischief."

"You're lucky to be alive," Derek said, glaring at me through narrowed eyes, as though it were my fault my family and friends were almost killed. Hell, maybe it was.

"Yeah, I get that," I muttered as I paced the floor of the hotel conference room the police once again had taken over as their temporary headquarters.

It was two hours later, after the Edinburgh CID had shown up to take over the investigation and the farmer had generously ferried us back to the hotel in his vintage Land Rover.

"And you're sure nobody saw anyone at the parking garage?" I asked for the third time. The hotel valets had parked Robin's rental van in the parking garage a block away from the hotel when she'd arrived two days ago.

The brakes could've been tampered with anytime in the last forty-eight hours, but the police were fairly certain someone had done it that morning. Otherwise, the brake fluid would've run out completely and the car wouldn't have made it all the way to Rosslyn Chapel.

Now I remembered Robin pumping the brakes when we first arrived there.

MacLeod sighed. "The garage is a four-story cavernous place with only one security man who doubles as the parking attendant. All the hotels in this part of the Royal Mile share the space. It's not well guarded, sad to say."

"No security cameras?"

"None." Frustrated, Angus raked his fingers through his unruly mop of hair.

Derek stood with his arms folded across his chest, watching the goings-on. He was dressed in an elegant black pin-striped business suit and deep blue silk tie that brought out the blue in his eyes. He looked almost criminally hot. The whole ensemble probably cost five thousand dollars, and I was reminded again how well the security business paid. Along that same line, I had to wonder just why he'd been here in Edinburgh this week. What was he doing? Besides looking criminally hot, of course?

"Is it our Miss Sherlock Holmes that's causing you to pull your hair out, Angus?" Derek asked, coming over and putting his arm around me. I leaned against him. He even *smelled* expensive.

The detective glanced at me, then Derek. "No, 'tis this case that's driving me to drink," he admitted.

"Not much of a drive there," Derek said with a wry grin.

"You've got the right of that, mate," he said with a rueful chuckle.

Derek tightened his grip on me as the two men talked and more was revealed about our close call with the haystack.

My life had been threatened, my family had almost been killed, and yet I couldn't seem to concentrate on any of it.

All I could process was the weight of Derek's arm around my shoulder and the warmth of his solid body against mine. For one insane second or two, I breathed him in, absorbing that all-male, autumn-and-leather scent and reveling in the warm security of his powerful muscles.

Oh, dear God.

Appalled by my pathetically needy reaction, I was nevertheless incapable of moving away from the heat of his touch. In a day or so, they would find my body completely melted in a pool of lust on the floor of this conference room. I hoped they would give me as nice a service as Kyle had received. With better music, please.

"You'd be right about that," Derek said, his head cocked as he gazed at me with curiosity.

I blinked. "What?"

"Where did you go, love?" he whispered.

I tried to speak, but my throat had dried up.

"Angus was saying you've made a formidable enemy," he said. The breath from his words tickled my ear.

I smiled up at him as I gently pulled away. My heart could no longer handle the spike in blood pressure, and my self-esteem wasn't doing much better. Sheesh, way to lose my cool in front of the head cop on the case.

"Uh, yeah," I said, pacing a few steps away until I could finally breathe again.

Derek was watching me with suspicion, and I could

feel my cheeks heat up. It just wasn't fair. I was in a weakened state or I would've stared him down.

"Brooklyn, Angus said you're no longer a suspect," Derek said.

I felt my mouth open, then close. Finally, I said, "Oh, is that what you were talking about? Sorry, my brain's going off in ten different directions."

"That's understandable," Angus said.

I could breathe again—in more ways than one. I was off the hook as a suspect in Kyle's murder, because after all, why would I cut the brake line in the car I was driving in with my family and friends?

"Did your men interview Perry McDougall about the brake line?" Derek asked.

Angus looked at me briefly before deciding it was all right to discuss the case in front of me. "He left his booth at the fair this morning and hasn't returned."

"Really?" I said. "That's suspicious, isn't it?"

"Aye, but witnesses say he was on his way to present a three-hour seminar on . . ." Angus checked his notes. "Appraising rare British ephemera." He gave me a puzzled look.

"Ephemera are printed items that weren't supposed to be worth anything but now they are," I explained. "Like a ticket to a Beatles concert at the Hollywood Bowl in 1964, for instance." I mentioned that because my mother still had hers in a scrapbook. The ticket price was five dollars, but she'd paid twelve dollars to a scalper. Those were the days.

"Rare British ephemera usually has to do with the monarchy," I continued. "Or the Beatles, as I said, or World War Two posters and brochures, baseball cards, that sort of thing."

"Ah," Angus said. "Well, he never showed up for the seminar."

"Any word on his whereabouts?" Derek asked.

"Nothing yet."

I didn't know whether to laugh or cry. If Perry had cut our brake line, then skipped town, he could be anywhere. Or he could be hiding somewhere in the hotel, waiting to attack again.

The chills were back. I rubbed my arms briskly, but it didn't help.

I suddenly realized it was getting late. "I've got to run. I'm supposed to do a three-o'clock workshop."

"Where?"

I had to think. "It's on the D level. I don't know the room number."

"I'll drop by," Derek said.

"Yes, I may do the same," Angus chimed in.

I would've felt warm and fuzzy with all the attention from the cute guys, but I figured their consideration had more to do with my possibly getting another unwelcome visitor than with their wanting to be near me. "Thanks."

They walked with me down the hall to the elevator.

"Will you be stirring up the crowd again?" Derek asked, his lips pursed in a smirk. I wished I didn't find that look so damned attractive.

"No, this is a book arts class."

"Sounds interesting," Angus said, clearly lying.

"It's arts and crafts," I explained. "Everyone gets to make a small, accordion-style album."

"Are there weapons involved?" Derek asked.

I thought about it. "If you consider X-Acto knives and bone folders weapons, then yes. Oh, and glue sticks."

"Ah, then I'll be there," he said.

I laughed. "Oh, good times for you."

"Be careful, Brooklyn," Angus said as the elevator door opened. "You've an enemy here who's growing more reckless by the hour."

With that happy thought, Derek and I stepped into the elevator and rode it up to my floor.

Once inside my room, he watched as I gathered my supplies and materials for the twenty participants who'd signed up for the class to make their own small, accordion-style album. I'd packed everything in one satchel: forty four-by-four-inch pieces of neutral book board; the acid-free paper used for the book pages, already scored; twenty sets of decorative Japanese papers for the covers, already cut to size; and ribbon to tie each album closed. In addition, I would supply all the tools necessary to complete the project, including twenty sets of glue sticks, X-Acto knives and bone folders, which were lightweight tools usually shaped like tongue depressors and often made from bone, that were used for folding and scoring paper and to give the fold a sharper, more professional crease. I also had plenty of scrap paper, pencils and rulers.

If the police didn't know I was teaching a bookbinding class, they would think I was carrying a small arsenal. I supposed a glue stick could be considered a dangerous weapon if you used it to poke somebody's eye out.

We rode back down to D level and Derek held the door to my workshop conference room open, then left me to my task. Alone in the room, as I set up individual places at the worktables with tools and supplies, I worried about Perry. Where was he hiding? Did he really have a legitimate alibi or had Minka been lying to the police?

And who else besides Perry and Jack had Kyle talked to? The number of experts in British history and Scottish poetry at this book fair probably ran in the hundreds. On a hunch, I pulled out my book fair program and checked the back pages, where the exhibitors were listed by their specialties. A number of names appeared under both categories, including Perry McDougall and Royce McVee.

Royce. It stood to reason that Kyle would've asked his own cousin for advice on the Burns book.

Had he killed Kyle to stop him from discussing the book? Had he wanted to gain control of the lucrative McVee businesses? If so, then finding out Kyle had a wife would really put a crimp in his style. And he'd been so angry about Serena, the "lying tart." I wondered if I should warn Serena that Royce might come after her. But did I honestly think Royce was capable of murder? He was so bland.

What did I know about Royce, really? During the blissful six months Kyle and I were dating, we'd had drinks with Royce a few times. He was a big man, not overbearingly big like Perry, but at least six feet tall. Realistically, he was probably strong enough to bludgeon a grown man with a hammer, but he seemed weak and insubstantial.

I hadn't seen him in a day or so and wondered if he had indeed stayed in Edinburgh. Had he had more words with Serena? Had he accused her to her face of lying?

And speaking of Serena, was she a lying tart or not? Something about her really bothered me. It probably wasn't *her*, specifically, but the simple fact that Kyle had had a wife all this time and I never knew. Either way, I didn't get a feeling of connection between her and Kyle. That bothered me, too.

I munched on chocolate buttons as I arranged each student's workspace with decorative papers and book boards. As I laid out tools and supplies on the third table, I had a sudden sick thought: If Kyle had been "promised" to Serena when he was dating me, had she known about me? Had she arrived in town and followed him to the castle? Had she seen him greet me with kisses and hugs, then watched as we popped into the nearest pub?

I stopped in my tracks. Was it hatred and jealousy of me that had driven her to follow me back to my hotel room, sneak in while I was sleeping off jet lag, and steal my tools? Jealousy was a powerful motive. If she was angry enough, she could've killed Kyle using my bookbinder's hammer and pinned the murder on me.

Could Serena be the one who'd called Kyle while we were at the pub together?

I shook myself out of those thoughts. But it creeped me out to think about how friendly Serena and Minka had become. How did they know each other? Maybe Minka had helped her do the deed. Minka would be up for anything that might ruin my life.

I decided I would track down Serena after my workshop and try to schmooze her. I needed to do the same with Royce. Maybe I could get one of them to reveal something. Anything. Just for my own peace of mind. I wasn't conducting an investigation. Just trying to find answers to a few burning questions.

I looked around the room. The four long worktables were now arranged with five workspaces each.

At the front of the room was a larger worktable with a conference-style tablecloth over it. It was set up on a platform to act as a dais of sorts.

I stepped up on the platform and started to lay out all my own tools and supplies I would need to instruct the students, but almost tripped over something sticking out from underneath the table.

It felt like a heavy pipe. Maybe someone had thought it would be okay to store it here, but I knew I'd break my neck if it stayed there. I tried to kick it back under the table, but it wouldn't budge. I could see myself tripping and tumbling off the platform in front of the class, so I knelt down to push it out of the way.

But it wasn't a pipe.

It was a foot, connected to a leg, connected to a dead body.

I scrambled to my feet, jumped off the platform and ran out of the room, screaming bloody murder.

Chapter 14

I would've slammed right into Derek in the hall, but he managed to escape being steamrollered by simply grabbing hold of me and crushing me to his chest.

I was still screaming.

"What is it?" he demanded. "What's wrong?"

"He's dead!" I cried.

"Who?" He shook me a little, and ordinarily I would've smacked him for that, but this time it stopped me from screaming and forced me to breathe.

"Oh, my God," I whispered. "Why does this keep happening to me?"

"Show me," he said. He took my hand and led me back into the conference room where I pointed a shaky finger toward the front of the room.

"Under the table."

"Stay here."

"No problem."

He walked over to see what the fuss was all about while I stood in the back sniveling like a scaredy-cat.

Derek stared at the foot, then knelt down and stared at the body for a good minute. Then he stood, pulled his cell phone out and made a quick call as he walked back to me.

"Who is it?" I asked. "Whose body is it?"

"You didn't see?" he asked.

I shook my head vigorously as he pulled me by the hand out of the room and shut the conference room door.

Out in the hall, he held my shoulders as he said, "It's Perry McDougall."

I gaped at him. "No way." I moved away to pace up and down the empty hall, muttering and swearing to myself.

"You do have a proclivity for finding dead bodies," Derek said. "It's almost as though somebody knew you'd be here."

"Damn it," I said for the tenth time. Was I being set up again?

"My sentiments exactly," Derek said "Guess we know where Perry McDougall disappeared to."

"Yes." I should've felt bad for Perry, but I confess I felt worse for myself. Perry had been the best suspect we had for Kyle's murder. Now what? Or more precisely, *who*?

"And why me?" I asked myself for the hundredth time.

Within five minutes Angus was running down the hall toward us like a wild-eyed Highlander, followed by a small phalanx of constables.

Seconds later, inside the conference room, Angus stared down at the body. He pursed his lips, then glanced across at me and Derek and said, "Curiouser and curiouser."

Without his warm Scottish accent, he never would've gotten away with using that silly *Alice in Wonderland* phrase. He looked around for his second in command and in a much more grim manner said, "Terrence, clear the outer hall area. We've got ourselves another crime scene."

As Terrence took off, Angus muttered, "We're going to bloody run out of tape."

The crime scene people made quick work of closing off the doorway to interested passersby and dusting every last surface in the room. Then several men picked up the heavy wood table and moved it to the side of the room.

Perry's body lay uncovered on the platform, ignored by the technicians who worked the scene, taking photographs and combing the carpet for possible clues.

I stared at Perry's exposed neck and saw for the first time the knotting awl sticking out of it.

"Oh, shit." Fumbling for the nearest chair, I slid down and sat with my elbows resting on my thighs, breathing deeply, trying not to look at poor dead Perry. Or the bloody knotting awl.

I knew it was a knotting awl because I used one all the time to pierce holes in paper before sewing them together to make books.

By now I should've been used to finding dead bodies, but I wasn't. And it wasn't even Perry's body that freaked me out as much as it was the blood that was pooling beneath his neck and spreading out into a tiny lake—or maybe it was a loch—around his head.

The sight of blood has always been an issue for me. I don't mind needles. Even spiders don't freak me out as much as blood. I'm kind of a wimp that way. And hey, that was how Derek and I met, which should've made it all touchingly romantic. But not even the fond memory of me fainting and waking up in Derek's arms as he smacked me back to consciousness could help relieve the wooziness I was feeling.

"What have we here?" MacLeod said, and knelt down next to Perry to study the apparent murder weapon stuck in his neck.

I had a really bad feeling about that knotting awl.

Clearly, so did he. Looking up, he said, "Miss Wainwright, can I ask you to come here?"

I grimaced. "No, thank you."

Derek sat down next to me. "I'll help you."

I looked at him beseechingly. "Please don't make me go over there. Remember that little issue I have with blood?"

Derek looked across the room at Angus. "She faints at the first sign of blood. You won't want to deal with that."

"Thanks a lot," I muttered.

"I'd like her to identify this weapon."

I frowned at Derek. "It's a knotting awl."

"She says it's a knotting awl."

"Can she describe it for me?" Angus asked.

"I can hear you," I snapped.

"Steady, love," Derek murmured close to my ear.

"Sorry, Angus," I said quickly. I was starting to shake but took some deep breaths and managed to stay upright.

"It's cherrywood," I began. "Very hard. Pear-shaped, with lines carved in waves. It's used to pierce holes in the folds of the pages of a book before they're sewn to linen tapes. It fits nicely in my hand. I've had it for years." My throat was closing up, so I stopped talking.

MacLeod grunted. He didn't have to say anything. I knew it was mine, knew someone had used my tool as a murder weapon in order to implicate me again.

I forced my hands to relax by splaying them on my knees. I imagined the awl in my left hand. I'd used it hundreds of times. It was an old favorite tool, an old friend. One of the woodworkers at the Fellowship had handcrafted it for me a long time ago. Over the years, I would occasionally hone the shaft to a perfect point, but that probably wouldn't help my case if I mentioned it now.

I had all different shapes and sizes of awls for use with paper and leather and boards, but this knotting awl was my favorite. It was actually designed to thread the knots in string between beads, thus the name, knotting awl. The shaft was narrower and more tapered than a typical bookbinder's awl, and that was why I liked it.

Evidently, the killer had liked it, too.

I was frustrated and angry. What was MacLeod going to do now that a second murder had been committed? There probably weren't that many murders in Scotland in a whole year, so I figured his superiors would be clamoring for an arrest. And I was looking better and better for it. And why not? Not only had my awl been used to kill Perry, but the police could make a case for motivation, as well. After all, with Perry dead, there was no one else to challenge my version of the Robert Burns book mythology.

Except for the killer.

Whoever that was.

I almost moaned in aggravation. Why couldn't Perry have been Kyle's killer? It would've been so much more convenient all around. I rubbed my face in frustration. I was all about convenience, damn it.

I'd racked my brain to figure out who would benefit from Kyle's death, and my only conclusion—before this moment—had been Perry. Perry had wanted Kyle to shut up about the Robert Burns legend. He'd attacked me almost before I'd made it through the door of the hotel. He was the perfect suspect. Damn it, I wanted to cry.

Now I had to start over, studying my suspect list for someone with enough motivation to kill twice *and* set me up to take the fall. And I had to find someone quickly, because there was no way I wanted to go to prison for someone else's crime.

I had a sudden thought: Maybe Perry *had* killed Kyle. Then somebody else killed Perry. And now someone else would kill that someone else and pretty soon everyone in Edinburgh would be dead.

Oh, yeah. That was plausible.

There was a hair-raising shriek out in the hall. Then the door banged against the wall and someone pushed through the guards.

"She killed him!" Minka screamed, pointing at me in an alarming case of déjà vu. "She killed Perry! She's a murderer, and it's not the first time!"

"Oh, jeez," I said, shaking my head in disgust. If I ever did decide to kill somebody, guess who my target would be?

Angus rushed over and took hold of her arm. "Ma'am, you're not—"

"Let go of me, you big oaf!" She managed to shake him loose, which was a testament to her frenzy, because Angus was a really big guy.

"Bloody hell," Derek said, and instinctively shoved me behind him for protection, then tried to cage me as I attempted to move around him and confront Minka. I'm not sure why I wanted to. She scared me to death. But Derek's caveman routine was too much. Maybe he thought I was going to kick the crap out of her. And what was wrong with that? She'd thrown a screaming fit once before, then smacked me in the face. I would've liked to have returned the favor, just once.

"She's like the angel of death," Minka cried. "Wherever she goes, someone dies!"

"Not fair," I countered. True, but not fair.

"Stay back," Derek commanded.

"No." I twisted around and managed to escape Derek's protective shield, then went for payback. "Angus, she was working for Perry. She had plenty of opportunity to kill him."

"Liar! I'll kill you!"

"I don't think so." But I knew the woman packed a wallop, so I threw my hands up to protect my face. Sure enough, Minka charged. As I prepared to take her down, Derek pulled me back.

"Hey!" I cried.

Angus caught Minka in a headlock at the same time. She squeaked like a bat and her arms flailed around as Angus held up his free hand and snapped his fingers. Two constables dashed over to grab Minka and lead her out.

"No! Not me," Minka griped. "She's the one."

"She's crazy," I said. As far as accusations went, it was weak, but I was wiped out. However, seeing Minka dragged out by the police went a long way toward making my day brighter.

Derek gave me a warning glance as he took my arm and drew me closer.

Minka saw the move. She whipped around and faced Angus, her lip curled in a sneer. "Oh, my God, you're going to let her go, aren't you?" She wiggled to escape the cops' grasp, but they held firm. "Dumb-shit cops are always swayed by blondes."

Really? Then why was I always the prime suspect?

"That's enough," Angus snapped.

"Fine, I'll go," Minka said, "but don't you dare release her! You'll be sorry. I'll report you!"

"Get her out of here."

The door banged shut behind her and there was a sudden silence.

"Well, she's an angry one," Angus finally said, brushing his hands off.

"Thank you for intervening," I said. "And I hope everyone noticed she threatened to kill me. Shouldn't you make a note somewhere?"

Derek chuckled.

Angus sighed. "She was just overwrought."

"She's a raving loon," I said pointedly. "And dangerous. It's not the first time she's attacked me."

"Yes, I saw you both tangling the other day."

"No, before that," I said. "Back in San Francisco. Never mind. Anyway, thanks."

"My job," he said, holding out his hands. "Besides, she's got no business in here. This is a crime scene."

"She really will try to report you." Minka wasn't the sharpest crayon in the box.

"She's welcome to try." Angus shook his head. "She seems more and more unbalanced every time I see her. We'll hold her for questioning."

"Good," Derek said.

Minka had blamed me for another death after Abraham was killed last month. She'd attacked me and accused the police of playing favorites. I was getting a little tired of it.

A little? I slumped into my chair as the adrenaline rush wore off. I felt like an idiot for behaving so wildly, but nobody in the world ticked me off like Minka did. Would I ever be free of her maddening presence in my life? I truly wished her dead.

Okay, erase that. My mother would call that tempting karma. I wasn't cynical enough to disagree, so I shook my head and quickly erased that thought. If only it were that easy, as if my brain were an Etch A Sketch and the screen were now blank.

So maybe I didn't want her dead, but I did want her to go away and leave me alone.

I considered that new change in thinking a sign of personal growth.

The crime scene investigators took over the room, and Angus moved our little group to the far corner. He grilled me again, implored me to search my mind for any other people Kyle might've spoken to about the Robert Burns book.

"And more important," he added, "who's most likely

to have stolen your bookbinding tools for the purposes of implicating you?"

"Exactly," I said emphatically. "That's the key to this puzzle."

I pulled out the book fair program and went down the list of exhibitors, pointing out the names of experts who might've given Kyle some feedback.

"I would've thought his cousin Royce would have an opinion of the book," I said, "but he seems completely uninvolved in that side of the business."

Angus flipped through his notebook. "Royce McVee was interviewed and had a strong alibi for the night his cousin was killed. He was speaking to a group of underwriters that afternoon, and everyone proceeded directly to a cocktail party and dinner that evening."

"Shoot," I muttered.

As he continued to read his notes, I stood and paced. It helped me think.

I felt a twinge of guilt but finally said, "Have you talked to Helen Chin's husband, Martin?"

"Martin?" He skimmed back over his notes. "Martin Warrington? I've got his name listed, but I didn't talk to him." He called Terrence over and asked him to track down whoever interviewed Martin. It turned out Martin had a number of people who'd vouched for his whereabouts the night Kyle died.

"Helen Chin was with you on the ghost tour," Angus said.

"Yes," I said. "But there's no way she could've dragged Perry under the table. And she was in our car on the way back from Rosslyn Chapel."

"Yes, it's doubtful she'd get in the car after sabotaging it," Angus said, frowning. I couldn't blame him, as we were running low on suspects.

"The cousin was also the partner, wasn't he?" Derek said.

"Yes, partner in a very lucrative company," Angus added.

"He had a lot to gain by Kyle's death," I mused aloud. "I would talk to him again. He might've started out at the meeting, then sneaked out, then returned for the cocktail party."

I looked up to see both Derek and Angus staring at me with some apprehension. Angus turned to Derek. "You did warn me."

"What?" I asked.

Derek shook his head. "It sounds like you're running your own investigation, darling. It almost got you killed once before, remember?"

"I'm just helping," I said defensively, then thought, *Screw it.* "In case you didn't notice, I've got a stake in the outcome here. Some clown is trying to frame me for murder."

Derek's lips twisted in a wry smile. "She has a point."

Angus scowled.

I felt tears of self-pity sting my eyes and sniffled and blinked a few times to get rid of them. But it wasn't fair. I'd just wanted to teach my book-arts class this afternoon. It would've been an easy, fun way to distract myself and forget my worries for two hours. I'd always loved teaching the craft. Showing someone how to take a few scraps of cloth and ribbon and paper and turn them into a tangible piece of art was immensely satisfying. The students' excitement and pride in their finished work were always a great high for me.

Besides, the Edinburgh Book Fair was supposed to be about books. Not murder.

Wherever she goes, someone dies.

I shivered and zipped my down vest as Minka's words played over in my head. Damn her for saying that. Even if it was true, it was so unfair. And in my precarious—okay, whiny—state, I wasn't quite capable of breezing over it.

I used my mental Etch A Sketch again to wipe away the thought that any of this was my fault. It was ridiculous and untrue, not to mention destructive to my psyche. After all, wherever *Minka* went, people died, too. It wasn't just me.

Still, it was disturbing to once more find myself in the middle of a murder investigation. Why? Was there something in my auric field that was attracting all this nastiness to me? Was I somehow paying for past sins by becoming a witness to violent death?

Maybe I needed a high colonic, after all.

Oh, hell, maybe I just needed a drink.

My book-arts class was postponed until tomorrow afternoon, so I took an hour and strolled through the book fair to relax. Derek was kind enough to walk with me, possibly afraid I might cause a scene or accuse somebody of murder if left to my own devices.

As we walked, I was surprised to realize I was starting to chill out.

Was it wrong of me to enjoy being in the hustle and bustle of book land with a gorgeous British commander holding my hand? Maybe I should've been off hiding in my room after discovering another body, or maybe I should've been in church praying for poor Perry, but the truth was, he just hadn't been a very nice man.

Strangely enough, even with the gruesome news of Perry's murder, the book fair was thriving. We passed booths where people talked in hushed tones, then stopped as I approached. I could only figure that Minka had spread the word about my finding the body, probably adding that I was about to be arrested for murder. The possibility should've annoyed me but it didn't.

No, for some reason, despite stumbling over yet another dead body, I felt good. Calm. I didn't think I could blame it on Derek's presence, because I rarely felt calm around him. More like fired up and ready to go. So maybe it was simply because I was in my element, surrounded by books.

I spied an illustrated *Alice in Wonderland* and rushed over to examine it. It was a 1927 edition in spring green leather, mint condition, with heavy gilding around the edges and on the spine. Ornate dentelles decorated the inside front and back covers. There was a wonderful gilt-tooled White Rabbit on the center of the front cover, checking his pocket watch, and a scolding Queen of Hearts on the back. It was delightful. Expensive, but worth it.

"Curiouser and curiouser," I said to Derek, grinning as I repeated Angus's words. "I have to buy this."

"Interesting how staring at books and paper seems to soothe your nerves," Derek noted.

"I was just thinking the same thing."

"I'd thought it was only food that perked you up this much."

"Food always helps." And since he'd mentioned it, I reached into my purse for the small bag of Cadbury Clusters I'd brought with me. I held out the bag to him, but he just rolled his eyes.

"More for me," I said, and popped one in my mouth.

I paid for the *Alice* and waited while the bookseller wrapped it for me. Then we continued walking. I stopped and introduced myself to a few booksellers I'd never met and handed out my business card. Derek ended up purchasing a small, leather-bound edition of *The Enchiridion* by the Stoic philosopher Epictetus. It was a handbook of aphorisms, he explained.

"Yes, I know," I said. "My parents have one at home."

"Ah, yes, no spiritual commune is complete without one."

"Right." I smiled. "Guru Bob gets all his best lines from the Stoics."

"I'll bet." He studied the book more closely.

"It's a beautiful binding," I said, admiring the rich, golden brown calfskin cover and matching cloth slipcase.

"Yes, it is."

"Sangorski and Sutcliffe does excellent work."

"I was given a paperback version of *The Enchiridion* by a favorite professor in school," he said softly. "I always admired its philosophy and practical application to daily life."

"Figures a former intelligence officer would find pleasure in Stoic philosophy."

"Indeed, looking inward to find truth and justice never gets old."

"That must be why my mother likes you so much. Careful, or she'll sign you up for one of her colon cleansings."

He actually shuddered.

I grinned. "So you've purchased a philosophy book while all I've got is *Alice*, a children's story. You're trying to make me feel shallow, aren't you?"

"Is it working?"

"Yes, but I should warn you, I'm perfectly comfortable with my superficiality."

He laughed and I quivered with some kind of joy at that sound. I was happy, I realized.

"You don't really believe *Alice in Wonderland* is a children's story," he said as we continued walking. "All that symbolism?"

I smiled. "Guru Bob believes that every character in the book is a different part of man's psyche."

"Ah, I knew you had a method to your madness."

I laughed again as we passed the large glass cabinet that displayed all the entries in the bookbinding contest. Derek stopped to look. I'd forgotten all about the contest and the fact that I had a book entered.

"Which is yours?" Derek asked.

I pointed it out, taking a moment to admire the work I'd done. Win or lose, I was proud of that book. Then I realized that tomorrow night was the annual dinner and awards ceremony. The week had gone by quickly.

"That's lovely work," he said, giving me a smile that dazzled my brain.

"Thank you."

"Did you design the cover yourself?"

"Of course." I had designed a stylized W and had sculpted it into the leather cover, then inlaid thin bands of gold and tiny amber stones to form the letter, and gilded the edges. It had taken me hours to get it right.

"It's stunning," he said after studying it for another few moments. "Well done."

My eyes widened. It was the first time Derek had truly complimented me on my bookbinding skills, and surprisingly, it meant a lot. "Thank you."

"But *Waverley*?" he said, staring at my navy blue, leather-bound version of Walter Scott's epic work. "I'm surprised. Not *Rob Roy* or *Ivanhoe*?"

"It wasn't my choice," I admitted. "I was going through some old books, looking for ideas, and this old, beat-up edition of *Waverley* called out to me."

"Did you read it, as well?"

"If I say yes, will you be impressed?"

He looked appalled. "Of course not. Horrible book."

"I read it," I said, laughing. It had taken me three long weeks. Slow going, to say the least. There wasn't a lot of action, but the story was romantic and the writing was lyrical. And by lyrical, I meant convoluted and wordy, but in a good way, really.

"Not as shallow as you appear," he said, eyeing me with suspicion.

"Don't be silly, of course I am."

Tucking my arm through his, Derek gazed back at the entries and pointed to another book on the lower shelf.

"Is that our own Minka's entry?"

"Yes."

Minka had chosen to bind a copy of *Robinson Crusoe* in padded black leather with palm trees embossed on the front and spine. I understood the use of palm trees based on the subject matter, but black leather? And padded? It suited Minka, but I wasn't sure it suited Defoe's classic work.

"Interesting choice," Derek murmured.

"Mm-hmm." What else could I say? I was feeling too good to go for the meow moment.

We were walking down one aisle, then up another, when I stopped and grabbed his arm.

"What's wrong?"

I angled my chin in the general direction of the nearby booth where Serena and Helen stood talking and laughing. What was even weirder was that the booth belonged to Kyle McVee's company. I wondered if Royce was somewhere in the vicinity, seething. Or maybe he was whooping it up with them. Stranger things had happened lately.

"I agree, that's an odd pairing," Derek said.

"It's totally weird," I said. "And it's not the first time I've seen them chatting."

Helen looked up, saw me and waved. "Hi, Brooklyn! Commander, come meet Serena."

"Tell her to stop calling me that," Derek grumbled.

"No way," I said as we approached the booth. "Maybe I can get her to salute you."

Helen introduced Derek to Serena, who said a shy hello.

"I'm sorry for your loss," Derek said. It didn't sound at all lame when he said it.

She clasped her hands at her breastbone. "Oh, thank

you, everyone has been so nice." Her voice was high and breathy, like a little British bird who'd run out of air. "I didn't think I would stay after Kyle ... Well, I'm glad I decided to stay and get to know the people in his world. I'm enjoying the book fair immensely. Royce has made me feel so welcome. Everyone has. Minka and Helen, and you, Brooklyn. You've all been so kind."

Really? Minka? Kind? And Royce? Welcoming? Were we all living on the same planet?

"That's great," I said, ill at ease with all the perky, shiny "aren't we all one big happy family" stuff. "Well, we have to be going. It was nice to see you."

Helen piped up, "I should probably go, too. But we'll get together later for a drink, right?"

"Oh, yes," Serena said, grabbing Helen's hand and squeezing it a bit too desperately before letting go. "Please, Helen, I would love that."

"I'll see you in the pub at five, then," Helen said.

"Super!"

Helen waved with real enthusiasm as we walked away.

I slipped Helen's arm through mine. Once we were out of Serena's earshot, I said, "Helen, isn't this getting a little awkward?"

"What do you mean?" she asked.

"You're acting like you're best friends with your dead lover's wife."

Helen swallowed. "But she's sweet. It's not her fault Kyle was a beast."

"I know, but don't you think it's a little odd that she's still hanging around? Her husband was murdered and she's here, going around making friends with everyone he knew."

"But she said she wanted to get to know Kyle's friends."

"Including his secret lover?"

Derek nudged my arm.

"Okay, okay," I said. "Derek thinks I'm being rude. And he's probably right. But honestly, don't you find it uncomfortable being around her?"

"You're so sweet to think of me," Helen said, and took my hand. "But she's an interesting girl, Brooklyn. And I know it sounds odd, but I feel like I'm connected to Kyle when I talk to her."

So Helen still wanted that connection to Kyle. Did she even realize what she'd just said? And what did that say about her future with Martin? I bit my tongue to keep from asking her.

Helen kept talking. "You and I didn't have a chance to hear Serena's eulogy at the memorial service, but everyone's been telling me it was heartbreaking. Did you know they've loved each other since grade school?"

"She mentioned something about that before."

"Right. Doesn't that just break your heart?"

"Not really. It seems kind of creepy."

She smacked my hand. "I'm serious. By the time they married, Kyle was traveling so much, and she's a kindergarten teacher, so she never got a chance to meet his friends. This weekend was supposed to be her entrée into his world; then they were going to have a long, romantic Scottish honeymoon. But then he was . . . you know. Killed."

"Yeah, I know."

"She's being very brave," Helen said, getting a little choked up.

"And so are you," I said staunchly. "Don't forget, you are the injured party through all of this."

That brought fresh tears to her eyes. "Your loyalty and friendship mean so much to me."

"Helen, please don't cry."

Derek stepped back a foot at the threat of tears, and I shot him an evil look.

"I'm okay," she said, sniffing back the emotion. "But I'm going to keep trying to get you two to be friends. She's really a dear, and I think you'll like her once you get to know her."

"You think?"

"Definitely."

"Well, good luck with that." As we passed a booth specializing in horror posters, I asked, "How did you meet her, anyway?"

She smiled. "The first time I met her in the hotel store, we both reached for the same package of mints. Then we laughed and introduced ourselves and she said she loved my hair, which was endearing, don't you think?"

Helen unconsciously played with the ends of her hair. She did have great hair, but good grief, here was a big secret: If you ever want to get a woman to do anything for you, just compliment her hair.

Was I being a bitch for suspecting that there might be an ulterior motive for Serena's complimenting her dead husband's lover's hair?

Maybe I was just jealous that Helen had a new BFF.

I thought about that for a few seconds but concluded that Helen's having a new BFF had nothing to do with it. The truth was, I was concerned that this Stepford person in front of me had done something with my friend Helen. I'd always admired her well-honed sense of humor, but that part of her was completely missing this time around. Maybe the trauma of Kyle's death had pushed her over the edge. Or maybe the last few years spent with Martin had dulled her ability to recognize irony when it stuck its tongue out at her.

"Well, Serena sounds like a peach," I said finally, trying for lightness. "I hope you have fun at the pub."

"Why don't you join us?"

I touched her arm. "Thanks, but Derek and I are having an early dinner. After that, I have to prepare for my workshop."

"Okay, but if you get free, come on by."

"I will." Not.

"So," Derek said when she was gone. "Where are we having dinner? Do we have a reservation?"

"Okay, I lied. But you were a good excuse, so thanks."

"I'll bet you say that to all the commanders."

We both watched Helen as she made her way down the wide aisle of book vendors.

"Derek," I said after a moment, "have you ever noticed that women can be really stupid?"

He put his arm around my shoulders. "And yet, they're generally smarter than men."

"That's a sad, sad statement."

Derek had to run off to some royal business function at the Palace of Holyroodhouse, and tonight was the night Robin had planned to take Mom and Dad on the ghost tour.

I had wanted to study the Robert Burns book in depth, in hopes of gleaning some clue from it, and it seemed I now had the time to do so. I stopped at the front desk and the clerk led me to the small, secure safety-deposit room, inserted the hotel key in the box, then left me alone. I inserted my key in the second keyhole and pulled the box down. Alone in the secure cubicle, I felt a chill along my spine. I glanced around. I was indeed alone. There were no two-way mirrors where someone could see what I had in the box. I attributed my nerves to finding Perry's body earlier and fought to shake off the feelings.

I pulled the book out of the long steel box and unwrapped it. I needed to see it, needed to touch the leather binding and assure myself that despite the furor circling around me and the book fair, the Robert Burns book was perfectly safe and unharmed. I hadn't taken a good look at it since before the attack in the National Library, and that seemed like ages ago.

It had all started with this book. The murders, the attacks, the questions. Could it possibly hold the answers to any of them? Was that putting too much pressure on one little book? But books didn't kill people. They didn't steal tools from your hotel room or try to run you off the road.

Pulling away the parchment paper, I gazed at the book and marveled all over again at the beautiful condition of the leather. The deeply etched gilding shone like new. Thistle and heather, Solomon's wheels, everything indicated that William Cathcart's own hand had created this masterpiece. His bindery's name was stamped on the leather lining of the inside back cover. So why was I suspicious of it?

Maybe because I was seeing it in the harsh light of the small room. In the bright light, I had to wonder, was it really a Cathcart? It would've been easy enough for a master bookbinder to duplicate Cathcart's work.

I'd once copied a rare Dubuisson binding, right down to the one-o'clock birds the revered seventeenth-century French bookbinder was famous for. I'd done a good enough job that the head curator of the Covington Library was completely fooled. Of course, he was my fiancé at the time, so maybe he'd been a bit prejudiced.

Had someone pulled off the same trick with this William Cathcart edition? There were a few ways to tell if this book was made over two hundred years ago or within the last year. I'd given the class in forgery just two days ago, so if anyone could find out the truth about the book, it would be me. Right?

With a deep sigh, I wrapped the book up and slipped it into my bag. I was still nervous. Taking the book with me was probably dangerous. After all, someone had been able to gain access to my room as easily as if it had a revolving door to it. The book would be safer in the lockup, but then I might never have the chance to determine whether it was the real deal or an excellent forgery.

Earlier, knowing I'd made no plans for tonight, I'd felt at loose ends and a little sorry for myself. Now, the thought of spending the evening alone in my room with a good book, a rare steak and a decent bottle of wine was extremely appealing.

Especially if I uncovered a forgery.

Chapter 15

"Hey!" someone yelled in my dreams.

Glass broke and footsteps pounded on the iron railing outside my window.

I sat up straight, threw off the covers and bolted from the bed. My hotel room was dark, but moonlit shadows flew around the walls from the curtains blowing and swaying across my window. Disoriented, I trembled in fear. Chills hit me in places I didn't know existed.

Suddenly a man jumped in through my window. More glass shattered in his wake. He pushed me back on the bed as he raced to the door. I could hear him fumble with the locks. Then the door opened and slammed shut.

"What the—"

Stunned and frightened, I leaped up, switched on the light and looked around. My eyes were blurry with sleep, but I couldn't see anything out of place. I focused on the clock next to the lamp. It was three fifteen.

What the hell?

Without warning, more heavy footsteps rattled the fire escape outside. I screamed and an instant later, another man jumped through my window. Taller, broader, dressed in black.

No. This couldn't be real.

"Where'd he go?" he demanded.

"Out the door!" I shouted, then lost my balance and fell back on the bed. Again. Probably from shock.

He stormed to the door, whipped it open and ran out into the hall.

I followed him to the door. He was pacing up and down the hall, swearing sharply. What was he doing here, and where in the world had he come from?

Then he stalked back into my room. It took another few seconds of creative swearing before he seemed to notice me again.

"Hey, babe," he said. "You're looking good." Then he bent over to catch his breath.

"Are you freaking kidding me?" I shouted. This wasn't a dream. I was wide-awake now, but still bewildered and slightly discombobulated. And yeah, angry.

He straightened up and let out another heavy breath, then raked both hands through his thick black hair. Talk about looking good. The man was gorgeous, if you like them tall, tough and sexy, with hair long enough to tie back and eyes greener than a Sonoma hillside.

He laughed, still breathing heavily. "Haven't climbed a fire escape in a few years. Call the police, would you?"

"Gabriel," I said. "What the hell are you doing here?"

He studied me frankly, from my toes up to my hair. Then he grinned, causing his eyes to sparkle and two adorable dimples to appear in his cheeks. "Saving your ass again. Not that I mind. It's a fine ass."

I looked down. Yes, I was still wearing my baggy plaid flannel pajamas. On the bright side, at least I was wearing something.

He, on the other hand, wore a black leather bomber jacket over a black T-shirt, boots and worn black jeans that perfectly accented his equally fine ass.

Gabriel—no last name, apparently—and I had met a

month or so ago when he helped save me from a psycho-pathic teenager who'd been hired by Abraham's mur-derer to kill me. And if that didn't make sense, welcome to my world.

After gaining my trust, Gabriel had later stolen an extremely rare copy of Plutarch's *Parallel Lives* from my apartment and given it to Guru Bob. Heck, if I'd known Guru Bob wanted the book, I would've given it to him myself. I didn't need some darkly handsome thief breaking into my place to do it for me.

And here he was. It was déjà vu all over again.

"Gabriel, what's going on?"

He'd moved over to the window and was checking the broken glass. "Call the police first. We can shoot the breeze after."

"Oh, yeah, we'll shoot the breeze." Not trusting him as far as I could throw him, I kept an eye on him as I picked up the phone and made the emergency call, asking the dispatcher to alert Detective Inspector Mac-Leod that there had been a break-in related to the re-cent murders.

I hung up the phone and stared hard at Gabriel. De-spite my mistrust, I knew I was perfectly safe with him. But that wasn't the point.

"What are you really doing here?"

"I'm here on business," he said, pushing the windows open and climbing out to the fire escape. He fiddled with the window locks, and it looked as if he were testing them for some reason. Then he pulled a handkerchief from his pocket and began to wipe down the locks and the window frame.

"Wait!" I said. "There might be fingerprints."

"Right," he said. "Mine." His generous mouth twisted into a frown as he wiped down the surface of the unbro-ken glass. "I don't need any trouble with the Edinburgh constabulary."

"But you didn't do anything," I insisted. "I'll tell them you came in to help me."

"I appreciate that, babe." His smile was so sweet, his dimples so delectable that I had a hard time remembering he was basically a thief. "Do you have another room you can stay in tonight?"

"Yeah," I said, thinking of Robin. I dropped into the desk chair and rubbed my face. I should've been more freaked out, but the truth was, I was just too tired to manage it. I knew without a doubt that it was the killer who had run through my room before Gabriel showed up.

"What happened?" I asked. "How did you come after this guy?"

"Just lucky," he said with a shrug. "I was crossing the parking lot and happened to look up and see him outside your room. I threw some rocks at him, then finally started up the fire escape after him. That's when he broke your window and escaped through here."

"Wow, lucky is right."

"Damn straight."

"Did you recognize him? Could you describe him for the police?"

"I couldn't see him that well," he explained as he crossed the room to wipe the door handle clean. "I basically saw a figure by your window and went after him."

I sat back in the chair. "Well, that sucks."

Gabriel moved to the desk and wiped it down. "I'd say he was probably my height, about six feet, maybe six-one. But that's about it. Sorry."

My shoulders slumped. I wouldn't be able to describe the guy either, except to say that he was definitely male. So much for my powers of observation.

"I'm just glad you were here," I murmured, shaking my head in amazement. "I still can't believe you were walking by and saw that guy." What would've happened if Gabriel hadn't been here? Would I be dead by now?

I couldn't dwell on that. It was meant to be that Gabriel had been in that parking lot at precisely the right moment.

I thought about that for a moment, then asked, "So let me get this straight: You were out in the parking lot?"

"Yeah," he said, his lips curved in a smile. "Some luck, huh? I was just leaving for the airport."

"At three in the morning."

He grinned. "A red-eye."

I studied him. "And how did you know the guy was outside *my* room?"

He smiled wickedly. "I get paid to know these things."

My heart thudded in my chest. He really was gorgeous.

And I really was a sap. "Oh, damn it." I jumped up and ran to the bed. "My book."

"What book?" Gabriel asked as he folded up the handkerchief and stuck it back in his pocket.

"The Robert Burns. Crap, crap, crap." It wasn't anywhere on the bed where I'd fallen asleep reading it. I pulled the bedspread completely off the bed and shook it. Nothing. I knelt down and searched the floor. Nothing.

"Let me help you," he said, and knelt down next to me. "What does it look like?"

"It's red. It's . . . it's . . ." He was so close, I could smell him. Clean, citrusy. Sexy. Whew.

Disgusted with myself, I concentrated on looking for the book, running my hands along the floor, around the nightstand. The bed was perched on a solid platform, so nothing could've slid underneath.

The book was gone.

But how? The intruder was in my room for maybe five seconds, and that was at a dead run.

"It's not here," I said finally, accepting the inevitable. "I'm so screwed."

"Sorry, babe."

I stood up and looked him in the eyes. "How could he have stolen it? I saw him race right through the room. He never stopped."

"Beats me, babe."

I stared at him as a police siren shrieked in the still night.

"The cops should be here soon," he said. "Maybe they can help you find it. I've got to get going."

"Probably a good idea," I said, blocking his way as I held out my hand. "But first, give me the book."

He smiled in sympathy. "Ah, now, see? You're all distraught."

"Give me the book, Gabriel."

"Honey, I would love nothing better." He pointed toward the open window, where the sound of the police siren grew more shrill. "But that's my cue to get moving."

"Gabriel, I know you have it," I said, slowly moving closer to him. "I don't know how you did it, but I know you've got it."

"Calm down, babe," he said, holding up both hands.

"Give it to me and I won't sic the cops on you."

He checked his wristwatch. "Look at the time. I should be going."

"Did you sneak in here earlier and take it?" I asked. "Then maybe a while later, as you were about to drive away, you happened to see the other guy up here?"

His eyes narrowed and he took a step back. "Yeah, and I saved your life."

"I appreciate that," I said through clenched teeth. "I feel truly blessed that you came along when you did, but I don't think it was a coincidence, now, was it?"

I was so angry, I pushed him.

He chuckled as he grabbed my wrists. "Babe, you're getting kind of violent, and I'm a peaceful man."

"See, I'm usually totally peaceful, too," I said, managing to push him again despite his hold on me. His chest was like a steel wall. "But you're making me so mad, I can't seem to help myself."

The blaring sirens came closer.

I held out my hand. "I want it now, damn it."

Gabriel sighed, unzipped his bomber jacket, pulled out the book and tossed it on the bed.

My eyes were wide as I stared at the book, then back at him. "Oh, my God, you really had it."

I punched him in the stomach.

"Ouch," he said.

"Oh, give me a break. You barely felt that."

"I felt it." Without any warning, he grabbed my elbows, tugged me close and kissed me. I was so shocked I let him. He angled his head and deepened the kiss. And I let him. He was really good at it. His lips were warm and soft, and when he finally lifted his head and stepped back, I almost sank to the floor.

But I didn't.

"Gotta go," he said, zipping up his jacket.

"Thanks for the book," I said, gazing right back at him.

"I'll see you soon, Brooklyn."

"In your dreams."

He laughed. "You got that right, babe." He winked at me, walked over to the window and was gone.

The police jammed into my room minutes later, but after all was said and done, they were no closer to finding the killer than they were before. All I could tell them about the man who ran through my room was that he was male. It could've been anyone.

With a broken window and fingerprint dust on every surface of my room, I packed a few things and went to spend the rest of the night in Robin's room.

I woke up four hours later feeling prickly again. I couldn't sleep another minute. Someone besides Gabriel had gotten into my room last night, and it was just a guess, but I was pretty sure their motive had been to either kill me or steal another weapon. Either way, that someone wanted me dead or rotting in jail, which was unsettlingly close to the same thing.

But who? And why?

I glanced at the other side of the king-size bed. Robin was still snoring softly. I got up and went to wash my face, brush my teeth and dress for the day. Staring at the mirror, I told myself it was time to shape up, regroup, make a new list of suspects and try to save my own damn life. Starting now.

At Robin's desk, I pulled out a hotel notepad and once again wrote down any and all possible suspects. The list wasn't very long. My best suspect was dead. I was running out of possibilities and I had to face facts. Rather than the two dead men, I was the one who seemed to be the common denominator. So everyone I knew went on the list, including Royce, Martin, even Winnie Paine, the elderly IAAB president, along with Helen, Serena and Minka.

I decided not to add Gabriel, since he'd had the perfect opportunity to kill me last night and hadn't done so—not that I'd ever suspected he was capable of it. I also didn't list Derek or my parents or Robin. But I did write down the names of my friends Peter and Benny and four other booksellers I was friendly with. I knew it hadn't been a woman running through my room during the night, but I was leaving no stone unturned. Maybe one of them had a male accomplice.

There was a knock on the door. Robin muttered into her pillow.

I shook her leg and said, "Get up, girlfriend. We have company."

She grunted as I answered the door. It was MacLeod

and Derek, and I was glad I'd changed out of my luscious plaid jammies.

"Come on in," I said, leading the way inside, where
I flung the curtains open and pulled the desk chair out.
"Have a seat. Robin, company's here."

Robin burbled some profanity, then rolled over,
opened her eyes and shrieked like a girl. She jumped
out of bed, ran to the bathroom and slammed the door.

Derek bit back a grin, but MacLeod's eyes goggled as
though he'd seen a vision. Robin did not sleep in plaid
jammies, to say the least.

"What's up?" I asked Derek, as MacLeod seemed incapable of speech.

"You had an interesting night," Derek said, leaning
one hip against the desk.

"That's one way to put it," I said as I sat down on the
edge of the bed.

"So much excitement, yet you didn't call."

Uh-oh.

I could tell he was offended. Crap, I hated that. But
what to say? I couldn't mention Gabriel.

"I called the police," I said, which was totally true. "I
wasn't thinking. I thought I'd lost the book and I was
searching around for it, and by the time I found it, the
police were knocking on the door. Then Robin came
down to help me pack...."

I was an idiot.

He probably thought the same thing as he listened to
me blather.

Angus's phone rang and he excused himself to talk
in the hall.

"I'm sorry, Derek," I said, almost ready to cry. And I
really was sorry. I couldn't believe I hadn't called him,
but to say I'd had a crazy night was putting it mildly.

"I should've called," I said, shaking my head. "I was
completely distracted and stupid."

He stood and walked over, pulled me into his arms and held me. "I don't quite have your trust, do I, love?"

I buried my face in his divinely warm wool jacket. God, he smelled like heaven. "I'm getting there."

He rubbed my back, then gave me a squeeze. "We'll work on it."

I pulled back and searched his face for some deeper meaning to his words. How would we work on it? Did we have anything to work on? We lived on opposite sides of the planet. Would I ever see him again after this week?

Robin walked back into the room still wearing her short, flimsy nightgown, but at least she'd added a short, flimsy robe. She looked disheveled and sexy, not exactly appropriate for a meeting with the police.

She noticed my expression of dismay and said, "Hey, you guys are in my room."

"Yes, and we should go," Derek said immediately, and turned to me. "We just came by to check your schedule. I don't want you going anywhere alone. If one of us can't be with you, Angus will call one of his men to accompany you wherever you need to go. Right, Angus? Angus?"

MacLeod kept trying to swallow, but he'd lost all ability to speak. It probably wasn't the first time a man was flummoxed by the sight of Robin in a silk nightie.

Ignoring him, I laid out my day's agenda for Derek. I had two seminars I wanted to attend, one on textile conservation and storage treatments, and another one, given by Helen, on Japanese paper-folding techniques. The first one complied with my continuing-education efforts and the second sounded like fun. I hoped I'd come away with a few new ideas for my own classes, especially the master bookbinding class I was scheduled to teach next month at the Bay Area Book Arts center, affectionately known as BABA.

Then after lunch, I'd be giving my rescheduled book-binding class.

Robin pulled me aside and warned me to listen to Derek and stay safe. "If I have to explain to your mother that you were tossed down an elevator shaft, it'll just piss me off."

"Thanks," I said. "Now I'll have that image in my head all day."

"Good, maybe you'll be more careful," she said, and gave me a fierce hug.

Derek and I dragged poor Angus out of the room, leaving Robin to dress for the day trip she and my parents were taking to St. Andrews.

The two men walked me downstairs to the textile conservation seminar on the conference level. At the door, I turned and faced my protectors.

"Thanks," I said, grateful for their presence.

"One of my men will be waiting out here when you're finished," Angus said, having regained his voice.

"Take care, love," Derek said, and in front of a few hundred of my closest, personal book fair friends, Derek planted a kiss on me that made Gabriel's really excellent efforts seem half-assed. My vision was blurred as I stood at the door and watched Derek and Angus walk away.

The textile conservation seminar was dull but necessary. Helen's paper folding class was fun, and she gave me some great ideas for my own classes. I asked her what she was doing for lunch, but she was already booked. Then afterward, she was running off to an invitation-only seminar up at the castle. I expressed my extreme jealousy and she laughed. We set a time to meet later on in the pub.

After she left, I grabbed a take-out sandwich from the lobby kiosk and ate it on the way to my rescheduled bookbinding workshop. Constable McKenzie caught up with me at the escalator and followed me downstairs.

As I stepped off the escalator, I saw Royce McVee coming out of another conference room. He waved me over and I gave him a light hug.

"How are you holding up?" I asked.

"Fairly well, thanks," he said with a tight smile. "I've managed to drum up some new business, despite my rather dour reputation."

"You'll do fine," I said. He asked where I was going, then walked down the wide corridor with me. The vigilant Constable McKenzie trailed several feet behind us.

"I had a chance to talk to Serena," I said after a moment.

"Ah, yes, the blushing bride," he said snidely. "Your thoughts?"

"I can't figure her out," I admitted. "My friend Helen—do you know her? Helen Chin? She's a paper and fabric artist. Anyway, Helen thinks Serena's story is heartbreakingly real and believes every word she says."

"Oh, Serena's story is certainly compelling," Royce said, his tone dripping sarcasm.

I chuckled. "Yes, isn't it? I can't believe it, but Helen is so wrapped up in it and actually wants to be friends with Serena, which is just ridiculous, seeing as how she herself was engaged to Kyle and didn't—"

"I beg your pardon?"

Oops. Had I really just blown Helen's secret wide-open? What an idiot I was.

"Go on, Brooklyn," Royce said calmly. "Tell me about Helen and Kyle."

Later I might chalk it up to the stress of the week, but right now I had some emergency triage to perform. So I laughed. "Oh, Royce, I shouldn't have said anything, and I hope you won't repeat it. It was nothing. Just a bit of a misunderstanding. You know how Kyle was with the ladies. Always flirting, making promises he had no intention of keeping. Helen knew he was pulling her leg."

I continued to chuckle, but Royce was no longer amused. Instead, he chewed his lip as his eyes narrowed. He looked as if he were contemplating murder. Not mine, I hoped.

"Look, Royce," I said quickly, "I just meant that Helen and Serena's becoming friends is odd because they both claimed to be Kyle's ... well, not really, but, you know ... hmm."

Oh, God, I needed an exit strategy.

"Oh, look, here's my workshop," I said brightly "Guess I'll see you later."

"Indeed you will," he murmured, and walked off.

The quietly observant Constable McKenzie watched Royce walk all the way back down the hall until he reached the escalator and disappeared. Then the good constable opened the door to the conference room and was kind enough to check around for dead bodies under the worktable, finally declaring the room dead-body-free. He said he'd wait outside and left me to arrange my supplies and tools for the class.

I made a conscious decision not to think about Royce McVee until the workshop was over.

The class filled up quickly and we went to work. I had to laugh at one point when an older woman named Millie glued her decorative cloth book cover to the worktable.

"Oopsie-daisy," she said.

"No problem, Millie," I said, prying open my supply case and pulling out an extra piece of Japanese cloth so klutzy Millie could start over.

Even with all the pieces precut and the instructions easy enough for a six-year-old to follow, there were always one or two people who just didn't get it.

But most of them did.

"Ooh, it's so pretty," one woman said, smiling. She'd finished the project and was tying the small album together with the purple grosgrain ribbon I'd provided.

"Beautiful job, Maureen," I said as I walked up and down along the tables, observing everyone's work.

The long day and the strange appearances of a possible killer and Gabriel during the night started to catch up with me, and I had to keep myself from yawning more than once.

Finally, the two hours were up and the class began to file out with their treasures as a young woman waded through the wave of departing students. She approached and handed me a small envelope.

"What's this?" I asked.

"You're Ms. Wainwright?" she asked as she straightened the royal blue vest she wore as an official book fair volunteer. She was breathing heavily.

"Yes. Are you okay?"

"I just ran from the castle? Anyway, that's for you?" She pointed to the small envelope she'd just handed me.

I absently noted her thinning, frizzy red hair and tendency to end sentences with question marks as I opened the envelope and read the note inside.

I know who killed Kyle. Meet me at St. Margaret's Chapel at 16:30. Be careful. Tell no one.

I shook the note at the volunteer. "Who gave this to you?"

She cowered at the demand in my voice. "Some lady up at the castle?"

"What did she look like?"

The volunteer screwed up her face as though I were an evil headmaster with a whip.

I took a deep breath and said calmly, "Can you describe her for me? It's really important."

"I don't know?" she whined. "Oriental? Dark hair? Short? Nice jacket?"

Helen.

"Thanks very much." I didn't want to make her cry by pointing out that the politically correct term was Asian, not Oriental. She hurried off and I was left alone in the small conference room with Helen's note and no clue what to do next.

I stared at the note.

I know who killed Kyle.

Had Helen called the police? Why would she take a chance and send a note about the killer to me?

Meet me at St. Margaret's Chapel at 16:30.

I assumed that meant four thirty. Helen had been born and raised in California, which was one more reason we'd bonded during that summer in Austin, Texas, when we decided that earthquakes were easier to live with than hurricanes. But she'd spent the last few years living with Martin in London, so maybe she'd acclimated to the British method of using the twenty-four-hour clock. Maybe.

More than likely, though, the note was a hoax and not from Helen at all. Which meant Helen was in trouble.

Unless Helen had killed Kyle. No, I would never believe that. But if she'd sent the note, then someone close to her was the killer. Martin? Serena? A dozen other people? Oh, hell.

I checked my watch. My workshop had officially ended at three thirty so it was now three forty. It would take me twenty minutes to walk up to the castle and another ten or fifteen minutes to reach St. Margaret's Chapel on the castle grounds. I figured I'd be perfectly safe in the middle of the afternoon at Edinburgh Castle, surrounded by hundreds of tourists, not to mention the Scottish Guard.

Besides, I wouldn't be going alone. I wasn't a complete idiot, despite my recent gaffe with Royce.

Royce.

Had he gone after Helen? But why? Why would he care if Helen and Kyle had been engaged? I could understand if he went after Serena. She stood to inherit Kyle's portion of the business, but Helen?

And what did Helen have to do with the Robert Burns book? Had Royce killed Kyle to keep him from presenting the book to the world, and now realized he would have to kill Helen to keep it quiet? But wait, he already knew I had the book.

I was driving myself crazy and wasting time wondering about Royce. I needed to find Helen. But first, I needed to find the police.

I stuck the note in my jacket pocket and rushed through the room cleaning up, stuffing tools and leftover supplies into my bag. When I walked out of the conference room, the corridor was empty. I wondered briefly where Constable McKenzie was, but figured I'd run into him on my way upstairs.

As I hopped on the escalator, I pulled out my cell phone to call Derek, hoping to convince him to go with me to the castle. He would think I was nuts, I realized, after I'd left a detailed message on his voice mail. Once in the lobby, I found a house phone and dialed his suite. No answer there, either, so I left another message.

I gazed around the lobby, hoping to see Angus or one of his constables. The police had been omnipresent from the beginning of the book fair, but now I didn't see any sign of them. Figured—you could never find a cop when you needed one. I asked the hotel operator to connect me with the police and had to leave another message, this one for Angus.

As I hung up the phone, I heard someone call my name and turned.

It was Serena standing not more than four feet away from me. Had she been listening to my slightly hysterical message for Angus?

"Hi, Serena."

"Hi, I thought that was you."

"It's me. Listen, I've got to get—"

She licked her lips nervously. "I was wondering if you'd seen Helen."

"Not lately, why?"

She wrung her hands. "You'll probably think I'm crazy, but I'm a bit worried."

"Why? What's wrong?"

"I saw her awhile ago. She was arguing with Royce and he was yelling."

"Arguing about what?"

"I don't know, but then that other man pulled her away and started yelling at Royce."

"What other man?"

"I think it's her boyfriend or something?"

"Do you mean Martin? Her husband? Tall? Blond? Kind of skinny?"

"That's him. He's her husband?" She looked embarrassed. "Ah." She shook her head, gave me a look of befuddlement, then waved off her words with both hands. "In that case, I'm sure everything's fine then. Well, he was mad and all, but as long as they're married, it's probably not—"

"Serena, what exactly did Martin do with Helen? And where's Royce?"

She went back to wringing her hands. The woman really was a basket case. "I overheard Helen tell her husband that she needed to go to the castle, so they left together. But they didn't look happy. In fact, he was practically dragging her out of here and she kept trying to pull away." Her chirpy voice rose higher and higher. "I called to her and she looked at me in complete and utter terror. I didn't know what to think. But if he's her husband, well, then maybe it's all right. Sometimes I worry too much. Maybe they were simply in a hurry to get somewhere. But then Royce ran after them. That was odd. But perhaps I misread the whole event. I tend to overdramatize things."

Shizzle. I had no time to think about what a complete moron Serena was. Martin must've written that note—or forced Helen to do so. And where was Royce? I needed to find a cop and get to St. Margaret's Chapel now.

"Yoo-hoo!"

I whipped around and saw my mother waving at me from the hotel entry. She was carrying several shopping bags, and Dad followed behind with several of his own. Robin trailed them both, wearing a new plaid beret and a tired grin.

I turned back. "Look, Serena, thanks for telling me about Helen. I've got to go."

Her face was a mask of tragedy. "I hope she's not in any trouble."

"Right, me too. See you later." I ran across the lobby to meet my parents.

"Mom, hi," I said. "Listen, I've got to—"

"We went crazy!" Mom said as she dropped all the bags on the carpet, then opened one up and whipped out a bright red Royal Stewart plaid skirt. "Matching kilts for your father and me! Kilt, jacket, sporran, shoes, socks, sash, the whole enchilada."

"Oh, my God," I said, momentarily stunned by all that plaid. "Dad, you sure you want to be seen wearing a skirt around Dharma?"

"I think the whole thing's a gas," he said, always up for a challenge.

"We'll have everyone wearing kilts within six months," Mom predicted.

"Right on." Dad grinned. "Let's go put this stuff away and hit the pub."

"I can't right now," I said. "I need to go to St. Margaret's Chapel up at the castle."

"You're going to church?" Dad asked, baffled.

"No, it's a . . . a meeting, up at the castle, and I'll be late if I don't leave right now."

"Let's all go," Mom said merrily.

I started to protest. "That's probably not—"

"Groovy," Dad said, ignoring me. "We'll leave everything with the bellman."

I sent Robin a pleading look. "Will you come, too?"

"More the merrier," she said, then added more quietly, "What's going on?"

"Looks like we're going to church."

As we walked quickly up Castle Hill toward the ancient fortress, I thought it might be just as well that my family was along for the ride. There was safety in numbers, after all.

I pulled Robin close. "Do you have Angus's phone number?"

"Yeah, should I call him?"

"I left him a message and another two for Derek, but I'd feel better if you tried Angus again."

"What's going on, Brooklyn?"

I pulled the note from my pocket. "Got this from Helen."

She read it and frowned. "Weird. Did she call the police?"

"That's what I wondered. It might be a trap, or Helen might be in trouble." I turned and saw Mom and Dad straggling half a block behind us. "Maybe we can drop them off somewhere and you and I can head over to the chapel."

"Good idea. Your mom might like to see the doggy cemetery."

"Perfect."

She pulled out her cell and got hold of Angus immediately. Hmm, guess she had his personal number.

After explaining the note to Angus, Robin held the phone away from her ear and looked at me. We could both hear him yelling. After a few seconds, she brought the phone back to her ear. "We appreciate your concern, Angus. So I guess we'll see you soon. Okay. Bye-bye."

He was still yelling as she disconnected the call. She looked at me and shrugged. "Guess we'll have backup."

"Good." I was glad to know not only that Angus would be there, but also that I was not the only one being lectured to lately.

Since it was teatime, there weren't many tourists wandering around. The air had turned bitterly cold, and the Scottish cadets walking the perimeter had to be shivering in their sporrans. Gray clouds huddled just overhead, and the drone of the wind across the stones sounded mournful.

We crossed the wide esplanade, passed the elegant bronze statues of Robert the Bruce and William Wallace, and walked briskly through the gatehouse. After paying the entry fees, we hurried through the Portcullis Gate and turned to face the treacherously steep and curving Lang Stairs that would lead to the Upper Ward and St. Margaret's.

"These may be too much for you to climb," I said.

"It's good exercise," Mom said.

"Yeah, let's go," said Dad.

We didn't speak as our boots scuffed against the rough stone stairs. To take my mind off what I might find at St. Margaret's, I counted steps and finally hit seventy. I knew now why they were called the Lang Stairs, as *lang* was the old Scots word for *long*. I'd made it to the top but hardly in triumph. I had to grip my stomach as I bent over, huffing and puffing and wheezing like an asthmatic smoker.

I was somewhat relieved to see Robin and my parents do the same, although Mom and Dad recovered quickly. What was up with that? Maybe there was something to all those purging and cleansing tonics they swilled.

Once we'd caught our breaths, I led Mom and Dad past St. Margaret's Chapel on the left, to the low wall that looked out over the lower levels of the castle and much of the New Town. I pointed out the lovingly tended pet cemetery on a small plot of lush green land that covered a lower terrace twenty feet below where we stood. Small headstones lined the curved wall, with colorful flowers planted alongside them.

"This is where the faithful companions of the castle's commanders are given their final resting places," Robin said softly, sounding just like the tour guide she was.

"How wonderful," Mom said, leaning both elbows on the thick parapet. "I want to read every miniature tombstone."

"That's a great idea," I said. "I've got a meeting in that little chapel right over there." I pointed to the small, ancient stone building just across the wide walkway.

"Oh, it's as small as a dollhouse," Mom said.

"Have fun," said Dad.

I started to walk away, then turned to face my parents. "Don't go anywhere. I'll be back here in ten minutes."

"Okay, sweetie."

"You don't want them coming in the chapel?" Robin said.

"No way." When I realized Robin had followed me across to the chapel, I turned and glared at her. "What are you doing? You need to stay with them."

"I'm coming with you," she said, her boots scuffing against the cobbled walkway. "They'll be fine, while you, on the other hand, scare the shit out of me."

St. Margaret's Chapel, the most ancient of all the buildings on the castle grounds, was covered in rough stone that masked the pristine jewel within. I remembered from my last visit that the chapel nave was minuscule, barely ten feet across and maybe fifteen feet in length, with a deep, wide archway that separated the nave from the tiny vaulted altar area.

"Aren't you going inside?" Robin asked.

"In a minute," I said, scanning the castle grounds. "Where the hell are the police?"

From where we stood at the railing outside the door leading into the chapel, the view was spectacular. We could see the entire city and surrounding hills from this point at the top of the castle grounds. White clouds scudded across a sky so blue it might've been a Boucher painting.

"Wow, it's beautiful up here," she remarked.

A scream pierced the air.

I raced up the ramp, yanked the chapel door open and stepped inside.

Chapter 16

"Helen?" I called.

"In here!" she cried. She had to be behind the wide arch. There was nowhere else to hide in here. The place was literally the size of a kid's playhouse.

I hesitated inside the nave. If this was a trap, I didn't want to be caught without an escape route. "Helen, the police are on their way."

"Fuck that!" a man yelled. "Get over here or she's going to die."

"Martin?"

I wasn't surprised. I'd never really believed that fake apology of his. What a snake.

"Move it!" he shouted.

I looked at Robin, who shook her head madly. "Don't."

"What else can I do?" I whispered.

"Who's there with you?" he shouted.

"No one," I said. "I talk to myself when I'm nervous."

"She's lying," a chirpy voice sang out from behind us.

Serena stood a few feet away, pointing a gun at us.

"Serena?"

"Surprise," she said.

Serena and Martin, accomplices? Curiouser and curiouser.

"Move it." She jerked the gun toward the altar, and we took that as a sign to get moving.

Robin grabbed my arm and we approached the altar, which was separated from the nave by a velvet rope extended across the archway. The small altar area was painted white and the ceiling was low and vaulted. I felt as if I were walking inside an igloo. Stained-glass windows illuminated the space, throwing blue and green shards of color across the stone floor. A font of holy water was suspended on the far wall, and covering the altar were layers of elegantly braided and embroidered blue, gold and white silk runners.

A body was sprawled under the altar.

"Royce?" I said.

Robin whispered, "Is he dead?"

"Not yet," Martin said menacingly. "But the day's not over yet. Now shut up and come over here where I can see you."

I unhooked the velvet rope and peeked around the arch. Martin had one arm around Helen's neck in a choke hold and was pressing a knife to her throat with his other hand.

"Martin, what are you doing?" I asked.

"I'm pouring tea, you stupid bitch. What do you think I'm doing?"

"I thought you loved Helen," I said. "Why are you hurting her?"

Helen squirmed and he struggled to adjust his grip. "This seems to be the only way to get my darling wife to cooperate."

"Really?" I said. "Because that technique never works for me."

"That's because you're a bitch whore."

"Well, that explains it," Robin whispered.

I turned to glower at her but met Serena's gaze instead. She didn't look so willowy and wrung-out now. She looked skinny and mean and surly.

"Helen's not like you," Martin said with a sneer, and tightened his hold. Helen began to gag and he let up slightly. "She can be taught to obey."

"Of course she can," I said, watching Helen, who stared back at me with wide eyes. Her chest rose and fell rapidly, and I knew she was scared to death. So was I. But to get us out of here, I was going to have to placate a psycho. Been there, done that. Hoped I'd learned something.

"She just needs to remember who's in charge," he said, emphasizing each word by jerking his arm against Helen's throat. "Am I right, Helen? There won't be any more talk of divorce, will there, Helen?"

Helen's eyes goggled.

"Stop," I said frantically. "Threatening her with a knife is not what love's all about."

"Shut up," he said. "You don't know anything."

"I know Helen still loves you," I said, pushing the truth, but desperate to make him reconsider his actions. "She, um, told me. And you told me you loved her, too."

He swallowed, then shook his head and grumbled, "I said shut up."

"Okay."

He didn't seem to know what to do next. Helen looked utterly terrified.

"So you killed Kyle," I said slowly, since I wasn't ready to shut up entirely.

"Yeah," he snarled. "And good riddance."

"Why?"

He stretched his neck and shoulders. "He thought he could fuck around with my wife. I warned him to stop, but he just laughed at me."

"You warned him?"

Helen's eyes met mine and I knew she was hearing this for the first time, her own husband verifying that he had killed her lover.

"Yeah, and he wouldn't stop." Martin waved his knife defensively as he spoke. "Said she was filing for divorce so she'd be free to go with him. Wrong!"

"What did you do, Martin?"

His chuckle was raw and evil. "It was so friggin' easy. What a posh ass. I got him into that room as easily as I got you to come here."

"You called his cell while we were at the pub," I said. "You told him you had Helen."

He laughed smugly. "Yes, and he came running, didn't he?"

Robin edged closer to me, obviously as creeped out by him as I was.

"So he must've loved Helen very much to go with you," I reasoned.

"No! He didn't love her. I love her, and no one else can have her."

I watched as Helen absorbed the words. Her face crumpled as she began to cry, began to realize that maybe Kyle had loved her, after all. I couldn't say that he had or hadn't, but if it helped in the moment to ease some of her pain, then it was worth it to say that yes, he'd loved her.

But oh, God, Angus MacLeod was right: Kyle's murder wasn't about a book at all. It was about Martin being insanely jealous of his wife's relationship with Kyle McVee. Martin had killed the man to get his wife back. I'd always known Martin was emotionally abusive, but I'd never really suspected he could be a killer.

My mistake.

I glanced behind me, considering the possibility of distracting Serena and grabbing Martin's knife.

I turned back and focused on the knife and Martin. That was when I realized he was holding *my* knife. My French paring knife with its two-inch-wide, flat, square blade. I'd sharpened it finely enough to split a hair, so even if he barely grazed her, he would draw blood.

I had to breathe, had to center my thoughts. Unfortunately, they were racing around in circles. "Why me, Martin? Why did you use my tools?"

"I saw you with him," he said, his eyes like lasers honing in on me. "On the street. I was following him, trying to trap him, and I saw him grab you. You kissed him. I knew you were a whore bitch."

Okay, that was getting old. Martin was undoubtedly insane. The signs might've been there all along, but I'd never seen them.

"He hates you," Serena explained.

"I get that," I muttered.

"He's not exactly speaking in code," Robin said, a smart-ass to the end.

"You shut up," Serena warned Robin. To me, she said smugly, "It was my idea to steal your tools. Martin wanted to make you pay somehow. He's always hated you, from the time he first met you in Lyon. You were so full of yourself. You tried to talk Helen out of marrying Martin. McVee tried to do the same thing, right, Martin? When you were all in Lyon, right? Seems he wanted Helen for himself, even back then."

Martin pressed his lips into a thin line, so Serena kept talking. "McVee acted like nothing was going on between him and Helen, even pretending friendship, offering to buy Martin a drink on occasion. He tried that a few nights ago when they first arrived. That was the last straw, wasn't it, Martin?"

Martin leaned against the vaulted wall, dragging Helen with him. Was he growing tired of all the talk? If he reached the end of his rope, would he let Helen go or would he kill her?

"How'd you get into my room to steal my tools?" I asked, not only to stall for time but because I needed to know.

Serena snorted a laugh, then chirped, "Housekeeping."

"You," I said, as realization dawned. "You were that hotel maid. The first day I was here."

"The girls prefer you call them housekeepers," she said acerbically.

Whatever. "Yeah, sorry."

"No wonder I could never get any towels," Robin murmured. She was acting cool, but her eyes darted back and forth between Serena and me. She wore an expression of both worry and revulsion with some impatience mixed in. Not a good combination.

Maybe I should've stopped asking questions, but I had to keep them both talking. "So I guess this means you're not Mrs. Kyle McVee."

Serena wrinkled her nose in disgust. "Me and that pansy toffer? Fat chance."

If she thought Kyle was rich and snooty, how in the world did she put up with Martin?

"So what does that make you and Martin?" I asked.

She grinned at Martin with affection, but he didn't seem to be paying attention. "He's my baby bro."

Her brother? I looked from one to the other. Why hadn't I seen the resemblance? Both tall, both thin, the wispy blond hair and pale blue eyes, same shape of the head. "I see it now. But Helen never met you before?"

"No, Martin was busy playing the toff, weren't you, bro? Didn't want his big sis coming around." She continued to keep a vigilant eye on her brother, but her gaze had narrowed a bit. "But baby bro ran into a little trouble up here." She shrugged. "So who ya gonna call?"

"Big sister," I said.

"Bingo," she said, waving the gun at me. "I hopped the train and got here in two hours. I've been here all week. Had plenty of time to play housekeeper. That's how I got those love letters inside Kyle's room."

"Love letters?" I asked.

She relaxed her grip on the gun and exhaled heavily, perhaps annoyed that I was so dense. "I suppose you'd call them poison-pen letters. Just wanted to pull his chain a bit, you know."

Kyle's poison-pen letters. I'd forgotten about them until now.

"Oh, for God's sake," Robin whispered under her breath. "They're both nuts."

Luckily, only I heard her and I squeezed her arm in commiseration. Serena saw the move and aimed the gun back at me.

"I thought people in England didn't use guns," I said.

Serena's laugh was harsh. "You haven't been in my neighborhood, have you?"

Mentioning her neighborhood reminded me of something that had bothered me from the very beginning. "How do you know Minka?"

Serena chuckled malevolently. "I needed a shill. She was in the right place at the right time and bought my sad-widow story, hook, line and sinker."

"Figures," I said.

"She has a good heart but not many brain cells," she added.

Out of the mouths of criminals.

"So, you're from a bad neighborhood?"

"It was all right," she said, and tossed her hair in a defensive gesture.

"It's just that I always thought Martin was wealthy."

She snorted a laugh. "There's a good one, eh, Martin?"

"But he owns a bookstore."

She winked. "He's a clerk. But the owners trust him, let him take care of the business. He wormed his way into their hearts, didn't you, darling?" She smiled widely. "No, he's not the toffer, but he knew how to look the part well enough to snag himself a rich bride. And our Helen's just the girl. Lets him take care of the finances, don't you, dear? We don't want to lose her, now, do we?"

She winked and I stared warily at Helen. She looked more than terrified now. She looked furious.

Serena continued to talk, but Martin was the one I watched. He hadn't loosened his grasp on Helen, whose eyes were completely focused on him. What was she thinking? Was she looking for the right moment to attack him somehow? She had nothing to lose. Martin seemed more than willing to kill her.

"Taking your tools was a piece of cake," Serena went on. "Martin told me he's always stealing things at these book fairs because people don't pay attention."

"That's enough, Rena," Martin said abruptly. "Just shut up and kill them."

"Me? What about—"

"Now!"

"In a church?" she said, taken aback. "And go to hell?"

Serena had standards all of a sudden?

"Do it!" he shouted.

"Wait," I cried, frantically stalling for time. "You . . . you cut our brake line. Um, how did you know we were going for a drive?"

"What?" He stared at me. He seemed to be losing focus. Maybe he was starting to realize the trouble he was in. Or maybe he was just nuts, as Robin had said.

"Are you okay, Martin?" I asked.

"He's fine," Serena said heatedly.

I turned to her. "He seems kind of spaced-out."

"He gets tired. He's not been well, worrying about things." Then she flipped her hair back in a contemptuous move. "Besides, what do you care, anyway?"

True. I didn't care about him at all, except that he was a murderer and was holding Helen at knifepoint. *My* knifepoint.

Martin shook his head like a wet dog, coming out of whatever daze he'd been in. "Everybody heard you," he snapped.

I looked at him. "Heard me what?"

"You and your people, making plans to go to Rosslyn Chapel the other night."

Oh, great. He'd overheard that freaky conversation with Mom and Dad outside the hotel pub, before they went off to do the conga. "So you cut the brakes in Robin's car yesterday morning."

"Yeah," he said.

"I guess it was quite a shock when you found out Helen was in the car, too."

"I blame you for that," he said, glaring at me. "She could've been killed."

Yeah, duh. "What happened to Perry?"

He frowned. "Perry saw me coming out of the auto garage, and later, when word got out that you'd crashed, he tried to blackmail me."

"Yeah," Serena said offhandedly. "He had to go."

"So you killed him," I said flatly.

"We did it together," Serena said, beaming. The family that kills together. Jeez.

"A shame," Martin said. "I always liked Perry."

He would.

"And you broke into my room last night. Why?"

He looked puzzled. "You're mad."

Now I was the puzzled one. "Are you saying you didn't break into my room last night?"

"Hell, no," he insisted, then looked at Helen. "I wasn't in her room, I swear."

The fact that Helen obviously couldn't care less didn't faze Martin, but I believed him. But if it wasn't Martin, then who broke in? Whom did Gabriel chase away from my room last night?

I had another realization. "You followed me to the National Library."

Martin chuckled. "Now, that was fun. That shelf fell like a big tree, and you never even saw me."

"Jackass," I said under my breath.

"I heard that," Robin whispered. "We need to get out of here."

"I know."

Without warning, Helen said, "Kyle was a wonderful lover."

"Uh-oh," Robin murmured.

"What?" Serena said in disbelief.

"Shut up!" Martin said, shaking his wife.

"Jesus Christ, Helen," Serena cried. "What kind of stupid cow are you?"

"Don't call her a cow!" Martin shouted.

"Easy, bro," Serena said, holding up both hands in acquiescence.

Robin swore under her breath. I had to agree; this was not going to end well. And where the hell was everybody? The police? The tourists? Was everyone off having tea or something? Had Serena locked the door behind her?

"You killed the only man I ever loved," Helen said, her voice strained and halting.

"I told you to shut up!" Martin roared.

"And I'll never do what you say," Helen said flatly.

Serena stared in disbelief at her sister-in-law, and I couldn't blame her. What was Helen thinking by taunting Martin? On the other hand, what did she have to lose?

Martin flexed his arm, putting more pressure on Helen's throat. It must've been the last straw, because she bent, then swung her leg and kicked him in the shin.

Martin grunted. "What're you—"

She kicked him again.

"Stop provoking him." Serena moved closer, clearly sensing trouble.

The kick didn't disarm Martin, but it distracted Serena long enough for me to grab the only thing within reach: the four-foot-high wrought-iron candle stand. I whipped it like a light saber at Serena's stomach and her gun went flying.

I heard the chapel door bang open then. "Yoo-hoo!"

"It's Mom!" I shouted at Robin. "Don't let her come in here!"

Robin took off. I went scrambling for the gun and so did Martin, relaxing his grip on Helen, who sprang loose and went after the only target available: Serena. Robin jumped on her back and started pounding the hell out of her.

"Go, Helen!" Mom shouted from the back of the nave.

"Get off me, you bitch!" Serena bucked, but Helen was too pissed off to care.

Martin yanked the gun out of reach, but I managed to scrape his arm with my nails. The gash drew blood and he swore ripely as it dripped onto his beige linen jacket.

"Shit," he cried. "You bitch!"

"Payback always is," I said, and backhanded him across the chin. Man, that hurt.

His head jerked back just as heavy footsteps pounded across the nave floor. Martin paid no attention, just shook off my attack and fought to aim the gun back at me. "I'll kill you, bitch."

"I don't think so," Derek said as he dived on top of Martin.

"Oomph." Martin's hand released the gun and it skittered away.

I managed to roll out of Derek's way, then scrabbled to my knees and claimed the gun. I wasn't entirely sure whom to point it at, so I held it up as if it were a trophy. Which it sort of was, I guess.

Derek jumped to a standing position, then shoved one foot onto Martin's back, forcing him to stay prone on the floor until a constable scurried in and handcuffed him.

Derek's eyes were dark with concern as he lifted me up, took the gun from my hand and pulled me close.

"Where the hell have you been?" I asked as I buried my face in his soft leather jacket.

"Just trying to quell an international incident," he murmured, wrapping his arms around me. "Sorry I was late."

I sagged against him, craving the warm strength he radiated. "Late? No, you were right on time."

"And the grand-prize winner of the Lawton-McNamara Bookbinding Prize is . . . Brooklyn Wainwright!"

As I walked up the aisle to the wide stage, I was vaguely aware of the announcer describing my work. A giant screen played a short video I'd shot of my gilding process. I think I made a speech, but mere minutes later, back in my chair and surrounded by the crowd of over two thousand of my peers, I had almost no memory of what I'd said.

But I had a gleaming Baccarat crystal plaque with my name on it to remind me that I'd won.

Later, during the champagne reception that followed,

I savored the rush of hugs from family and friends, the joy of my work being recognized, and the admittedly shallow but nonetheless thrilling shock of victory. I was pretty sure I'd never forget it as long as I lived.

The sight of my parents dressed in matching tartans almost brought tears to my eyes. It was safe to say that the one thing they would never be called was subtle.

My mother ran up and hugged me. "I'm so proud of you, honey."

"Thanks, Mom."

She looked me up and down. "We should've bought you a kilt, too. You look so serious in your black suit."

"I was trying for understated elegance."

"And that's exactly what you achieved," she said with a generous smile.

I laughed. I knew I would never be as flamboyant as my parents—or Robin, for that matter, who stood a few feet away wearing a short gold sheath that fit her like skin. But I thought the black silk pants and slim matching jacket I'd chosen suited my mood tonight. Just hours before, I'd struggled for my life with a homicidal maniac and his sociopathic sibling. Serena and Martin had been led away in handcuffs, and Helen had collapsed in the arms of the first constable on the scene and been taken to the hospital for observation.

I saw Royce across the room, having an animated conversation with the small group gathered around him. He wore a tuxedo and a rather rakish bandage around his head. Earlier, he'd made the mistake of arguing with Helen in the hotel lobby when Martin came looking for his wife. Martin had immediately concluded that Helen and Royce were also having an affair and decided to add Royce to his kill list.

I shook off those awful thoughts and instead watched Robin flirt with Angus. He'd also dressed in full kilt regalia for the occasion—or maybe for Robin, who'd expressed more than a passing interest in seeing him kilted to the max.

I'd had a debriefing session with Angus directly after the St. Margaret's standoff. He'd relished the fact that Martin's purpose in killing Kyle had been that oldest of motives, jealousy, pure and simple.

"Nobody kills over a book," he reiterated.

I didn't take it personally because he was right—this time. But who was to say that books couldn't kill?

I took another sip of champagne as Mom and Dad discussed stopping at Stonehenge on the way back to London tomorrow. I was about to comment when I heard a whining voice somewhere close by, behind me. I focused my attention on the snippet of conversation.

A man was saying, "Why, it's simply wonderful work, excellent inlay, superior gilding and the best example of—"

"But did she have to win first prize?" Minka whined.

Another woman asked, "Have you seen her book?"

"I saw it, I saw it," Minka groused. "What's the BFD?"

"One merely has to observe the outstanding use of—"

Minka interrupted with a sound of pure disgust and stomped away.

Ah, sweet. "More champagne, please," I quipped, perky in victory.

"That's my girl," Dad said, happy as a man could be when dressed from neck to knees in red plaid wool.

A passing waiter stopped and held his tray steady as I traded my empty glass for a flute filled with sparkly liquid.

After the tense confrontation of that afternoon, the party atmosphere was infectious. I reveled in the laughter and cheer and made plans to meet friends in Lyon in the summer and the Lisbon fair next fall.

As I sipped champagne and shared an air kiss with

the woman who ran the book-arts center where I taught classes back in San Francisco, a commotion erupted nearby. From out of the crowd, two men approached.

"Stop pushing me."

"You'll apologize now and be done with it."

It was Tommy and Harry from the Robert Burns Society, my kidnappers from earlier in the week. They stopped in front of me and Tommy nudged Harry. "Now, tell her you're sorry."

Harry rolled his eyes. "Hello, Brooklyn."

"Hi, Harry," I said. "Hi, Tommy. What's going on?"

A waiter sailed by. Harry grabbed a champagne flute from the tray and drained it in one gulp.

He wiped his mouth, then blew out a heavy breath. "I'm to apologize for frightening you last night, miss. I thought I could get inside, grab the book and be done with it. Seems I was wrong."

I gaped at him. "It was you?"

"Aye, it was me," Harry grumbled, shooting a dirty look at Tommy. "And I'd've done it clean and quietly without causing you any pain and suffering if it hadn't been for that other bloke. Where'd he come from, anyway? Bugger all, the man took ten years off me life."

"You were going to steal the Robert Burns book?"

"Aye, he was," Tommy said, shaking his head. "But it was for the greater good, love."

"You frightened her very badly," Derek said sternly. "I would strongly urge her to press charges."

"You would?" I said, looking at Derek.

"Oh, now, miss," Harry said in a rush. "That won't be necessary. I admit it was a foolish thing I did, and I've learned my lesson."

"He'd had a snootful in the bar with the boys," Tommy whispered loudly. "He did it for Rabbie."

"For Rabbie," I said, and sighed. "I'll let it go this time, Harry, but don't ever do anything like that again."

"Ach, no worries, miss. As I said, I've learned my lesson."

"We'll be off now," Tommy said. "It was a pleasure to see you again, Miss Brooklyn."

"Likewise," I said, and watched as Tommy nudged Harry toward the bar.

The chandeliers glittered, the champagne flowed and the big-band music brought a sophisticated flair to the festivities.

Derek checked his watch, glanced around, then leaned in close to me. "Can I drag you away from the celebration for a moment, love?"

"Okay," I said, then was struck that this might be the last night I ever see him. And wasn't that depressing? I forced myself to smile as I added, "I have no plans to do anything other than swill champagne and bask in the glory of the big win."

"That's my girl." He was tall, dark and tempting in a beautiful suit that fit his wide shoulders and narrow waist to perfection. He took my hand and a little shiver of excitement passed through me. Was it the touch of his skin? His accent? His strength and virility? Something about Derek Stone always gave me a little thrill of anticipation, and I doubted the feeling would ever get old.

I sipped my champagne as we walked to the front desk. Derek asked for his package and the clerk handed him a small wrapped parcel.

The Robert Burns book.

I turned on him, miffed. "I left that in the safe. What are you doing with it?"

"Giving it to you," he said, and handed me the book.

"Oh." I held the book close to my chest. "Hmm. I'm not sure what I should—"

"Let's go outside, shall we?"

Taking hold of my elbow, he walked me out to the

valet area, where a deep purple Bentley limousine was parked. It was solidly built, like a Sherman tank.

The blacked-out back window slowly rolled down and a woman inside extended her expensively gloved hand out the window.

Derek turned to me. "May I have the book?"

"You're kidding," I whispered. I recognized the woman wrapped in shadows in the Bentley's backseat.

"I never kid," Derek said.

I stared at the Robert Burns book, its red gilded cover radiant in the reflected light of the old-fashioned streetlamps that lined the hotel's drive. Then I met Derek's gaze. "Are you sure it's the right thing to do? The world should have a chance to see this book and read its contents."

"This is the right thing to do," Derek assured me.

Why wasn't I convinced? "It doesn't matter what I think. The book belongs to Royce McVee."

"Yes, I spoke with him earlier. He's thrilled to be rid of it, and when he heard who the buyer was, I thought he would spontaneously combust."

"Oh. Well, that settles it." Reluctantly, I gave the book to Derek and he turned to face the woman in the car. He placed the book in her open hand and bowed from the waist.

"Thank you, Commander," she said crisply. After handing the book to a man sitting beside her, she gave me a minute nod and a queenly wave of her hand. The window began to rise and the Bentley drove off.

"Whoa," I said, staring at the car as it reached the end of the drive and turned left. "That was intense. So you told her about the book?"

Derek watched until the Bentley disappeared over the ridge. "No."

"But how else would she know? She must've heard

the whole background thing with Robert Burns and the princess."

"Not from me," he stated. "Do you honestly think I would repeat the story of a seditious eighteenth-century Scots poet illegitimately fathering a royal princess's baby? I'd be laughed out of the palace. It obviously never happened."

"But—" A movement across the street caught my eye. I glanced over and saw Gabriel leaning against a stone wall, watching me. His arms were folded across his chest and he was laughing. A black taxicab pulled up and Gabriel gave me a salute, then climbed into the cab and was whisked away.

"What were you going to say?" Derek said.

I blinked a few times. Had I imagined him? No, and I hadn't imagined his laughter, either. So now I had to wonder if Gabriel had tried to steal the book in order to sell it to the very person who now owned it. I couldn't blame him for laughing. Maybe I should've just let him get away with the book.

"Love?"

I focused on Derek. His eyes twinkled with laughter and his lips were twisted in that mocking half smile I grew more and more fond of every day, despite my best intentions.

"So you're saying," I began, "that all of a sudden, out of the blue, the queen of England gets a bug up her butt for an old book of coarse, sentimental, impossible-to-comprehend Scottish poetry."

He flexed his shoulders. "If you don't mind, we Brits prefer not to think that members of our beloved monarchy have bugs." He shrugged. "Or butts, for that matter."

"Sorry to offend. But . . ." I stared down the street, where I'd last seen the Bentley driving east toward the palace. Then I glanced in the opposite direction, where

Gabriel's taxi had gone. I wasn't sure what I'd learned from the *Flaxen'd Quean* and Kyle's death, but I knew I was not quite as unhinged and tattered as when I first arrived in Edinburgh. In fact, I felt a lot better. I turned to Derek and asked, "What do you think will happen to the book?"

He eased his arm around my shoulders and I caught a trace of his scent, an intoxicating mix of leather and citrus and pure masculinity. "I think it'll make for hours of royal bedtime reading."

"I doubt it," I said, shaking my head. "I can't help but worry that she'll take that book and its secrets to her grave."

"Darling Brooklyn," he said with an affectionate squeeze. "That surely won't be the only secret she takes with her."

"Aha! So you admit she'll be taking the secret with her, which must mean that you believe the story is true."

"That's quite a leap, and you're sadly mistaken."

"No, I'm not. I think . . ."

He stopped in the shadow of the hotel wall. The night was cool, but I didn't feel it as he held me at arm's length and patiently studied my features. "The stress has finally gotten to you, hasn't it, darling?"

"I'm not stressed at all," I said, biting back a grin. "I feel great."

He touched my cheek, pushed a thick strand of hair behind my ear and kissed me there. "But you're obviously delusional, aren't you?"

I laughed, then almost moaned as he moved his lips along my hairline and down to skim across my jaw. I should've asked him if this was his idea of a kiss-off, or if he intended to finish what he was starting. Instead, I decided to do as Guru Bob would do and simply live in the moment.

"What was the question?" I whispered when I could speak again.

"Ah, your memory is impaired as well," he murmured, his warm breath stirring the tiny hairs along my neck. "I suspect you've conked your head on some hard surface. That can be dangerous. I'll have to watch you very carefully from now on."

"If you insist," I managed to say as he turned his attention to my earlobe.

"Oh, I do, sweetheart," he said. "I really do."

You're invited to read an excerpt of
the third Bibliophile Mystery

The Lies That Bind

Available from Obsidian in February 2011

Layla Fontaine, executive artistic director of the Bay Area Book Arts Center, was tall, blond and strikingly beautiful, with a hair-trigger temper and a reputation for ruthlessness. Some in the book community called her a malevolent shark. Others disagreed, insisting that calling her a shark served only to tarnish the reputation of decent sharks everywhere.

Since I had business with the shark, I arrived at the book center early and parked my car in the adjacent lot. Grabbing the small package I'd brought, I climbed out of the car and immediately started to shiver. It was dusk and the March air in San Francisco was positively frigid. I seemed to be in the direct path of a brisk wind that whooshed straight off the Bay over AT&T Park and up Potrero Hill. Huddling inside my down vest, I jogged quickly over to the front entrance and climbed the stairs.

I almost whimpered as I stepped inside the warm interior and rubbed my arms to rid myself of the chills. Looking around, I grinned with giddy excitement. It was the first night of my latest master-bookbinding class and I, Brooklyn Wainwright, Super Bookbinder, was like a kid on the first day of grammar school. A nerdy kid, of course: one who actually looked forward to spending the day in school. I couldn't help myself. This place was a veritable shrine to paper and books and bookbinding arts, and it was all due to Layla Fontaine.

As head fund-raiser and the public face of the center, or BABA as some affectionately called it, Layla had her finger—and usually a few other body parts—on the pulse of every well-heeled person in the San Francisco Bay area. She was willing to do, say or promise anything to keep BABA on firm financial ground, no matter how shaky the legalities seemed. Hers was a higher calling, she claimed, right up there with Doctors Without Borders and Save the Children, and anything was fair game in the nonprofit sector. While that might've been true, the fact remained that Layla Fontaine was a snarky, sneaky, notoriously picky, manipulative bitch.

But Layla had one true saving grace, and that was her pure and abiding appreciation and devotion to books. She had an extensive collection of antiquarian treasures that she displayed regularly in the center's main gallery. And miracle of miracles, she'd managed to turn BABA into a profitable enterprise and a prestigious place to visit and contribute to.

Most important, she'd hired me a number of times to do restoration work on her books, which meant that I was more than willing to give her the benefit of the doubt when it came to her questionable behavior. Yes, I could be bought. I wasn't ashamed to admit it. After all, a girl's got to make a living.

Walking down the ramp into the central gallery, I spied Naomi Fontaine, Layla's niece and the coordinator for the center. She was busy assembling a display of vintage children's pop-up books.

"Hi, Naomi," I called out. "Is Layla in her office?"

She bared her teeth at me. "She's in there and she's a total bitch today. Good luck."

"Thanks for the heads-up," I said, wondering, not for

the first time, why Naomi stayed on at the center. She would never get the respect she deserved from her aunt Layla, and would always stand in her shadow. Naomi was a true bluestocking who, in another era, might've been just as happy as a cloistered nun. She was pretty in an understated way, and talented enough, but she lacked the dynamic personality it took to appeal to the high-society types with whom her aunt Layla hobnobbed.

Still, it was wise to keep on Naomi's good side. She was the person to talk to if you wanted to get anything done. If Layla was the brains behind the center, Naomi was its heart and soul. She had her faults, but everything ran smoothly because of her.

I crossed the gallery and headed down a wide hallway toward Layla's office. I was anxious to show her the restoration work I'd done on a rotted-out copy of an illustrated nineteenth-century edition of Charles Dickens's *Oliver Twist*. She'd given me the decrepit old book to restore, and if I said so myself, I'd done a fabulous job for her.

Layla planned to use the book as the centerpiece for BABA's weeklong celebration of the one hundred seventy-fifth anniversary of the publication of *Oliver Twist*. She was calling the festival "Twisted." Layla was always throwing lavish parties to celebrate obscure anniversaries such as this one. Anything to drum up sponsors and visitors to the center.

I was grateful for the work, and figured that as long as Layla was willing to provide me with books to restore, I was willing to believe she had a heart buried somewhere in that size-double-D chest of hers.

As I reached the end of the hall leading to Layla's office, I could hear voices. Her door was closed, but the angry shouts penetrated through the thick wood. I was about to knock when the door flew open. I jumped back and missed being hit by an inch.

"You'll be sorry you crossed me, you bitch," a furious man declared, then stormed out of Layla's office. I stood flat against the wall as a handsome, well-dressed Asian man stomped down the hall, across the gallery and out the front door.

I took a moment to catch my breath, then peeked around the doorway to make sure Layla was all right. She sat at her desk, casually applying red lipstick and looking as if she didn't have a care in the world.

"Are you okay?" I asked.

She glanced at me over her mirror. "Of course. Why wouldn't I be?"

"Oh, I don't know. But that guy sounded really annoyed."

"Men." She waved away my concern, swept her cosmetics into her top drawer, then stood and rounded her desk. She was dressed in an impossibly tight short black skirt and a crisp white blouse unbuttoned to show off her impressive cleavage. In her five-inch black patent-leather stilettos, she looked like an overeducated Pussycat Doll.

"Give me the book," she demanded.

I hesitated, feeling a bit like a mother wavering at the thought of handing a beloved child over to a stern East German nanny. Yes, the woman might make sure the child was fed, but she wouldn't *love* it.

"Brooklyn." She snapped her fingers.

I don't know why I faltered. The book belonged to Layla. Aside from that, she was my employer. I exhaled heavily and carefully handed her the wrapped parcel, then had to watch as she ripped the brown paper to shreds to reveal the *Oliver Twist*.

"Oh, it's perfect," she said greedily as she turned the book over and back. "You did a good job."

"Thank you." Good? It was a great job, if I said so myself.

She stared at the elegant spine, studying my work; then she glanced inside and stared at the endpapers. Turning to the title page, she murmured, "No one will ever suspect this isn't a first edition."

I laughed. "Unless they know books."

She glared at me. "Nobody knows that much about books. If I say it's a first edition, then that's what they'll believe."

"Probably," I conceded.

Then she jabbed her finger at the date on the title page. I tried not to cringe, but I could see the dent she'd made in the thick vellum. "It says right there, printed in 1838. The year he wrote it."

"Right," I said slowly. "But that doesn't mean anything. We both know it's not a first edition."

Her left eye began to twitch, and she rubbed her temple as she leaned her hip against the edge of her desk. "True. But no one's going to hear the real story, are they, Brooklyn?"

Her tone was vaguely threatening. Was I missing something?

"Are you saying I should lie about the book?" I asked.

"I'm saying you should just keep your mouth shut."

"But what's the big deal? The festival is all about this book, and it's got an interesting history."

To me, anyway. It seemed that Charles Dickens was doing so well with the serialization of *Oliver Twist* that his publisher went behind his back and published the manuscript, using Dickens's pseudonym, "Boz." That first edition included all of the illustrator Cruikshank's drawings.

Dickens was displeased because he'd intended to use his real name once the book was published. He was also unhappy with one of Cruikshank's drawings in the book, calling it too sentimental, according to some accounts. He insisted that the publisher pull that edition and revise it to his specifications. It was done within the week.

A true first edition of *Oliver Twist* written under the pseudonym of Boz, with Cruikshank's unauthorized drawings, was beyond rare.

Layla's book had Charles Dickens listed as author on the title page, and the Cruikshank illustration was missing. So, officially, it didn't count as a first edition.

"I don't want you going around telling people about this book—do you hear me?" Layla pushed away from the desk, drew herself up to her full height and glared down at me. She was only an inch or so taller than I, but it was a good attempt at intimidation. "For the purposes of the festival, this book is a first edition. Got it?"

I looked at her sideways. "So you want me to lie?"

"Isn't that what I just said?"

"It just seems like the real story would be more interesting to people."

"Jesus, do you ever give up?" she asked. "Nobody cares about your stupid book theories, and if you like working here, you'll say what I tell you to say. *Capice?*"

I sucked my cheeks in—something I tended to do whenever I wanted to chew somebody's ass but needed to hold my tongue instead. After a long moment, I gritted my teeth and said, "Got it."

Casually slapping the exquisite nineteenth-century volume against her hand, she said, "That's what I thought you'd say."

"You know what?" I turned toward the door. "I've got to go get my classroom set up."

She pointed her finger at me as though it were a gun and she'd just pulled the trigger. "Good idea."

I rushed out of her office and made it back to the central gallery before the urge to strangle her took over.

Naomi took one look at my face and snorted. "Glad I'm not the only one she's picking on today."

"Yeah, lucky me." As I headed toward my classroom, I couldn't decide what annoyed me more: the fact that Layla hadn't given me enough props for my work, or the idea that I should lie about the whole first-edition issue. The lack of props won out. I'd done a spectacular job of restoring the book, but she was just too screwed up and snotty to allow me more than that pitiful "good job" comment she'd grudgingly given me. I would have to think twice if she offered me any more restoration work.

But Layla was forgotten as a sudden bone-deep chill settled over me, as if someone had just walked on my grave. My mother used to say that, but I never knew what it meant until that moment.

"Well, if it isn't the black widow herself," a woman said in a familiar high, whiny tone that was purported to cause dogs' ears to bleed. "Wherever she goes, somebody dies."

Minka LaBoeuf.

My worst nightmare. To think I'd been so happy to be here only a few minutes ago.

I turned and glared at her. "So maybe you ought to leave, just to be on the safe side."

"Very funny," she said, tossing back her overprocessed stringy black hair. "I should think they'd be afraid to let you in here with your record."

I ignored that. "What the hell are you doing here?"

"I'm an instructor now," she said, jutting her pointy chin out smugly.

"What?" I might've shrieked the word. I couldn't help it. Minka was the world's worst bookbinder. She destroyed books. She was like the bubonic plague to books. Who in the world had hired her to teach anyone bookbinding? "You've got to be kidding."

"Minka, darling," Layla cried as she rushed forward and gave Minka a big hug. "I thought I heard your voice."

Not surprising, since yapping puppies in the next county could hear Minka's voice.

"I'm so pleased you could join our faculty," Layla gushed, winding her arm through Minka's. Then she turned to me and her eyes gleamed with amusement. "Don't tell me you two know each other. Isn't that perfect? Brooklyn, you'll be able to show Minka around. I know you'll make her feel comfortable and welcome here."

Minka smirked in victory. Over Minka's shoulder, I saw Naomi roll her eyes. Good to know it wasn't just me who thought that Minka working here was a really bad idea.

I gave Minka a look that made it clear that hell would freeze over before I would show her anything but the back door. My former good mood plummeted even further as I realized I'd have to spend the next three weeks trying to avoid both Layla's caustic bitchiness and Minka's toxic stupidity.

I thought of Minka's first words a minute ago, about people dying whenever I was in the vicinity. I hoped her words wouldn't come back to haunt us, but I had to wonder how long it would take before someone in that room turned up dead.

Also Available from

Kate Carlisle

Homicide in Hardcover

A Bibliophile Mystery

The streets of San Francisco would be lined with
hardcovers if rare book expert Brooklyn
Wainwright had her way. And her mentor wouldn't
be lying in a pool of his own blood on the eve of
a celebration for his latest book restoration.

With his final breath he leaves Brooklyn a cryptic
message, and gives her a priceless—and
supposedly cursed—copy of Goethe's *Faust*
for safekeeping.

Brooklyn suddenly finds herself accused of murder
and theft, thanks to the humorless—but attractive—
British security officer who finds her kneeling over
the body. Now she has to read the clues left
behind by her mentor if she is going to
restore justice…

**Available wherever books are sold or
at penguin.com**

Kate Collins

The Flower Shop Mystery Series

Abby Knight is the proud owner of her
hometown flower shop. She has a gift for
arranging flowers—and for solving crimes.

Mum's the Word
Slay It with Flowers
Dearly Depotted
Snipped in the Bud
Acts of Violets
A Rose from the Dead
Shoots to Kill
Evil in Carnations
Sleeping with Anemone

"A sharp and funny heroine."
—Maggie Sefton